Chemistry & Chaos

❧

JC Conrad-Ellis

CHEMISTRY & CHAOS

Copyright ©2022 by JC Conrad-Ellis
Cover Design ©2022 by Valerie Connelly

For information about Provision Press please
visit our website at www.blackdiamondseries.com.

Library of Congress Cataloging-in-Publication Data

Conrad-Ellis, JC,

CHEMISTRY & CHAOS/ JC Conrad-Ellis
ISBN 13: 978-1-957593-02-9
Teen Fiction

Copyright Registered: 2022
Published by Provision Press in the USA

Printed in the USA

January 2022

10 9 8 7 6 5 4 3 2

DEDICATION

To my Mother,
LMC

Thank you for reminding me to
"Seek ye first the kingdom of God and all
these things shall be granted unto you."   Matthew 6:33

With love, JTC-E

ACKNOWLEDGEMENTS

I'd like to thank:

God for my story telling and writing ability. I pray that my words bring pleasure and enjoyment to you, but glory and honor to him.

My husband, Brian, and our three amazing children for allowing me the leash and space to write, rewrite, edit and re-edit and for loving and encouraging me through every page.

Nia Feaster and Ashlynn Thompson for patiently awaiting the arrival of each book in my series. I am glad that I know you. You are destined to become amazing women.

Karyn Roelke, my neighbor, friend, and the best copy editor a cup of coffee can buy! Thank you for sharing your gifts with me. I miss our walks and chats.

My vast network circle and patchwork quilt of women whom I turn to for friendship, guidance, comfort, encouragement, love, nurturing and support. You know who you are, and you are in my life for a reason. I'm glad that our season is still flourishing. I love each of you!

The women in my family, the mothers of Jack and Jill of America, Inc., The women of Delta Sigma Theta Sorority, Inc., the members of Mississippi Boulevard Christian Church, and the MBCC Blvd East Collierville Life Group, the members of Covenant United Church of Christ, the women of the Links, Incorporated Memphis (TN) chapter, and my kind and nurturing publisher, Valerie Connelly and the team at Nightengale Press, especially Mike Connelly, my patient webmaster.

My readers, without you reading and enjoying my work, my writing is just words on a page. Thank you for allowing me to be a part of your lives.

In loving memory of

Doristene "Gramsy" Neeley

CONTENTS

*"Commit to the Lord whatever you do,
and your plans will succeed."*
Proverbs 16:3
NIV Study Bible
New International Version

Chapter 1

The Cat's Meow

The glassware complete, she took a swig from her mug, and prepared to hunker down for a long afternoon. The hot liquid felt good against the back of her throat. Her tongue expertly tucked ice chips into the pockets of her cheeks, like a squirrel hoarding acorns for the winter. She'd captured four ice chips with this swig. She crunched noisily, savoring the hint of peppermint that clung to the melting ice. Her friends teased her about drinking hot chocolate in the middle of August, but she enjoyed the smooth taste of the drink year round, adding ice to the hot liquid during the summer months. Peppermint hot chocolate was her comfort food. She ran her tongue along the rim, carefully tracing the outline of a small crack in the mug. She tucked her hair behind her ear and grabbed another section of the aged <u>Chicago Tribune</u> newspaper. The china dinner plates needed to be wrapped with care.

Fighting back tears, she thought about the upcoming move from Newberry East. Justine couldn't believe that her mom had actually continued with her plans to find a new job. The process from application to offer had taken less time than it seemed it would take to pack the kitchen. Her mother, Andrea Wellington, would soon be the Resident Head Nurse in the Surgical Intensive

Care Unit at Evanston Memorial Hospital in Evanston, Illinois. Justine was moving sixty six miles away from her friends.

Just weeks before, she and her mom had driven to the Waukegan area to find an apartment.

"Justine, this is it," Mrs. Wellington grinned. She parked the car in the small parking lot and walked up to a three story apartment building with a sign out front that read "Rental Office."

Justine inhaled deeply. "Well, it's an apartment. It's going to be smaller than the townhouse we have now," Justine replied agitatedly. "Have you thought about that, Mom? Our current house is barely large enough for all of us." Justine wanted to cry.

Mrs. Wellington sighed loudly and rubbed Justine's arm. "I know baby, but it's what I can afford right now. Your brothers can share a room for a while. And at least you'll still have your own room. Since your dad lost his job at the shoe store, he won't be paying child support until he finds a new job. Don't worry, if I invest and save, with the extra money that I'll be making from my new job, we should be able to afford a house in about a year or so."

They walked into the rental office and were greeted by a woman wearing a gold Coldwell Banker name badge that read Kathleen K.

"Hi. I'm Kathleen Kelly, you must be Andrea," Kathleen chirped. She took a swig from a white Styrofoam coffee cup before extending her hand. Her red hair was pulled into a severe ballet bun, and small wisps of hair hung loosely around her round freckled face. She wore a white blouse with a string of pearls around her neck. The blouse was tucked neatly inside her khaki slacks which had a crisp, freshly laundered pleat that hung over the top of the maroon penny loafers that she wore sans hosiery.

"Yes, I'm Andrea Wellington, and this is my daughter, Justine."

"Hello, Hello! Welcome to Waukegan! Let's go see the unit!" Kathleen escorted them up three flights of stairs to the third floor.

The hallway was well lit with sconces that hung to the right of each apartment door. Kathleen headed to her left at the top of the stairs. Justine peered to her right and counted six sconces, three on either side of the corridor's hallway.

Kathleen slowed her pace when she realized that Mrs. Wellington was not directly behind her. "There's a small service elevator down the hall, but it's really only for deliveries and moving in or out," she explained. "The tenants in the building take the stairs to get to their units."

"Well, I could certainly trim down a little climbing up three flights of stairs every day!" Mrs. Wellington stated. "I'm terribly out of shape." She rested at the top of the landing to catch her breath.

Kathleen led them down the small corridor and opened the door to Apartment 306.

Justine entered last. She bit her lip, and surveyed her surroundings while her mother chatted with Kathleen. The apartment had a total of five rooms including the kitchen. The small foyer led into a small dining area that was connected to a small galley style kitchen. The kitchen had two pass through areas with one connecting to the dining room and the other to the living room. The living room and dining room were combined and shaped like an L. The living room area had two sliding glass doors leading to a small balcony. To the left of the dining room was a hallway leading to the bedrooms. The smaller bedrooms were side by side with a small bathroom across from the first bedroom. The master bedroom had a separate bath with a walk-in closet. The floors were covered in shiny black tile.

Mrs. Wellington reappeared with Kathleen. "Justine, what do you think?" she asked hopefully.

Justine shrugged her shoulders without responding. She knew that if she spoke, she would cry, and she didn't want to cry in front of this stranger.

Knowingly rubbing Justine's back, Mrs. Wellington spoke to Kathleen. "By the way, we have a cat," she said casually. "That's not going to be a problem is it?"

Kathleen shook her head slowly from side to side. "Oh dear, I'm sorry, but the building doesn't allow pets." Kathleen bit her lower lip and fiddled with the cap of her pen.

Justine's ears perked up. "I didn't realize that, it didn't state that in the information," Mrs. Wellington said.

"I'm so sorry. I thought you knew that this was a no pet building. It's in the bottom of the ad, in very small print, but it's there." Kathleen stated as she carefully folded the paper in her hand.

Justine saw her opportunity. "Mom, we can't get rid of Fudge! He's part of the family." She felt the tears that she'd been suppressing slowly rolling down her cheeks.

"I know, sweetie," Mrs. Wellington agreed. She turned to address Kathleen. "Our cat is seven years old, and he's part of the family. My children have been through a lot this summer. I couldn't imagine getting rid of the family pet. Thank you, but it looks like we can't take this unit. We'll have to find a place that accepts pets," she finished.

"I'm so sorry. I know you would have really liked it here," Kathleen explained. But if we made an exception for one tenant, other tenants would expect exceptions," she finished.

"No, I understand. I should have read the fine print," Mrs.

Wellington sighed slowly as she jiggled her keys.

Justine exhaled a sigh of relief. Kathleen led them into the hallway, making small talk about the summer heat and other possible buildings in Waukegan that she thought accepted pets. As they walked to the car, Justine spoke.

"Mom, what about all of those apartment buildings that we saw near that cemetery along Sheridan Road? I saw at least three or four people walking dogs as we were driving up here, and I saw a bunch of For Rent signs. On the way back, let's stop and look at one of those places," Justine suggested.

"We may as well look since we drove all the way up here, and it's on the way home anyway. This is the only place that I saw that I liked in Waukegan, but since I didn't get that job at Waukegan General, this would be a long commute to Evanston Memorial every day," she sighed. "Rents are more expensive in Evanston, but it doesn't hurt to look."

The sun scorched the asphalt parking lot and glistened from the silver door handle, which burned their hands as they opened their car doors.

They climbed into the hot car and headed east back to Greenbay Road. Justine admired the beautiful homes that lined the picturesque community. She wondered what the area looked like in December when it was decorated for the holiday season. Mrs. Wellington guided the car along Greenbay Road and headed south along Sheridan Road. As they drove through the suburbs of Winnetka and Wilmette, Justine again marveled at the majestic estates lining either side of the road. She'd never seen homes this grand before. She wondered where Grace's maternal grandparents had once lived.

When they entered Northwestern University's campus, she

admired the beautiful limestone buildings and wondered why there were so few students wandering along Sheridan Road.

"Why aren't there more students walking around on campus, Mom?" she asked.

"Oh, that's because school hasn't started yet, sweetie. Northwestern is on the quarter system. Their fall quarter doesn't start until the third week in September. They have three quarters that are ten or eleven weeks in length instead of two sixteen week semesters like most universities," she explained. "A lot of the colleges on the East coast are on quarters. And I think Stanford and the University of Chicago are on quarters too. Most of the large state universities are on semesters like the University of Illinois," she continued. "Anyway, some people say that all of the "major" universities or Ivy League caliber schools are on quarters. My school was on quarters. I liked it better, because you could take more classes during the year and you didn't get bored with studying a subject for sixteen weeks. But some people don't like quarters because you have to start preparing for midterms almost immediately, and the pace of study is a tad more rigorous."

Mrs. Wellington continued her diatribe on the benefits of quarters vs. semesters as Justine stared out the window. She twirled a rubber band that she wore on her right wrist and pretended to listen to her mom. As they wound through Evanston and passed a curve on Sheridan Road with Lake Michigan on their left and a cemetery on their right Justine sat upright.

"Mom, this is where I remember seeing all of those signs," she explained.

"This is where I thought you meant, baby. I'll park on one of these side streets and we'll see what we can find." Mrs. Wellington parallel parked along Jarvis Street across from a nursing home and instinctively grabbed Justine's hand as they waited at the stop light to cross the busy street.

"Mom! I'm fifteen! You don't need to hold my hand to cross the street." Justine jerked her hand away.

"I'm sorry, honey! It's just a force of habit," her mother smiled.

Justine noticed several Open House signs as they waited for the light to change. They headed north along Sheridan Road and entered a walk-up building that was across the street from a gas station. The building was well maintained with blue and white balloons flying in the breeze. There were crocuses planted in the built in flower pots lining the walkway. As they entered the courtyard, they noticed a man in a suit tying more balloons to a nail at the top of the doorway.

"Excuse me, sir. Can you tell me where the Open House is?" Mrs. Wellington asked.

"I sure can. I'm Bob, the rental agent. The unit is in this building. I'll take you up to see it as soon as I get this last balloon to stay put." Bob wound the balloon string around the nail and dusted off his hands, reaching to shake Mrs. Wellington's hand.

"Thanks, Bob. I'm Andrea Wellington, and this is my daughter, Justine," she said.

Bob picked up a manila folder that he'd placed on the stoop and removed a sheet of paper.

"Here's a write up on the unit that's for rent." He handed the paper to Mrs. Wellington. "This is a condo building, but the owner rents this unit as an income property. He's a doctor on staff at Northwestern Memorial Hospital," he continued. "Dr. Griffin is a really nice man. He lives in Wilmette, but his handyman, Willie, lives on Howard Street which is just a couple of blocks away. If there are any problems with the unit, Willie takes care of it right away."

"Thank you. Bob, does this building allow pets?" Mrs. Wellington asked.

"Absolutely! Dogs, cats, gerbils, birds, you name it. It's a menagerie in this building. Almost all of the owners have at least one pet. But you should know that a city ordinance was recently passed, and you are now required to pick up your pet's poop in this area," he cautioned.

"No problem. We have a cat anyway. By the way, I know this isn't Evanston, but what's this area called?" Mrs. Wellington smiled at Bob.

"This is the Rogers Park neighborhood, so you're still in Chicago, but on the other side of that cemetery is Evanston. This building feeds into the Chicago Preparatory Magnet School that's two blocks over across Sheridan Road which is the busy street right out front," he explained.

"I've heard about that school. They post great test scores and have a high college admissions rate," Mrs. Wellington said. "The courtyard is pretty. I'd like to go up and take a look at the unit."

They entered the building and walked to the second floor. There were two units on the floor, one on either side of the hallway. The door to the left of the stairway was open and blue and white balloons hung from the doorknob. Bob entered the unit first.

"Feel free to walk around. I'll meet you in the kitchen and can answer any questions that you may have," he offered. "The unit really sells itself, so enjoy your tour!" Bob walked down a long hallway and disappeared.

The apartment had hardwood floors and period detailing including mahogany wainscoting and white crown molding in the ceilings. Once inside, a wide foyer connected to a large living room that fed into an attached sun porch with an unobstructed view of

Lake Michigan from the east facing window and a view of the gas station and cemetery from the remaining windows. One wall of the living room was a fireplace with built in bookcases on either side. The master bedroom and bath shared a wall with the living room and was entered from the front foyer.

"This must be the master bedroom since it has a bathroom connected to it," Mrs. Wellington surmised. She walked into the bathroom with Justine on her heels. "It's small, but it'll do."

A long hallway led to two additional bedrooms that were connected by a Jack & Jill style bathroom in the center.

"You and the boys could share this bathroom," Mrs. Wellington suggested.

"This reminds me of the Brady Bunch bathroom," Justine said. She walked through the bathroom and entered a room that was slightly smaller than the other adjacent bedroom. "Mom, did you notice how small the closets are? I don't think all of my clothes would fit in this closet."

"That's one thing about older homes, the closet space is always lacking. There are two small closets in the hallway, so we could use those for our clothes, and we could also buy an armoire to store sweaters and winter coats," she suggested.

The hall ended at a large dining room on the right connected to a small sun porch that overlooked a well kept backyard and large garage. "I wonder if the unit comes with a garage space," Andrea stated hopefully. Across from the dining room, an eat-in kitchen connected to a smaller room with a tiny powder room adjacent to it.

Mrs. Wellington peeked into the tiny room adjacent to the kitchen. "This must have been the maid's quarters," she suggested.

"You're absolutely correct." Bob peered over Mrs. Wellington's shoulder. "Back in the 1920's when this apartment was built, everyone had live-in help, and this would have been the maid's room. It can't really be counted as a bedroom under today's standards since it doesn't have a closet, but you can fit a twin bed or a daybed in here easily or it could serve as a nice office or study." Bob walked into the kitchen and twirled around. "Dr. Griffin just had the kitchen remodeled last year, so the cabinetry, countertops and appliances are new. He also had them redo the plumbing and installed a stackable washer and dryer in the pantry. And last but not least, the unit does have access to one of the spots in the garage out back which is really nice because parking in this neighborhood is very tricky."

Andrea smiled widely. "This place is really nice. I'm a nurse, and I'll be working at Evanston Hospital in a few weeks. We're moving so that I can be closer to work." Mrs. Wellington rubbed her hand along the counter. "I'm also going through a divorce," she said softly.

"I'm sorry to hear about the divorce, but congratulations on the new job. This is a great building, and the school that it feeds into is one of the best in the city. Plus, you're only a quick train or bus ride from downtown. The CTA 151 bus depot is right in front of the building, and the Howard Street train stop is just two blocks away. It's close, but you don't hear the train," he explained.

Mrs. Wellington studied the flyer. "The rent seems reasonable," she stated. "It's only a little more than the place we just saw in Waukegan, and it would be nice to be closer to work in case there was an emergency with one of my kids. I have two sons, as well. One is nine and the older is eleven," she offered.

"Great! There's another family in the building that has a son and a daughter who are in fourth and sixth grade. The unit just became available last week, because the Loyola professor who was renting it accepted a tenured assignment at Washington University in St. Louis. I don't want to pressure you, but since this unit has a lake view from the front sun room, I know it's going to go quickly. You're the first person to see it since I put the Open House sign outside. This is a very popular neighborhood, so you may want to decide today. Why don't you give it some thought, and I'll meet you in front."

Bob whistled as he walked down the hall.

Mrs. Wellington whispered to Justine. "Justine, what do you think?"

"Mom, I like this place much better than that place in Waukegan. Much better. You'd be a lot closer to work, and we'd be closer to downtown. I could jump on the train and meet my friends at Water Tower Place or Marshall Field's. Plus, it would be easier for them to visit me here than way up in Waukegan. I think we should take it, Mom," she pleaded.

Her mother took a deep breath and bit her bottom lip. She jiggled the keys in her hand nervously. "I like it too," she admitted. "It's older, but it has so much character, and I've always admired older homes. Let's do it!" Mrs. Wellington squeezed Justine in a bear hug and speed walked to the front of the unit to speak with Bob.

"Mom, ask Bob if we can paint the rooms!" she shouted.

The sound of her brothers coming into the house, snapped Justine out of her daydream. She wrapped more newspaper around the plate in her hand, staring sadly at her ink stained hands. The vintage apartment on Sheridan Road would soon be her new home.

Chapter 2

It's Just Hair

Grace bent at the waist and brushed her long golden locks from the back to the front. She stood and tossed her hair over her shoulders, splattering the mirror with water from her long tresses. Her hair was now well past the middle of her back. Shaking her head like a dog shakes his fur after a bath, she watched as hair streaked the mirror with tiny lines and fell limp down her back. Grace called this her Breck girl shake. She'd seen the Breck shampoo girl shake her hair like that on television. She grabbed her thick mane and twirled it into a tight French twist, piling it on top of her head and studying her profile in the mirror. She sucked in her cheeks and eyed her reflection.

She admired her features, studying her delicate cheek bones and small ears. She definitely had her mother's eyes and mouth. But her nose troubled her. It wasn't huge, but it wasn't perky. It protruded from her face and ended in a pronounced point. In third grade, Bobby Snider had called her beak nose. She'd come home in tears, but her mother had assured her that Bobby probably just had a crush on her, and that boys often teased girls that they liked. It was part of the mating ritual. Fortunately, the nickname hadn't stuck, and the other kids in school hadn't joined Bobby's playground chant. Years later, Grace still remembered the silly song.

Beak nose, beak nose, Gracie has a beak nose. Worms for breakfast, worms for lunch, Gracie's nose is big enough to munch!

Grace wanted to smack him, but her mom had encouraged her to just ignore him, which she had. But she had glared at him with a death stare and twirled her arms like she'd seen on Bewitched. She was pretending to cast a hex on Bobby. She slanted her eyes into slits and glared at him, not saying a word. He continued his chant and Grace continued her icy stare. When Bobby's teasing failed to stir a reaction in Grace, he walked away to play touch football with the other boys at recess. Her mom's advice had worked. He teased her a few more times, but when she didn't react, he would walk away defeated.

Years later, Grace agreed with Bobby Snider. Her nose did look like a bird's beak. She wondered if she had her father's nose. She brushed her hair again and thought about getting a haircut. Her hair had always been long, but she felt the urge to go with a different, shorter style. She'd admired Dorothy Hamill in the winter Olympics and thought about getting her hair cut into a feathered pixie style.

Grace walked into the living room and saw her mom stretched out across the sofa watching Soul Train.

"Hey, Mom. Who's on Soul Train today?" Grace's mom didn't look up from the television. "Mom!" Grace shouted.

"Hey, honey! Did you say something? I must have dozed off," Mrs. Dudley yawned.

"I said who's on Soul Train today?" she repeated.

"I have no idea. I was half watching. I just like to see Don Cornelius." Mrs. Dudley sat up on the sofa. "Half the time I don't even recognize the guests that he has on the show anymore. It's not the same as it was. When it first came on, he always had all of the big stars like Stevie Wonder, Gladys Knight and the Pips, Smokey Robinson, The O'Jays, Roberta Flack. It's gotten so now I don't know who any of these young people are," she moaned before continuing. "And the clothes that they wear are shameful. They used to dress up to be on Soul Train, but now these kids just show up in shorts, bathing suits and jeans and what not. When I was growing up, only poor people or farmers wore jeans. Now they want to charge you fifty dollars for a pair of blue jeans! It's absurd. Things have really changed," Mrs. Dudley complained.

Grace's mother slowly pulled the grey rollers from her hair, carefully placing the pink pins on the coffee table. She patted her head to ensure that she'd removed all of the curlers and counted them for good measure. Her mom always slept with eleven curlers in her hair. If she misplaced one, she tore the house apart until she found it. Grace and her dad once spent forty minutes searching for a wiry grey curler that had rolled under the recliner in the living room. Somehow the curler had gotten stuck to a piece of tape at the bottom of the chair. The family had almost given up, and Mr. Dudley was prepared to drive to the store to purchase a new package of curlers, when Mrs. Dudley lifted the small recliner and Justine saw the curler stuck to the bottom of the chair. Apparently, Mrs. Dudley had fallen asleep in the chair, and the roller had slipped between the cushions. Ever since that episode, Mrs. Dudley always counted the curlers as she took them out of her hair. She tied them in her satin sleep scarf and tucked them under the coffee table.

Grace shook her head as she watched her mom perform her daily routine. "Where's Daddy?" Grace asked.

"Huh? Did you say something, baby?" Mrs. Dudley asked.

"I said, where's Daddy?" Grace said louder this time.

"Daddy? He's in the back fooling around with the sprinkler hose trying to water the garden. You know how he gets to tinkering with stuff. I keep telling him that the money he spends trying to water that garden and buying fencing to keep those rabbits out, he could have bought a whole summer's worth of collard and mustard greens, but he insists that they don't taste the same," she explained. "Now you can buy greens at the store that are already picked and washed, but he still wants me to grow collards out back. He's an old fool. But ain't no fool like an old fool, that's for sure." Mrs. Dudley chuckled at her joke and sat upright. She stretched her arms over her head.

"I tricked him once and bought those store bought collard greens to see if he could taste the difference. He couldn't. I knew he wouldn't know the difference," she chuckled.

Mrs. Dudley rubbed her hands together. "I don't know how much longer my old arthritis is going to let me clean greens, so I'm glad he can't tell the difference between my greens and those store bought greens."

Grace smirked as she watched her mother move on to a different subject. She picked up the remote control and turned down the volume.

Mrs. Dudley was sixty two years old, and her hearing was deteriorating. Grace sat down next to her mother and patted her thigh. She loved how her mother always rocked her knees whenever she sat. Perpetual motion, her mother called it. She either rocked one leg by raising her heel off the ground or twitched both knees in rapid fashion. She said it relaxed her. Grace often found herself shaking as she sat and watched television with her mother. The perpetual motion was contagious. When she was younger, she thought that it was hereditary, but now she knew that she couldn't have inherited the quirk from her mother.

Grace leaned her head onto her mother's shoulder and spoke directly into her ear. "Mom, do you mind brushing my hair?"

"Sure, baby. Go get the brush," she said.

Grace picked up the hairbrush from the bathroom counter. She came out and sat on the floor between her mother's legs.

"Do you want me to grease your scalp too?" Mrs. Dudley parted her long nightgown and patted the sofa.

"No. I just washed my hair, so it's fine now," Grace said.

"Okay, but you know you have to grease your scalp at least every other day. Even though your hair is fine like mine, you still need oil in it. I remember when your mama died, and I didn't know what to do with your hair. It looked like white people's hair, but then it was thicker than their hair," she reflected. "I just didn't know what to do with it." She brushed with long gentle strokes. "I took you to one of those fancy salons in Glen. Alan Marc is what it was called I think. Anyway, I asked them if they knew how to take care of your hair, and if they could give me some professional tips on how to care for it at home. Well, they took one look at me and thought I was a white woman, and then looked at you and knew that you were mixed. They said I should just cut it off and you should wear an afro like the rest of your people," Mrs. Dudley coughed into her hand. She reached for her water glass and took a long sip.

"I couldn't believe it," she continued. "This was over fifteen years ago, and people weren't too happy about the races mixing back then. To tell you the truth, they're not too happy about the races mixing today," she paused. "So anyway, I took you outside to wait for me and then I went back in there and gave those prejudiced people a piece of my mind and then I strutted on out of there. I know when I opened my mouth they knew I wasn't no white woman then! I used some words I know they ain't never heard before!" Mrs. Dudley gently brushed Grace's long hair, and Grace rested her eyes as her mother retold the story. "Luckily, Mrs. Perkins helped me care for your hair and showed me how to make plaits. I never did learn how to make those French plaits. I think you kids call them French braids. But when I was coming up, we called them plaits. My hair was too fine to plait, but I learned how to do yours." She worked the brush through Grace's long hair in a slow and deliberate pattern. "Does it itch anywhere?'

"No. It's fine." Grace spoke in a loud voice to avoid repeating herself. She decided to test the water. "Mom, I was thinking that I wanted to get my hair cut."

"Do you need your ends trimmed? I'm sure Mrs. Perkins can trim them for you."

"I want to get it cut short like Dorothy Hamill." Grace braced herself for her mother's reaction.

"Who is Dorothy Hamilton?" Mrs. Dudley pulled the brush through Grace's hair in long, loving strokes. Having her hair brushed by her mom always relaxed Grace.

"Dorothy Hamill," Grace corrected. "She's an ice skater. She skated in the Olympics. She won a gold medal. Anyway, her hair looks really cute," Grace said loudly.

"Stop shouting, sweetie. I can hear you just fine. How short is her hair? You know your daddy don't want you cutting off this hair. He thinks ladies are supposed to have long hair," Mrs. Dudley explained.

Grace turned around to face her mother. She sat up on her knees. "Her hair is pretty short. It's up to her ears, and it's feathered. It's really cute." Grace traced her fingers along her ears and held her breath.

"Now you know your daddy is not going to go for that, Grace. You'll look like a boy. Uh, uh, he ain't gone have that." She patted the sofa with the hair brush. "Sit back down so I can finish brushing."

Resting back on her knees, Grace's tone hardened, and she raised her voice. "That's not fair, Mom! It's my hair! I'm tired of all of this hair!" She tugged at her long locks. "It just hangs down my back, and it doesn't even have a style!"

Mrs. Dudley stared at Grace with steely eyes. "Little girl, have you lost your mind? You don't raise your voice at me," Mrs. Dudley scolded, her voice barely above a loud whisper. "I will knock you into next week. I don't know what's gotten into you. Now you better talk to me like you have some sense or this conversation is over." Mrs. Dudley patted the brush in her hand.

"I'm sorry, Mom," Grace apologized. She sat back on her heels. "It's just that I want to start the school year with a new look. It's just hair, and if I don't like it, it will grow back. Can you please talk to Daddy for me?" Grace pleaded.

"Do you have a picture of this Dorothy Hamilton person so I can see what her hair looks like?" Mrs. Dudley asked.

Grace's face brightened. "I have a picture of her in my Teen magazine. I'll go get it."

She raced to her room and grabbed the Teen magazine from her dresser and raced back downstairs. She pointed to a picture of Dorothy Hamill.

Mrs. Dudley studied the magazine and studied Grace's face. "Well, your face is pretty enough to wear a short hair style. You have the high cheekbones and everything, but I don't know," she paused. "You're going to lose almost eighteen inches of hair, Grace. I don't know if I can convince your daddy to go along with this idea."

"Mom, please talk to him. I really want to get my hair cut. I'm fifteen now, and I've never had my hair cut," she pleaded. "I've had long hair all of my life, and I'm tired of it. I've been through a lot this past year. Finding out that I was adopted last summer was really hard for me. I just feel like a new look would help me accept my new reality," Grace sighed. "Come on, Mom. If you tell Dad it's a good idea, he'll go for it. Please!" Grace batted her eyes at her mother. She sat up on her knees with her hands under her chin and panted like a puppy.

"I'll see what I can do. But I can't make any promises. When does school start again? I don't remember," Mrs. Dudley yawned.

"We go back to school August 28. I really want to get my hair cut next week so I can get used to it," she explained.

Mrs. Dudley fingered Grace's long hair. "Gracie, your hair is so pretty. Are you sure that this is what you want?'

"Positive!" Grace clasped her hands in a prayer posture.

"Well, I guess it is just hair. And you have had a rough year. I can see why you might want a fresh new look." Mrs. Dudley exhaled and handed Grace the hairbrush. "But if your daddy says no, that's it. I'm not going to have my household upset over no haircut, you hear me?"

Grace shook her head rapidly up and down. "No problem, Mom! But if you tell Daddy you think it'll be good for me, he'll let me do it. He always listens to you when it comes to me."

"Okay, now shush they're about to start the word scramble on Soul Train. I can hardly hear the television as it is. Where's that remote control?" Mrs. Dudley tossed the pillows and squinted.

Grace handed her mother the remote control. "Please talk to him today, okay? I'm going to the mall with Maria, Tanisha, Lori and Rashanda. We're chipping in to buy a going away present for Justine," Grace explained.

Her mother reclined on the sofa and squinted at the television. Her sight was going bad too, but she refused to wear her glasses for anything except reading.

Beaming from ear to ear, Grace raced to her room to get her wallet knowing that her mother hadn't heard her.

Chapter 3

Help Yourself

"This is just not enough money, Mother! The jeans that I want cost fifty dollars, and I won't have enough to buy a shirt to match if you only give me sixty dollars!" Maria stared at the money in her hand like it was diseased.

"Maria, you just bought new jeans last week. Money does not grow on trees," Mrs. Wesley explained. "And don't call me 'mother.' It sounds so old fashioned."

"But Mom, I called the store, and they have the jeans that I really want in my size now. They're holding them for me. They didn't have those jeans last week," Maria explained.

"Well, you should have saved your money to buy the jeans that you really wanted. Better yet, return the jeans that you bought last week and use that money toward the jeans that you want." Mrs. Wesley continued reading her newspaper. She took a sip from her coffee mug and blew across the top to cool it off.

"I can't. I've already worn them," Maria groaned. She walked toward her mother. "What's the big deal, Mom?" She put her hand over the newspaper. "Why can't you just give me twenty more dollars?"

Mrs. Wesley stared at Maria. "Maria Wesley, the big deal is this. First, you are spoiled." She counted off on her fingers to emphasize each point. "Second, you have a closet full of clothes. And third, you do not need another pair of designer jeans. I gave you sixty dollars. Now, you can save that money or you can spend it, but I am not giving you any more money this week. And that's final."

Maria was not thwarted. She hadn't heard a word her mother said. "Mom, why don't you just give me your charge card?"

"Because the last time I let you use my charge you spent almost one hundred dollars more than you were supposed to spend," Mrs. Wesley scolded. "Maria Chantal, you'd better take the sixty dollars that I gave you before I take it back." Her mother took a tiny sip from her coffee mug.

Maria couldn't believe what was happening. Her mom was cutting her off. Tears welled in her eyes. She sobbed quietly.

Mrs. Wesley looked at Maria skeptically and laughed. "Don't even try it, Maria. You have nothing to cry about. If anything, I should be crying. I'm the one who needs new clothes, but I sacrifice so that you and your brother can have nice things and a college fund for school. When I was growing up, I got new clothes only when my clothes were tattered and torn or too small. I didn't get new clothes every time my little heart yearned for something. You need to learn that life is tough! If you want extra money for clothes, then you can earn money by babysitting the neighbor's kids on the weekend and saving your money," she encouraged. "I'll tell you what. If you start making money and saving it, I'll match what you earn every week," she suggested. "Fifty cents on the dollar."

Maria glared at her mother. "I'm not trying to watch those neighborhood brats on the weekend. Besides, if I'm babysitting, I won't be able to see my friends."

"Maria, you need to get your priorities straight. Learn from your friend Tanisha. Doesn't Tanisha still work at Save Mart? How does she still manage to hang out with you guys and have a job? Mrs. Wesley asked.

"Mom, we don't call her Tanisha anymore. She goes by Teenie now. And yes, Teenie works at Save Mart. She was able to get that job because her family is poor. We're not poor," Maria stated.

"Excuse me. I can't keep these nicknames straight with you and your friends." Mrs. Wesley shook her head from side to side. "You're right, we're not poor, but we're not rich either." She folded her paper and stared at her daughter. "Maria, you got what you're getting, now scoot so I can finish studying for my exam."

A student at the state university in Newberry East, Mrs. Wesley was one semester away from completing her bachelor's degree. She'd dropped out of the University of Illinois – Navy Pier campus to get married and had quickly gotten pregnant with Maria. She was completing studies toward a Bachelor of Arts degree in Human Learning and Development. Sighing loudly, she folded the newspaper and settled into the sofa scattered with school books and papers. Mrs. Wesley could hear Maria mumbling under her breath as she picked up her study pen, chewed on the tip of it, twirled her hair and opened her textbook.

Maria balled the bills in her fist and stuffed them into the pocket of her jean shorts. She rolled her eyes at her mother as she walked upstairs to her room. I can't believe she is being so cheap! All I want is twenty more dollars. She doesn't understand my life. I have a fashion reputation to maintain! I can't buy new jeans without buying a new shirt to go with them!

At the top of the stairs, she saw her mother's purse strewn across her bed. Maria peeked into her brother's room. Neal wasn't there. Maria remembered that he was playing basketball with the neighbor. She heard her mother shuffling papers in the family room. She quickly walked into her mother's room, and pulled her wallet out of her purse. She counted three twenty dollar bills, two ten dollar bills, one five dollar bill and six one dollar bills. Maria slipped twenty dollars into her pocket and placed the wallet back in her mother's purse. She stopped again to listen for her mother before walking into her room. She picked up the phone and called Lori.

"Hey girl! I'm ready whenever you are," she said. "In fact, I'll just walk to your house now and wait for Rashanda's mom to pick us up." Maria spoke quickly into the phone.

"Are you sure?" Lori asked. "It's over ninety degrees outside. But if you're up for a walk in the heat, that's cool. Come on over."

"I'll be right there. My mom, Liz the lizard, is working on my last nerve, so I want to get out of here before she goes postal. She's all worked up about her school work." Maria glanced at her watch. "I'll be there in ten minutes," she explained.

Maria hung up the phone and applied a liberal slathering of Vaseline to her lips. She decided to change into a freshly ironed pink tank top and white shorts. She carefully removed the cash from her pocket and transferred it to her purse. She reapplied her deodorant and patted baby powder under her arms and in between her small breasts to absorb some of the perspiration from the ninety degree heat. She brushed her long hair and decided to pull it back with a head band to keep the hair from sticking to her face in the heat.

Maria bounced down the stairs and popped her head into the family room. "Mom, I'm going to the mall with my friends. Rashanda's mom is taking us and Lori's mom is picking us up. I'll be back in a few hours," she smiled.

"Okay, sweetie. Have fun!" Mrs. Wesley sang.

"We will. And thanks for the money, Mom," Maria said. She gave her mother a peck on the cheek before leaving the house.

"You're welcome, sweetie. Have fun at the mall." Mrs. Wesley smiled and squeezed her daughter's small waist. Maria patted the money in her pocket and giggled as she closed the door and walked into the sweltering heat.

The air was thick, and the humidity clung to Maria's hair like a magnet. She could feel the curls loosening as she walked down the sidewalk. She quickened her pace to get out of the heat as fast as she could.

This wasn't the first time that Maria had taken money from her mother's purse. A few times she had taken a couple of dollars to enhance her weekly allowance, but she had never taken as much as twenty dollars. Normally, her mother only had ten or fifteen dollars in her wallet by the end of the week. Maria paused on the sidewalk to think.

Maria knew her mother's routine. After her weekly Saturday excursion to the grocery store, Mrs. Wesley wrote the check for twenty or thirty dollars over the register amount. She called this her "weekly walk around money." Maria knew that the most you could write above your grocery bill was fifty dollars. Mrs. Wesley had already given Maria fifty dollars and still had over ninety dollars in cash in her wallet. Maria used the back of her hand to wipe sweat from her forehead. Why does my mother have so much money in her wallet?

Chapter 4

The Metamorphosis

Inhaling deeply, she wrapped the leather belt around her tiny waist, slowly exhaling before securing it into the smallest hole. It's tight, but I can breathe. She admired her reflection. The black belt looked perfect in the new faded jean shorts. Her caramel skin glistened against the white tank top tucked neatly into the shorts. She wore one white sandal on her left foot and one white sneaker with a white sock on her right foot. White was her favorite color. As she stood in front of the floor length mirror, she placed one foot in front of the other. Her toenails were painted a bright pink and looked good against her tan skin. She paused and decided that the socks made her thin legs appear shapelier. She flopped on the bean bag chair at the foot of her bed and unfastened the sandal. The grandfather clock in the living room chimed 11:45.

As Rashanda fingered her new haircut, she remembered to apply deodorant and then quickly sprayed cologne on her neck and wrists. Next, she carefully applied eyeliner and lipstick, lining her lips like Maria had demonstrated. Scowling at the pink eye glass case on her dresser, she opened the top drawer and tossed it inside. Her small almond shaped eyes looked much larger with eyeliner. She sashayed down the hall and into the kitchen.

"Mom! Are you ready?" Rashanda grabbed a handful of grapes from the fruit bowl on the kitchen table and shoved them in her mouth. "I told everyone we'd pick them up at noon," she whined.

Rashanda's mom slowly chopped an onion. "I'll be ready in two minutes, just let me finish chopping this onion for the crock pot. Who am I picking up again?" Mrs. Jordan asked.

"We have to pick up Maria, Lori, Grace and Teenie. But Lori just called and Maria's already at her house so we just have to make three stops." She chewed her grape hungrily.

Mrs. Jordan wiped her hand on a dish towel and stared at Rashanda. "Look at you. I'm still not used to you without your glasses. And that make-up! Do you really have to wear make-up to go to the mall, Rashanda Rochelle? Don't you think you have on a little too much of that black stuff around your eyes? I mean, really! You look like a raccoon," Mrs. Jordan scolded.

"Mom, I do not. It's called eye liner and this is how everyone wears it. And you may as well get used to me without those glasses, because I'm never wearing those big pop bottles outside of this house again," Rashanda stated firmly. "The only reason I'm not tossing them in the trash is I might need them if I lose a contact."

"Well, everyone in our family wears glasses." Mrs. Jordan pushed her glasses up on her nose. "And I'm just worried about you putting those contacts on your eyes every day. I think you should just wear them for special occasions, honey."

"I'll be fine, Mom. Are you ready?" Rashanda popped another grape in her mouth as her mother continued to chop the onion.

For her fifteenth birthday, Rashanda had pleaded with her parents to let her get contact lenses. She'd deliberately broken her glasses and when they visited the optometrist for a replacement pair, she'd pleaded her case.

⁓⁂⁓

"Mom! I'm fifteen! Contacts are perfectly safe for someone my age. And they're cheaper than these glasses that keep breaking," she begged.

Dr. Page pretended to write notes on his pad. He'd seen this stunt before with teenage patients. As young as twelve, the female patients would somehow manage to break their glasses and beg their parents for contacts.

"Rashanda, glasses are safer for your eyes than contacts, and they're better for your eye sight too. Isn't that right, Dr. Page?" Mrs. Jordan asked. Rashanda slouched in her seat.

"Actually, contacts are very safe for someone Rashanda's age, Mrs. Jordan. In fact, the contact lens package carries replacement insurance in case one of the lenses is lost or scratched. We don't offer such insurance for the eye glasses," Dr. Page winked at Rashanda. "I've noticed that the frame that Rashanda chose tends to break at least once a year."

Rashanda's face lit up like a Christmas tree. Dr. Page was lobbying with her! She sat upright in her chair. "Mom, if you let me get contact lenses I will be so careful with them, I promise. And if I lose one, I'll pay for the replacement from my allowance. Please, Mom! We can say that they're my birthday present. I am so tired of wearing those glasses!" she exclaimed.

Rashanda placed her hands in the prayer position before continuing. "Please Mom. Please let me get contact lenses."

"Well, I should ask your daddy. He thinks we're getting glasses," Mrs. Jordan said.

Dr. Page stood up and walked toward Mrs. Jordan. "Here's an idea. Rashanda's prescription is pretty standard, so I can send you home with a free trial pair of contact lenses to see how they fit. And you can discuss it with your husband. We'd have to order the frames that she chose for the glasses anyway, so at least this way she'll go home with vision assistance today," Dr. Page suggested.

"Okay, but Rashanda, your dad and I have to discuss this," Mrs. Jordan reminded.

"I'll have my assistant fit Rashanda for the trial contact lenses and show her how to put them on, clean and sterilize them," Dr. Page finished.

۞

The memory made Rashanda smile. She ate another grape. Her parents had already told her that she could start getting her hair relaxed and wear lipstick and eyeliner when she turned fifteen.

Between the make-up, new hairdo and contact lenses, Rashanda felt like a new woman. Her friends hadn't seen her makeover, and she couldn't wait to get their feedback.

In the kitchen, Mrs. Jordan wiped her hands on her apron and untied it. *My mother is the only mother in the world who still wears an apron. She's so old fashioned!*

Rashanda's father was in their bedroom watching television. "I'm taking Rashanda to the mall," Mrs. Jordan yelled toward the back of the house before grabbing her purse and heading to the garage.

"Mom, can we take the Lincoln?" Rashanda asked.

Mrs. Jordan kicked off her slippers and slipped on her loafers. "No. Your daddy may want to go somewhere so I'm just going to drive my car."

"Why can't he drive the Torino if he wants to go somewhere? You'll be back in twenty minutes. How come you never get to drive the Lincoln?" Rashanda asked.

"The Lincoln is your daddy's car. He works hard, and his

car should be available to him if he needs it. Did you use the bathroom?" Mrs. Jordan asked.

Rashanda ignored her mother's question. "Well, you work hard around the house too. And why is the Lincoln his car and the Torino your car? What's up with that? Why do you have ownership of vehicles? You should be able to drive any car you want to drive whenever you want to drive it. If he wants to drive the Lincoln during the week, that's cool, but on the weekend, you should definitely be able to drive it if you want to. It's not fair that Daddy gets to style and profile all week, and we have to schlep around in that beat up old Torino," Rashanda argued.

Mrs. Jordan laughed. "Rashanda, one day when you get married you'll understand."

"No, I won't. My husband and I will share two cars and we'll switch cars whenever we need to," Rashanda insisted. "In fact, I'm going to liberate you. I'm going to ask Daddy if we can take the Lincoln." Rashanda raced up the stairs two at a time before Mrs. Jordan could respond. "Daddy!" she yelled.

Rashanda tapped at the open door and walked into the bedroom. Mr. Jordan was watching NASCAR racing. "Daddy, do you care if mom drives the Lincoln to take my friends and me to the mall?"

"I don't care, Pumpkin. Does the Torino need gas or something?" Mr. Jordan stared at the television. The cars whirred around the track at breathtaking speeds.

"No. I just want to ride in the Lincoln." Rashanda didn't understand how her dad could watch racing. It made her dizzy.

"That's fine. If I need to go somewhere I can just take the Torino. Doesn't make me no never mind," Mr. Jordan waved her off.

Rashanda bounced down the stairs. "It's all set. Daddy said we can take the Lincoln."

❧

As Rashanda walked down the hall, Mrs. Jordan glared. She'd heard the entire exchange. She spoke through clenched teeth. "Rashanda Rochelle, get your narrow tail in my car right now before I change my mind."

Rashanda paused before speaking. "Didn't you hear me? Daddy said we can take the Lincoln."

"Don't make me repeat myself, Rashanda Rochelle! Get in the Torino or we're not going!" Mrs. Jordan barked.

Rashanda climbed into the front seat of the Torino. Mrs. Jordan climbed into the driver's seat and faced Rashanda, resting her hands on the steering wheel.

"Let me explain something to you. Your father and I have been married for seventeen years. Our marriage does not need your input. We have a system that works for us. He drives his car, and I drive mine," she said. "I decide when I want to make a change in our system, not you. I don't need you to ask your father for permission for me to do anything. I know fully well that I could drive either car, but I choose to drive the Torino. It's my choice, and I don't need to explain my choice to you." Mrs. Jordan put the car in reverse and backed out of the garage.

"I'm sorry, Ma. I just wanted to ride in the Lincoln," Rashanda explained.

"Well, you need to learn when to stop minding other people's business," Mrs. Jordan said. You should be grateful that you have a ride to the mall. When I was growing up, we had to walk everywhere or take the bus." Her tone was softer.

Rashanda had never seen her mom so angry with her. She was stunned speechless and rode in silence the three short blocks to

Lori's house. Mrs. Jordan had scarcely put the car in park, before Rashanda jumped out to ring Lori's doorbell.

Lori stood in the foyer and stared at Rashanda through the screen door. "Oh my God, you look great!" Rashanda stared at her friend with a puzzled expression. She had forgotten about her makeover. Lori's greeting confirmed that Rashanda's new look met with approval. "Maria, come and check out Rashanda," Lori squealed.

Rashanda twirled slowly in the foyer, as Maria walked out of the kitchen drinking a glass of water. Maria gave a construction worker whistle. "Hubba, Hubba!" Maria giggled. "You look great, Rashanda. Your parents finally let you get your hair relaxed, huh?"

"Yup! I got my hair relaxed yesterday, and I got contacts two days ago. I wanted to surprise you guys," Rashanda confessed. "I feel like a butterfly that just busted out of an ugly cocoon."

"You weren't ugly, Rashanda, but your glasses were a little too big for your face.   Now everyone can see how pretty your eyes are. You look great!" Lori offered.

"And now I won't have to hide my glasses in my purse and rely on you guys to be my eyes when I walk around the mall," Rashanda said.

"Hallelujah to that! I felt like a service dog leading the blind walking around with you!" Maria placed her glass in the sink and joined the girls in the foyer.

"You're very funny! My mom had to plead with my dad, but once they sent me home with the trial pair there was no way I was going back to wearing those glasses again," Rashanda wiped her hands together. "Are you guys ready to go?"

"Let's go. Teenie has to work at Save Mart tonight from five to nine so we only have a few hours to hang out at the mall," Lori said.

"Did you call Grace and Teenie and let them know we're on the way?" Maria asked.

"No, but I'll do that right now. You guys go on outside, and I'll meet you in the car," Lori suggested.

Maria peeked out the window. "Rashanda, why does your mom always drive that old Torino? How come she hardly ever profiles and drives the Lincoln?"

"I only wish I knew. By the way, she's not in the best mood today, so don't mention the Lincoln to her." Rashanda rolled her eyes into the top of her head and traced her finger at her ear in a circular motion several times, the universal sign for cuckoo or crazy.

"It must be a mother thing. Liz was tripping today too." Maria popped a stick of Juicy Fruit gum in her mouth and spoke while chewing. "They're probably on the rag. You know how older women get when they're on their period," Maria exclaimed.

"Maybe you're right. But I'm glad we'll be hanging at the mall all day." Rashanda took a piece of gum from Maria. "I'm so glad I got my braces off and I can enjoy gum again," Rashanda beamed. "Lori, tell Teenie and Grace to make sure they're ready because I'm starving."

Lori held up a finger to silence Rashanda. "Hey Teenie, Mrs. Jordan is here so we're on our way. We just have to scoop Grace so we should be there in ten minutes." She stared at Rashanda and shook her head. "Since when are you not hungry?" she asked and hung up the phone. "And you know Teenie will be ready. She's always waiting for us curb side."

Chapter 5

Dime Store Therapy

Tanisha hung up the phone and raced into the bathroom to brush her teeth. She rubbed baby oil on her arms and legs and sprayed her body with her new Lauren cologne. She'd grown tired of her signature Love's Baby Soft scent and had treated herself to a bottle of Lauren and a bottle of Halston. Just two more weeks, and she would be a sophomore at River North High School. She wanted to make sure that when she walked the halls of River North she didn't smell like a junior high school girl. She smelled her wrist and smiled, grabbing the bottle again to quickly mist her neck and inner thighs. A daytime mall outing to cruise for cute boys requires a floral scent. She sniffed her wrist again and smiled.

She checked her watch. It was 12:09 p.m. She knew that Grace would probably make them wait at least five minutes. She decided to use the bathroom. She didn't want to have to pee at the mall. She hated public restrooms. The sight and smell made her squeamish. She tried to avoid using public restrooms at all cost, but with her tiny bladder, it was often necessary. Fortunately, the toilet seats in the employee lounge at Save Mart were white, so Tanisha was able to use the restrooms at work without being reminded of her public restroom phobia. She'd never completely gotten over a scary encounter with an oversize black toilet seat that happened when she was five years old. Whenever she saw a black toilet seat she had to push the scary memory from her mind.

⸎

"Mommy, I can't hold it!" Tanisha whined.

"Tanisha, I told you to go to the bathroom before we left!" Billie Mae was pregnant with Allen as they walked through Evergreen Plaza.

"I did go. But I have to go again, and I can't hold it!" Tanisha squeezed her knees together and placed both of her hands over her crotch area.

"Tanisha, we're going to miss the bus!" Billie Mae exhaled loudly. She looked around quickly and tugged her daughter by the elbow. "You can just use the bathroom in Kresge." They walked swiftly to the back of the discount drug store.

"Hurry up. I'm going to buy a pack of gum. Meet me at the front when you're done." Billie walked to the front of the store, checking her watch and shaking her head.

Tanisha entered the dimly lit restroom and rushed into the nearer of two stalls. She pushed the door to the first stall and wrinkled her nose at the sight of feces and urine floating in the toilet. She gagged. She walked to the next stall and prayed that the stall was clean as she squeezed her legs together to avoid wetting her pants. The large black toilet seat was splattered with urine but the bowl had been flushed. Tanisha grabbed toilet tissue and quickly wiped the seat dry, sitting down just as the urine stream started to slowly slip down her small thighs. She relieved her bladder as her feet dangled in front of her. As she reached for the toilet tissue to wipe herself, she lost her balance and slipped into the toilet. Her buttocks touched the cold water in the bowl as she struggled to pull herself out of the toilet. Tears streamed down her cheeks as she wiped herself dry with toilet paper and quickly washed her hands in the sink.

She walked swiftly to the front of the store and found her mother near the checkout lanes.

"Mommy, I fell…" Billie interrupted her. "What took you so long? I just saw our bus go by. Now we'll have to wait another twenty minutes!" Billie pulled out a pack of cigarettes and fumbled in her purse for her lighter. She dropped the lighter on the ground but was unable to pick it up because of her large pregnant belly. Her face wet with tears, she picked up the lighter and handed it to her mother.

∞∞

Tanisha wiped her hands dry and fluffed her hair. She was almost sixteen years old and still remembered that incident as if it were yesterday. Tanisha glanced at her watch. It was 12:13. She smiled as the time on her watch was her birthday, December 13th.

She carefully folded a pair of khakis and a white golf shirt and placed them neatly in her backpack. She was glad that Mrs. Perkins had already agreed to drop her off at Save Mart after the mall. Tanisha's friend Vicky was working until nine o'clock so she could bum a ride home with her. Tanisha tossed a few quarters into her purse so that she could rent a small locker at the mall for her back pack.

She tugged at one of the fringe strings from her cutoff shorts and smoothed her red and white checkered halter top before racing down the stairs and slipping on her well worn loafers. The checkered halter top reminded Tanisha of the lining of a wicker picnic basket. She ran back up the stairs and remembered to toss a bra in her backpack to slip on at work.

The house was empty save the family's new pet Butch, who rolled around in the living room and wrestled with a tennis ball. The puppy ran up to Tanisha with the wet tennis ball in his mouth and dropped it at her feet. At nine months old, he had already mastered the game of toss and fetch.

Billie had paid two hundred dollars for the pure bred Old English Sheep dog puppy, buying him from a colleague at the cable company where she worked. The family dog named Strongest had never been found, and Billie had decided that the family needed a replacement pet. She'd paid her colleague twenty-five dollars each pay period, for four months, for the expensive puppy.

Unlike Strongest, who was often sullen and temperamental, Butch had quickly won over everyone in the family, including Tanisha, who was in love with the pet. She grabbed the soaking tennis ball and tossed it into the dining room. The puppy raced into the room as the tennis ball rolled into the open faced bookshelf. His oversized body slammed into the bookcase jostling the knick knacks that were displayed. Butch grabbed the squishy ball in his mouth and raced back to Tanisha, dropping it at her feet.

Tanisha glanced at her watch again. It was 12:14. Her friends should be pulling up any minute. Butch could play fetch for hours. She decided that she would toss the ball one more time. She tossed it again and smiled as Butch obediently raced to the ball and brought it back to her feet. She patted him on the head and rubbed under his snout before leaving to wait for her friends outside. She sat on the front porch and watched an ant carry a popcorn kernel through the grass. The kernel was three times the size of the ant. Tanisha smiled as the ant skillfully pulled the oversized morsel through the grass. The popcorn kernel made her think of David Barton's birthday party a year earlier. Tanisha's thoughts drifted to that day.

❦

Tanisha finished in the bathroom just as David walked down the hall with Belvedere. She immediately patted Belvedere's head and nuzzled his nose in her face. She giggled as he licked her cheek and wagged his body excitedly.

"Hey there, buddy! I can't believe that your owner didn't invite you to the party. And you're his best friend!" Tanisha cooed in a voice that was considered baby talk. "He should be ashamed of himself for leaving you upstairs all alone."

David leaned against the wall with his arms folded and smiled at the natural chemistry between Teenie and Belvedere. "I know. I feel so guilty. But Patty has really bad asthma, and Belvedere triggers it, so I always put him away when she comes over. But I'll just close the door to the laundry room and he can hang out back here," David finished. Tanisha kissed Belvedere on the top of his head and she and David walked down the hall to join the party. They bumped into Patty near the kitchen.

"There you are, birthday boy! Where've you been? I was looking all over for you," Patty whined. "I introduced Andre to Kim like you suggested, and they hit it off! I think I've made a love connection." Patty rubbed her hands together and smiled at David. Tanisha noticed that Patty beamed as she gazed into David's face. Tanisha felt invisible for a brief moment.

"Patty, let me introduce you to Teenie. Patty, this is Teenie. Teenie, this is Patty," David explained.

Patty turned her head to the side and looked at Tanisha. "Hello." Patty's gaze turned steely as she stared at Tanisha. "Teenie? That's an interesting name. Is that your real name?" Patty's eyes roamed Tanisha from head to toe.

"Hi, Patty. It's nice to meet you. Actually, my real name is Tanisha. But some of my friends started calling me Teenie recently." Tanisha smiled at Patty warmly.

Patty did not return Tanisha's smile. "How do you two know each other?" Patty asked nervously, slowly twirling the strap of her small brown Gucci purse. She directed her question to David, but carefully eyed Tanisha's outfit as she awaited David's response.

"How'd we meet?" Tanisha repeated. "I'll answer that, David." Tanisha maintained eye contact with Patty. She tilted her head to the side and placed her index finger to her lip as though deep in thought. "Hmm! Let me think." She smiled to herself. Was Patty threatened by her? Patty carried a three hundred dollar designer purse, but she felt threatened by a fourteen year old. Tanisha felt empowered.

"Oh, I remember," she said. "I met David through my friend Leslie on a John & Judy ski trip. He gave me some ski pointers. We've hung out so much since then that I almost forgot how we met exactly." Tanisha giggled, grabbing David's bicep and squeezing his arm. "He's such a good skier. I felt like Suzy Chapstick after just one lesson with him. I'm a quick study right, big guy?" Tanisha gazed at David and gently rested her head on his chest and batted her eyes, wrapping her arms gently around his waist.

David stood speechless. "Yeah. You caught on pretty quickly," he stammered.

Patty swallowed and dropped her eyes to the floor. Tanisha thought that Patty was going to cry. "He's like a big brother to me," Tanisha continued. She held her head on his chest for another second before finishing. "He's told me all about you, Patty. David, you told me that Patty was pretty, but you lied. She's gorgeous," Tanisha offered.

David clenched his jaw and steadied his gaze at Tanisha. His eyes were as big as saucers.

Patty raised her head. "He's a play brother to you?" Patty repeated, a smile creeping across her lips, the sigh of relief audible and her confidence restored. "He described me as pretty?" she beamed. "Oh, you're so kind. Thank you." Patty tossed her long hair and smiled at David. The sparkle was back in her eyes. "He told you about me? I hope it was good stuff."

"Of course it was good stuff," Tanisha assured. "He told me that you guys went to prom together, and that he was your debutante cotillion escort. I bet you guys looked great all dressed up."

"I think so. I think the pictures came out nice," Patty's smile widened. "I'm sorry, what did you say your name was again?"

Tanisha could almost feel the air deflate from Patty's lungs as she exhaled.

"It's Tanisha. Tanisha Carlson," Tanisha repeated.

"Well, Tanisha, if you're like a sister to David then let me give you a hug." Patty reached out and encircled Tanisha in a lukewarm hug. Tanisha returned Patty's embrace.

"By the way, that's a great sundress. I saw that dress at Field's, but they didn't have it in my size. You have good taste," Patty complimented.

"Thanks, Patty." Tanisha smoothed her hands over the fabric of her dress and smiled again.

"Patty, I'll meet you by the pool. Why don't you find Leslie and let her know that Teenie, I mean Tanisha, is here. Tanisha wanted some popcorn so we'll be outside in a few minutes," David explained.

"Okay. It was nice to meet you, Tanisha." Patty swung her hips and walked confidently down the hallway.

"Ditto." Tanisha waved goodbye to Patty.

David gently grabbed Tanisha's arm and pulled her into the kitchen. "What was that about? I've never told you about Patty," David whispered.

"Ouch! You're pinching my arm, whacko! Sure you did." Tanisha rubbed her bicep. "You just told me about her on the driveway."

"What's with the performance? First, you act like you're flirting with me, squeezing my arm and laying your head on my chest, and then you make it sound like I talk about Patty all the time like she's my girlfriend. What are you doing?"

Tanisha bit her bottom lip. "I didn't like how she was giving me the once over so I just wanted to mess with her head. But then I felt bad, because she looked so sad. Actually, she looked like she was going to cry." Tanisha giggled and shook her head. "She seems nice, a little pretentious and insecure, like most Homer Glen High School girls, but she warmed up once I told her that you were like a brother to me. Besides, what was I supposed to say?" Tanisha made quotation marks in the air. "I'm fourteen, and he's biding his time waiting until I'm old enough to date? That's a bit too much information don't cha think?" Tanisha lightly tapped her fingers into David's chest.

David stared at Tanisha and cut his eyes, pointing a finger at her chest. "Well, you could have just said we were friends."

Tanisha shook her head from side to side. "You just told me that you and Patty were just friends and when she met me I could tell by the way she was studying me like a textbook that she felt threatened. She was eyeing me like I was the competition trying to move in on her man," Tanisha said. "At first, I was going to let her keep sweating, but that would have been mean, so I decided to say something that would make her feel better. Besides, if she thinks you're like a brother to me then we can pal around, and she won't try to spike my Kool-Aid with anti-freeze!"

David laughed. "You kill me. That's pretty quick thinking for a fourteen year old. You are definitely an old soul like your friend Maria said."

"I'm pretty quick on my feet if I do say so myself," she giggled. "But really, I just know how girls think. And now that we've redefined our friendship, you will be like a brother to me. You're going to help me weed out losers like Byron Bird," Tanisha whispered. "By the way, he's not here is he?"

"No, he's in Mississippi visiting his grandparents for the summer,"

David assured. "Speaking of Maria, Todd's here. He's probably getting his flirt on, so give him some space if you see him, okay?" David instructed. "And for the record, I'm going to weed out everybody. A brother is going to have to be like Superman to pass my screening test to get to know you." David pounded on his chest.

Tanisha laughed. "First of all, Todd is so Todd absorbed that he probably won't remember me. But if I see him getting too out of control I may have to notify my girl Maria. I can't just openly watch her boyfriend flirt with other babes and not tell her. That's not how I operate." Teenie slanted her eyes at David. "And as for you Superman, we just made a deal on the driveway, remember? You get to do your thing, and I get to do mine. Lest we forget, I just saw you almost trying to kiss Patty and I'm not tripping. And if you act like a lunatic, I won't introduce any perspective suitors to you," she threatened.

"Too late princess. You set the rules, and now you have to play by them," David said.

Teenie giggled. "I have created a monster. But I'm not worried because you'll be in college next year anyway."

"But I have a whole year to keep some of these deadbeats away from you." David raised his eyebrow.

"That's if you can find me." Tanisha rubbed her hands together and slanted her eyes.

"I know where you work, and I know where you live and go to school, remember?" Tanisha stared at David and opened her mouth to speak. She was interrupted by a loud squeal.

"Tanisha! What are you doing here? I thought you had a blind date?" Tanisha turned around as Leslie and Vicky entered the kitchen together.

"That's my cue. I better go back to playing host since I am the birthday boy." David patted Tanisha on the shoulder. "Teenie, I'll talk to you later."

"What about my popcorn?" Tanisha asked.

David slowly turned around. "You know where everything is, your highness. Feel free to have at it and make some if you want. Save me some if you make it." David sauntered toward the door. He turned around slowly and winked at Tanisha. "I'm glad you made it to my party, Teenie."

Leslie and Vicky stared at each other and eyed Tanisha curiously. Vicky spoke first. "How is it that you know where everything is in David's kitchen, little Miss?"

"Why does he call you Teenie, and why did he just wink at you?" Leslie continued.

Tanisha shook her head from side to side. "It's an inside joke. I picked up the nickname Teenie at Student Government Leadership Camp this summer, and I love it. So feel free to call me Teenie from now on," Tanisha continued. "Let's go outside, and I'll point out my blind date and fill you in on that disaster. By the way, are there any cute boys here?"

☙❧

The ant placed the popcorn kernel on top of the mound. Seconds later, the yellow kernel was covered with small black ants. Teenie's watch read 12:22.

The Jordan's car turned the corner just as Teenie's thighs were beginning to sweat from the heat. She bounced off the stoop and reached the car as Mrs. Perkins pulled into an empty stall in front of her house. Teenie greeted Mrs. Perkins and climbed into the back seat. As she settled in, she inhaled and whispered. "All right, I smell Lauren cologne, which one of you babes copied my scent?"

Chapter 6

A Mother's Secret

Twenty years later, the small barn looked the same as she remembered. The once brilliant red paint was now weathered and chipped after years of neglect and decline. She carefully tugged at the large barn door, wishing she'd worn gloves to protect her freshly manicured nails and hands from splinters. She slowly pulled the door open and peered inside, anchoring the heavy door in the dirt. Sunshine streamed into the barn as though it had been knocking and waiting patiently for an invitation to come inside.

Before entering, she hesitated several seconds, just enough time to allow any frightened mice to scatter and hide. Although not afraid of mice, the scampering of a four legged creature with a skinny tail still startled her from time to time. She was grateful that the sun shone in the sky like a bright yellow ball, and the sunshine created a small pathway through the door. She flipped the light switch. Nothing. No surprise there. I don't know why I thought the light would work. She expected that the light bulb had been burned out for years. Her eyes scanned the barn, and she wondered why there was no light coming in through the windows. She stared harder and noticed that the windows were all covered with black construction paper. Probably to discourage theft. She chuckled to herself. Only her father would view these discarded items as valuable and worth protecting and concealing. Who would steal this stuff? Maria's mom, Liz Wesley, snickered as she walked into the dusty barn.

Her father, John Willard was president of the block club and had been the eyes and ears of the Chatham community for a lifetime. He knew every person who lived within three blocks of his home in either direction. He walked the neighborhood every day for exercise and made a point of speaking and introducing himself to anyone who was outside. John Willard was the first to welcome new neighbors who moved into the middle class enclave. His peers called him John to his face, but when referencing him, he was always Mr. Willard. The teenage boys called him "The Mayor" behind his back, but to his face, he was Mr. Willard. He took pride in the fact that his neighborhood boasted the lowest crime rate in Chicago, and he enjoyed his role as head of the block club. He knew his nickname was The Mayor, and it didn't bother him one bit.

It's best to know the people in your community so you can keep the rifraff out. Communities lose their neighborly feel when you don't know the people living next door to you. When trashy people move in, it affects the thread of our community and ultimately our property values. I'll look out for you and you look out for your neighbor and so on and so on. If we all do a little bit of looking out, we'll all be all right. Liz remembered her father repeating this to new neighbors who moved in. It had become the neighborhood creed.

Her father had been president of the block club for as long as Liz could remember. Once, a new neighbor tried to run against Mr. Willard for block club president. He only received one vote, at the block club meeting, his own. Every year after that, Mr. Willard ran unopposed.

The Willard family had a small garage in the back of their property that was shaped like a traditional barn, so the family always referred to it as the barn. The barn was even painted red. Mr. Willard preferred to park his car in the front of his home, so he could visit with the neighbors who sat on the front porch in the evening. He'd had traditional barn doors installed on the side of the barn facing the house and had replaced the car entry door of the barn with drywall and two small barn windows. In its heyday, the tiny garage truly resembled a bright red barn.

The barn had been used as the neighborhood storage shed for many years and now served as a graveyard for broken or unwanted tools and equipment. There were six or seven lawn mowers, pieces of rusted lawn furniture stacked neatly in the corner and a dozen children's bicycles lined against the north wall of the barn. The neighbors didn't hesitate to ask Mr. Willard for use of the barn as storage.

Mr. Willard, sir, would it be okay if I put my lawn mower in your barn temporarily? I promise to get it out of your way come spring. I'll pay you a small rental fee if you like.

Now that won't be necessary. That barn is sitting out there taking up space. You go right ahead and put whatever you need in there. Now I won't be held liable if something happens to anything in there, but you can store whatever you like. That's what neighbors are for.

Word spread quickly on the block that Mr. Willard's abandoned barn was available for storage, and the occasional lawn mower morphed into outgrown bicycles, rusted patio furniture and broken tools. The spring retrieval promise was made year after year, yet spring came and went and the items remained in hibernation usually replaced by newer, fancier models. It was as though the bicycles, lawn mowers and lawn furniture mated during the winter, producing offspring of more rusted bicycles, lawn chairs and rusty garden tools. Mr. Willard didn't mind. He took the time to organize the items by category, even labeling the items with small identification tags. As the storage grew, he thought it wise to cover the windows facing the alley with black construction paper and place a lock on the barn door to discourage neighborhood pranksters and thieves. As the years passed, the neighbors forgot about the items, sometimes moving away and abandoning their stored possessions. It never occurred to Mr. Willard to discard or sell any of the items. He periodically dusted them and removed the cobwebs that collected.   He relished his role as the neighborhood storage purveyor.

Liz grinned as she noticed a small John Deere riding lawn mower nestled in the corner. Half of the tractor was covered with a green tarp. She walked over and peered underneath the tarp.

She remembered that her dad had just purchased the rider the previous summer. That was the summer when his arthritis would no longer allow him to mow his small plot of land with a self propelled gas mower. Every neighbor on the block offered to mow Mr. Willard's lawn, but his pride would not allow that, so he'd bought the expensive riding mower. Liz rubbed the rider as a tear slid down her cheek.

It had been three weeks since they'd moved her dad into a senior citizen's building. A hip replacement and arthritic knees made it nearly impossible for him to manage the stairs. Plus, an enlarged prostate pressed on his bladder which increased his desire to urinate. Mr. Willard refused to even consider having a chair lift installed to ferry him up the stairs to the only bathroom in the house. After three puddle episodes on the stairs, he decided that it was time for him to move into an apartment. Liz had begged him to move in with her family in Newberry East, but he had adamantly refused.

"I am a man, and I will not live in another man's house. I will not have you install one of those stair lift things like I'm an invalid. I'm not an invalid. I just move up the stairs slower than I did before," Mr. Willard insisted.

"But Dad, Neal wants you to move in with us. It's no problem, we've already discussed it and it will be fine," she coaxed.

"Elizabeth Jane, I appreciate the offer, I really do. And Neal is kind to even consider it, but I will not move into your husband's home, and that's final. Now, there's a senior citizen building that I've looked into, and they have a unit in there that I can rent. It's not too far from you so you can check on me whenever you want. But I am not going to move in with you and your family, and there will be no more discussion on this issue."

Liz knew better than to continue badgering her father. When she was sixteen and her mother died, she saw her father's strong will intensify when he refused to allow her mother's sister to raise her and her brother. "Flora Ann, these are my children, and I will raise them. If I need your help I will ask for it," he'd insisted.

Her brother Emmett was thirteen years old when their mother died. Liz became a mother figure to him. She ensured that his homework was done, made his breakfast in the morning, and packed his lunch. When her mother died, the neighbors adopted their family and at least three or four times each week a different neighbor brought dinner to their house, a practice that continued nearly two decades after her mother's death. Liz loved taking care of Emmett and chose to attend the University of Illinois at Navy Pier so that she could live at home to be near her brother until he finished high school. She cried tears of joy when Emmett graduated from Whitney Young High School. She beamed like a proud parent when they learned that he was accepted to Stanford University in Palo Alto, California. He'd fallen in love with the west coast and was now raising a family in California.

Liz missed her brother immensely, but she felt proud that he had moved on with his life. She was glad that she'd played a part in his upbringing, and had helped him cope with the grief of losing his mother as a teenager. Through prayers, counseling and the church family that surrounded them, they had all learned to accept the loss of Mrs. Willard as God's will.

"Now, Liz, I do need your help with a special project," Mr. Willard said.

"Anything Dad, I'll do whatever you need me to do," Mrs. Wesley replied.

"I'm going to sell the house, and I'm going to need you to help me get it ready to be sold. We're going to have to go through forty years worth of my collectibles, and I'm going to have to have a rummage sale. I think they call it a garage sale nowadays, which doesn't make any sense to me since I don't have a garage. But anyhow, we'll tag and sell the stuff that I can't fit in my new apartment and anything that you and Emmett don't want. Now, I'm not going to sell the stuff in that barn just yet because I want to give the neighbors a chance to come back and claim their things. I think that's only fair."

"Goodness gracious, Dad. Do you really think people are going to come back and claim any of that stuff after all these years?" Liz asked.

"Well, it's not for me to say. But I'll try to reach them and give them that choice. What I need you to do is to help me organize stuff so that the place looks nice and then label stuff for the rummage sale. Can you do that for me, baby girl?" her father asked.

"Of course, Dad. I'd be glad to help." Liz smiled at her father's term of endearment. She was in her mid thirties, but she was still her father's baby girl.

"Now, I know you're in school and you're busy with your own family so I plan to pay you for your help. In fact, whatever money I make from the rummage sale, we'll split fifty-fifty. I'm also going to put your name on my bank accounts in case something happens to me. This way you and your brother won't have any problem getting to any of my money when I pass on," he continued. "And since we're talking about money, I've decided to start spending some of my money now. Heck, I can't take it with me." Mr. Willard chuckled. "In fact, I'm going to send you and your brother a little money every month. I'm going to send you a little more because I want you to know that I appreciate how you took care of your brother after your mother died. I know you missed out on a few things taking care of Emmett, and I never really showed you how much I appreciate what you did. That was a lot for a young girl to take on, and you made me proud. I'm not going to be around forever so I want to lighten your load a little bit now," Mr. Willard explained.

"Dad, stop talking like that! Nothing's going to happen to you," Liz said. "I don't like to hear you talking like you could die any day."

"I'm just saying. You never know. I'm not a young man anymore," Mr. Willard reminded.

"But Dad, Neal and I are doing just fine. You don't need to help us out," Liz protested.

"I know baby, and I don't want to offend your husband, but

you're my daughter and I want to do this for you, and I insist. You don't even have to tell him about the money if you don't want to, you can just spend it on Maria and Neal, Jr. if you'd like," he paused. "Now understand, I don't believe in keeping secrets from your husband, but I respect Neal, and he may not understand my need to do this for my only daughter. Besides, I think a woman should always have a stash of mad money that she can get her hands on. So when I open my account at the bank, I'm going to open one for you and add money to it every month. Now you can tell Neal about it if you want to, that's up to you, but I don't want to hear another word about it. It's done."

True to his word, Mr. Willard had opened an account in Liz's name and placed twenty five hundred dollars in it, setting up an automatic deposit into her account from his in the amount of six hundred dollars each month. She'd shared the existence of the account with her husband Neal who encouraged her to spend the money however she chose. She decided not to share the inheritance set-up with Maria and Neal, Jr. as she and her husband struggled to teach their children the value of money and the sense of accomplishment that came from earning money. Even though she hadn't earned the money, Liz enjoyed the liberating feeling of having the extra cash. It relieved the guilt she sometimes felt each week when she wrote her check for thirty or forty dollars over the grocery costs. This weekly habit had always made her feel as though she were giving herself an allowance. Now with the money she received from her dad, she treated herself to weekly manicures and was able to indulge Maria's designer jean addiction, although she was trying to wean Maria from her shopping habit.

Liz had become Mrs. Neal Wesley at the tender age of nineteen and had delivered Maria two weeks shy of her twentieth birthday. As more women began to enter the workforce in larger numbers, Liz found herself desiring a career of some sort now that Maria and Neal were teenagers. However, with no marketable skills, she knew that she needed to finish her education in order to get a job outside of the retail arena. The money from her dad had become her educational trust fund. The six hundred dollars that he placed in her account each month more than covered the cost of the college courses that she took. She was only a few credits shy of her degree and would finish college within the year if she maintained her current pace of study.

Her eyes studied the barn from top to bottom. The barn always reminded her of her mother. She missed her mother.

As a teenager, the barn had become her private sanctuary and meditation place, a respite from watching her mother's body deteriorate as the inoperable cancer grew inside of her. Liz would retreat to the barn to cry in private as her mother lay in bed growing weaker and frailer each day. Mrs. Wesley had smoked for twenty years and had developed emphysema and lung cancer. The cancer was stage IV inoperable when it was diagnosed, and it had metastasized into her stomach lining. The doctors gave her six months to live. The neighbors and family prayed for a miracle. Candlelight prayer vigils were held in front of their house every week. When an oxygen tank was brought to their home for her mother to use around the clock, Liz knew that the end was near. Her mother lived seven months from the date of the original diagnosis. They were all at her bedside when she breathed her last breath. Emmett wept openly, as did her dad, but Liz couldn't cry. She just stared at her mother's lifeless body and held her frail hand. She crawled into her mother's hospital bed and snuggled on her chest until the nurse admonished her that it was time to leave. Her father had to pry Liz from her mother's body. But still, she did not cry.

After the funeral, when the mourners returned to the Willard house for the repast, Liz ran to the barn to be alone. When she closed the large barn door she lost control. She threw bicycles against the wall and created chaos in the otherwise organized barn. She cried and screamed in the barn for nearly twenty minutes before her father came out to check on her. When he walked quietly into the barn, she sat huddled on the floor gripping her knees and sobbing hysterically as she rocked back and forth on her heels. "Why did God take my mother, Daddy? Why?" she moaned.

Mr. Willard's voice was soft and controlled. "Liz, I don't have an answer for you, but God does not make mistakes. Your mother is in heaven now, and she is no longer suffering. She will always be with us in spirit. She went to make a place for you and Neal and me in her Father's house where there are many mansions. She will always be with you, now more than ever." Mr. Willard's tone softened. "Lizzie, I loved your mother with all my heart, and I thank God for the time she was here with us. But baby, we're going to be okay. We will get through this together," he assured. "God will get us through this difficult time." He lifted her up and held her in his arms and squeezed her tightly, walking her into the house arm in arm.

Liz shook her head to come out of her daydream and smiled as she felt her mother's spirit in the barn. She wiped the tears from her face. The memory of her mother's funeral always made her cry. Her father had been right. Her faith in God had pulled her through her grief. She and Neal had gone to grief counseling, but it was the support from her church family that really comforted her through the loss of her mother. She knew that her mother was still with her. She felt her presence in her daily life. She heard herself sounding like her mother as she raised her own children, and she saw her mother's delicate features in Maria and Neal.

The rummage sale was two weeks away, and she and her dad had a lot of work to do. They had decided to sell all of the items in the barn. Mr. Willard had reached only two or three neighbors who assured him that they didn't mind if he sold the items that they'd stored in his barn all these years. Liz had convinced him that he was under no obligation to send them the money that he made from the sold items since he'd stored the items in the barn without charging them a storage fee. She surveyed the barn items again and decided that with the exception of the new John Deere rider mower, the items in the barn would be labeled and sold as best offer. Anything not sold would be donated to the local salvage yard. She hoped that her father was in an agreeable mood and would consent to her recommendation.

She closed the barn door and walked back into the house to help her dad clean out the cluttered basement. She stepped into the kitchen and back tracked as her eyes wandered to a peg board attached above a work bench. A pair of new garden gloves hung from a hook on the enclosed back porch. Liz smiled at her dad's incredible sense of order. She popped off the price tag and slid the oversized men's gloves over her manicured hands.

Her dad's voice bellowed from the kitchen. "Liz, were you taking a nap in that barn? We have a lot of work to finish today. Don't forget, I'm paying you for your time, and you're on the clock, young lady!"

Liz shook her head and smiled. "I'm coming, Mr. Mayor, I'm coming!" Liz laughed and walked into the house.

Chapter 7

Family Business

Teenie squeezed into the backseat, wondering if it had been wise to politely decline Mrs. Perkins' invitation to sit in the front. She wriggled her thin frame snugly between her four friends, and managed to squeeze one buttock onto the seat, the other cheek preening on Lori's lap as her torso leaned into Rashanda's. Giggling, the girls settled in like a row of brown sardines.

"Are you sure someone doesn't want to sit in the front, girls?" Mrs. Jordan repeated, glancing and scowling at the girls from the rearview mirror.

"We're fine, Mom," Rashanda groaned.

Lori was the first to speak. "RJ is the one who copied your scent, TC. She needed a new perfume to go with her new look. Doesn't she look great?"

Recently the girls had started referring to each other using their initials or just their last names: RJ – Rashanda Jordan, LP – Lori Perkins, TC – Tanisha Carlson, MW – Maria Wesley, GD – Grace Dudley, JW – Justine Wellington.

"I almost didn't recognize you, RJ. You look amazing!" Tanisha gushed. "Your hair looks so cute like that!" Tanisha ruffled Rashanda's hair. "And your eyes are so pretty without those glasses."

"What's in the back pack, TC?" Maria asked. "I know that's not your lunch."

"You are too funny, MW. It's my work clothes." Teenie looked at Lori. "LP, I hope you reminded your mom that she has to drop me off at Save Mart when she picks us up."

"I forgot to remind her, but I'm sure she won't mind at all. It's on the way home, anyway." Lori shifted her weight as the five girls tried to get comfortable in the back seat of the car.

"I don't know why one of you just doesn't sit in the front seat," Mrs. Jordan observed. "You look like little sardines all squeezed back there."

Rashanda rolled her eyes into the top of her head. "We're fine, Mom."

Lori fingered Grace's long hair. "Did you just wash your hair, Dudley?"

Maria played with the gum in her mouth. "I thought we were using initials today, or do you want to switch to last names?" Maria asked.

"My fault. Let's use initials. GD, your hair smells so good," Lori corrected.

"I think my mom is finally going to let me get my hair cut," Grace giggled excitedly.

Lori wound a strand of Grace's long blonde hair through her fingers. "Don't cut your hair, GD. It's so pretty!" she complimented.

"I agree! I wish I had your hair," Tanisha said. "It looks like the hair from the Johnson's Baby Shampoo commercial. When I was little I used to put a yellow towel on my head and pretend that I was the Johnson's Baby Shampoo model. I remember begging my mother to buy that shampoo, hoping my hair would turn yellow and silky like that girl's on television," Teenie sighed.

"Girl, we all did that. I wanted my hair to be blonde like that girl's too," Maria agreed. "That's because there weren't any black people on television commercials back then. Shoot, I remember how excited we used to get when we saw a black person on television doing anything. We would all run into the room to see the person. It was a big deal," she continued. "My parents were so psyched when Good Times came on and then The Jeffersons," she finished. "My dad thinks those shows aren't realistic, but at least there was black people in them," she finished.

"I know. I don't know anyone who lives in the projects like Good Times, but our family was just happy to see black people on television too," Lori agreed.

"My aunt lives in Beverly Hills, California, and they have a maid that lives with them like Florence on The Jeffersons. But they live in a big mansion not a condo," Maria explained. "In fact, my cousin works for the Norman Lear production company that created The Jeffersons. She's a production assistant, and she's the only black person who isn't part of the custodial or secretarial staff. Anyway, they never ask her for advice on what it's like to live in a black household which is stupid because she could give them some realistic material on how black people actually live. It's a trip how white people try to write about the black experience without asking black people," she continued. "Now what were we talking about?" She rubbed her head. "Oh, GD's hair. GD, I think you should go for it and get it cut into a cute style. What style did you have in mind?"

"I think I want it really short like Dorothy Hamill," Grace said. "But my mom is going to have to do some smooth talking to get my dad to go for that one," Grace said. "If he won't let me get it cut that short, then I'll get it chopped to just below my neck, like

Kate Jackson's length on Charlie's Angels."

"Kate Jackson's hair is cute," Lori offered in agreement. "Girl, if I got my hair cut that short, it would probably take ten years to get it back to my neck. But with your white girl type of hair, it will probably grow back quickly if you don't like it short."

Grace's eyes darted downward and she stared out the window.

Rashanda elbowed Lori in the ribs.

"Ouch! What was that for?" Lori winced.

Teenie tilted her head in Grace's direction and mouthed "white girl comment."

Lori squeezed her eyes shut and grimaced. "GD, I didn't mean to hurt your feelings," she whispered. "I just meant that your hair is so fine and silky that it will grow back easier than mine," Lori explained.

"I know what you meant. I know I have white girl hair, it's no big deal," Grace shrugged.

Lori bit her lip. "I'm sorry, GD. I really am. I didn't mean anything by it. Your hair is beautiful."

"It's no big deal, LP. Don't even worry about it," Grace smiled.

Lori sank into her seat, stared out the window and remembered.

✺

"Ma, can you believe it? Mr. and Mrs. Dudley are Grace's adoptive parents! Her real mother's name was Lydia Moore, and she was white!" Lori gasped. "No wonder Grace has that long strawberry blonde hair. I always wondered where she got that hair from. Mrs. Dudley is very fair like Grace, and she has a nice grade of hair, but her hair isn't blonde. Her hair is jet black." Lori continued in an animated voice, barely pausing for breath in between sentences.

Mrs. Perkins listened intently, trying desperately to demonstrate the proper emotion for a story that she already knew.

She decided to smile and nod. "That's big news. How is Grace handling it?"

"Well, she's thinking that she may try to find her birth father in a few years, but she's not ready to deal with it just yet," Lori explained.

"I can imagine. That's a lot of information for a teenager to handle," Mrs. Perkins offered.

Lori studied her mother's expression. "Ma, you don't seem too surprised? Did you know that Grace was adopted?"

Mrs. Perkins exhaled slowly and bit her bottom lip. She hesitated slightly before responding. "Yes, I knew that Grace was adopted," she sighed.

Lori's eyes got wide. "Ma, you've known all this time that Grace was adopted, and you never said anything?"

"You know that I don't believe in spreading other people's business, Lori. I knew that eventually the Dudleys would tell Grace about her mother and they did."

"Did you know her real mother?" Lori asked.

"Lori, Mrs. Dudley is Grace's real mother. She is the only mother that Grace knows. Lydia Moore was her birth mother. And yes, I knew her birth mother," Mrs. Perkins revealed.

"What was she like and how did you know her?" Lori asked excitedly.

"Well, you know that I've known Ethel Dudley for years. When Lydia came to live with them, Ethel told me what was going on. I felt so sorry for that child, being disowned by her own flesh and blood just because she was having a baby by a black man. But things were different back then. Anyway, Ethel introduced us, and once Lydia had Grace I told her that she could come by so you two could play. She brought her over quite a bit, and you two played on the floor all the time. I taught her how to braid and comb Grace's long hair, and showed her how to apply a little bit of oil to her scalp. Grace's hair isn't really as fine as it looks. It has a lot of body and texture to it, and her mother didn't know how to manage it. When Grace was a baby, her hair would get really curly after it was washed," Mrs. Perkins sighed. "Lydia was a sweet woman, she really was. That girl died way too young, but I know she's in a better place. She's smiling down on Grace and the young lady that she's become." Mrs. Perkins closed her eyes and hummed Amazing Grace as though eulogizing Lydia Moore with her voice.

Lori knew better than to disturb her mother when she was humming a gospel tune. She listened and waited for her mom to finish before continuing. "Ma, did she ever tell you about Grace's father?" Lori asked.

A fly buzzed around the bed, pausing in the path of warm air that blew in from the window fan as if drying perspiration from its gossamer wings. Mrs. Perkins rolled up the Ebony magazine that rested on her nightstand and swung at the fly. She missed. The fly would live another day. Mrs. Perkins stared at the spot where she'd swung at the fly.

"I hate flies! They are the nastiest creatures on God's green Earth! Any animal that lands on animal dung and then lands on your food deserves to die as far as I'm concerned!" Mrs. Perkins said.

"Ma! Did she ever talk about Grace's father?" Lori repeated.

"Yes, sometimes she would talk about Grace's father," Mrs. Perkins said.

Lori pounced on her mother's bed excitedly. "Give up the dirt! What was he like? All Grace told us is that he was a professor at Northwestern University, and he was black. Mr. and Mrs. Dudley said that Grace's mother never talked about him."

"Well, I remember once she said that Grace had his eyes and chin and that she hoped that Grace would be tall like him."

"So he was tall! That's why Grace is so tall! Did Lydia Moore have any siblings?" Lori asked.

"No. She was an only child," Mrs. Perkins said.

"Did she ever tell you anything else about Grace's father, like where he was from and if he had any brothers and sisters?" Lori asked.

"Lori, that was a long time ago, and she wasn't over here a lot. She probably came over a total of six or seven times before she died. I don't remember too many details, but I do remember her saying that Grace's father was from the south. I think she said that once he mentioned that his mother was from Arkansas. I wasn't paying that close attention, but I do remember that she mentioned a little town called Strong, Arkansas. That stuck with me because I thought it was an odd name for a town. I always wondered how a town could come to be named Strong. If you came from Strong, did that mean that you were strong?" Mrs. Perkins laughed with a deep guttural laugh that made her ample frame jiggle, shaking the bed.

She coughed into her hand and continued. "That's all I remember. She may have mentioned some other things, but at the time, I didn't realize that she had never told Greg and Ethel Dudley about him, so I didn't pay that close attention. She didn't talk about him all the time, but she said that she was in love with him. I do remember that. When she told me that he was a married man, I remember saying something to her about adultery being against God's will and a violation of the commandments and telling her that she needed to confess her sin to God and ask for forgiveness.

She didn't say much after that and left pretty quickly. I think she thought that I was judging her for having an affair with a married man," Mrs. Perkins sighed. "My tone was probably judgmental," she confessed. "But I was trying to get her to repent so that she could be forgiven. I wasn't judging her. Romans chapter three verse twenty three says that all have sinned and fall short of God's glory, and are justified freely by his grace through his son Jesus Christ," she paused. "Lawd knows I've committed my fair share of sin. I have not had a blameless walk, but I know that God forgives me when I confess my sins to him. I believe that to my core," she continued. "I still feel guilty about that."

Tilting her head, Lori stared at her mother. "Guilty about what, Ma?" she asked.

"I still feel guilty that she left my house feeling judged when I was just trying to lead her to Christ," Mrs. Perkins explained. "But I was younger then, and now I know how to spread God's word without making people feel condemned," she sighed. "After that, I think I only saw her one more time before she died. Now that was sad. She was way too young to die, but God must have believed that she had suffered long enough on this Earth and called her to heaven. He knew that Grace would be in good hands with Ethel and Greg Dudley. After Lydia died, I learned that she'd never told Greg and Ethel anything about Grace's father. She'd told me more than she'd told them. I told Ethel what I remembered, the stuff I just told you," she shared. "But I don't think they bothered to try to find him. Ethel Dudley stepped up and raised Grace the best she could. But you know they're older, so I knew eventually they would have to tell Grace that she was adopted, because she would be able to do the math and calculate that Ethel had been too old to have a baby when Grace was born."

Lori was preparing to ask her next question when Mrs. Perkins raised one hand to silence her like a crossing guard stopping traffic. She rolled up the Ebony magazine tightly and slammed it down on the window ledge with great force. "Goodbye you little nasty fly!" She grabbed a tissue and pressed her thumb down, squeezing the last ounce of life from the writhing fly.

"Strong, Arkansas," Lori repeated. "Well, at least we have a little more information to go on. It's probably a small town, and I bet if she did some research she could probably learn something about him or someone in his family."

"Lori, sometimes it's best to let sleeping dogs sleep. I hope Grace doesn't rush into anything trying to locate her birth father. She's still a child, and that's a lot of information to digest. Sometimes when you turn over stones looking for treasure, you just find dirt and worms."

Lori ignored her mother's comment and continued. "Ma, how do you feel about the fact that Daddy doesn't have a high school diploma?"

Mrs. Perkins slanted her eyes at her daughter. "Where on earth did that come from, Lori? One minute we're talking about your friend Grace, and now you're talking about your Daddy?"

"I just wondered why you never encouraged him to get his General Equivalency Degree," Lori said. "Does it bother you? He doesn't even have a G.E.D."

Mrs. Perkins sat up in her bed. She stared out the window and rubbed her hands together. "It doesn't bother me anymore. But there was a time that I wished he would finish high school. It was right after we first got married. But he had to help his family after his daddy died, so he couldn't go to school anymore, and I understood that. He did what a man is supposed to do. He took care of his family. And now that we have four children, he doesn't have time to worry about high school. He keeps a roof over our heads, food on our table, and we don't usually want for anything." Mrs. Perkins took a long breath. "Having said all of that, I guess it doesn't bother me that he never finished high school." Mrs. Perkins lay back down in the bed. "Now, go on back downstairs so I can take a nap."

Lori obediently went downstairs and sat on the living room sofa. She casually flipped through one of the photo albums under their glass coffee table. She smiled at the baby photos of her and her siblings. She stared for a long time at a faded photograph of her dad's mother whom they called Gramsy. Lori traced her finger over the photo of Gramsy.

Lori's parents had been high school sweethearts. When his father died, Mr. Perkins dropped out of high school to get a job and help his family care for his sick sister. Lori's parents were married shortly after Mrs. Perkins graduated from high school. They'd both worked two jobs and saved every penny to buy their home in Newberry East. Their home was a small three bedroom split level with a family room in the lower level. Their landscaping was simple, just a neat row of hedges lining the front window. Perched in the center of their lawn was a plastic white swan with its neck outstretched pointing north as if searching for its missing life partner. Lori learned in science class that swans mate for life. She wished they could find a swan statue to match the lawn ornament.

Mrs. Perkins believed that education was important and encouraged her children to do well in school. But so far, Lori was the only child to demonstrate academic promise. Lori's older sister Charlotte had recently taken her ACT exam and posted a single digit score out of a possible score of thirty six. She retook the exam and scored one point less the second time. Lori teased Charlotte mercilessly about her anorexic ACT score, taunting her that a monkey had taken the exam and scored a thirteen! Lori wasn't sure if that was true, but she teased her sister with this nonetheless.

Lori excelled in school and tried to encourage her dad to receive his general equivalency diploma.

"Dad, there are a lot of places that will help you study for the G.E.D. Tanisha told me that Delta Sigma Theta Sorority has an adult literacy program that helps adults pass the test," Lori pleaded.

"I can read Lori! I ain't illiterate!" Mr. Perkins barked.

"I know you can read Dad, but the G.E.D. component of the program is under their literacy program. Tanisha's aunts are Deltas and I could get some more information from her if you want."

"I don't want you telling your friends that I ain't got a high school diploma, Lori. That ain't nobody's business, but family business. I have a good job down at the plant, and I make good money. It don't bother me one bit that I don't have no high school diploma. You ain't said nothing to nobody have you?" Mr. Perkins asked.

"I told Tanisha, but she's cool, she wouldn't tell anyone. I was just going to have one of her aunts call you with the information," Lori explained. "It's nothing to be ashamed of Dad," Lori finished.

"Well, I like Tanisha. I just don't know how I feel about that just yet. Let me think about it," Mr. Perkins said.

Lori decided that she'd try one last tactic. "Dad, since Charlotte will be graduating from high school next year, wouldn't it be nice to get your G.E.D. before she finishes high school? The whole family would be so proud of you."

She braced herself for his response. Seconds ticked by, and he stood silent. The whir of the white living room box fan was the only sound. A few more seconds passed, and Mr. Perkins took a deep breath, chewed his jaw and hummed. Mr. Perkins often chewed the inside of his jaw and hummed different tunes. It reminded Lori of the way a cow chewed its cud. It was never a recognizable tune, but Lori found the sound very relaxing. She knew from his humming that the conversation was finished.

∽∾

Maria snapped her fingers in Lori's face. "Earth calling, LP! Earth calling, Lori! Snap out of it. I swear, between you and TC, you two daydream too much! What were you thinking about?"

Lori shook her head and snapped out of her trance. "I was just thinking about my dad and a project I'm trying to help him finish. What did you ask me?" Lori smiled at Maria and stared her squarely in the face.

"I asked you what you thought we should get Justine as a going away gift," Maria repeated. She pulled her finger as far as she could to crack her knuckles, a disgusting habit that she'd recently started.

"Stop popping your knuckles, Maria!" Lori scolded. She smacked Maria's hand. "That's a good question. I hadn't really thought about any gift ideas. I thought we'd just get inspired once we got to Jefferson Mall," Lori paused. "But she could probably use some stationery so she can write us," Lori offered. "What do you guys think we should get her?"

"That's a good idea, Lori," Grace agreed. "I thought about stationery too, especially since Justine likes to write. If we have enough money we could also get her a matching shirt so she can still feel like part of our posse," Grace finished. She smiled at Lori.

As Lori smiled back, she could hear her mother's voice in her head. "Sometimes it's best to let sleeping dogs sleep." This was one dog that Lori couldn't let sleep. She knew what she had to do. She was going to help Grace find her biological father! But first she had to help with her own family's business.

Chapter 8

The Story of Grace

I have white girl hair. I have white girl hair. Grace stared out the window, and thought back to the story that she'd learned when she was fourteen. I should have white girl hair. My mother was white.

Grace wiped the tears from her eyes and stared aimlessly at her mother's mouth. She could see her lips moving, but the noise coming out was inaudible. It reminded her of the sound that the teacher from the Charlie Brown Halloween specials made when she addressed the class. "Wa wa wa waaa waa wa waa. I know this is a lot of information. But we love you so much. Wa waaa wa waa waa wa wa wa. I know this isn't the best time to tell you, especially learning about Justine, but there is never going to be a perfect time. You may not have questions today. If you do have questions later, we'll try to answer them as best we can," she paused. "We've always planned to tell you, Grace. We even wrote down the story in case something happened to us, so you would know," her mother said. "We've written it down." Grace's mother handed her several sheets of paper. "You can read it later in case you didn't hear all of what we said," she continued. "Grace, we love you so much, and we're here for you." Her parents hugged her but the hugs felt hollow. So much had changed in less than one hour. She was adopted. Her mother was white and her father was black. Who was she?

She glared at the clock on her dresser and traced her finger around the clock's face. The hands read 9:36. She pulled her hair into a tight ponytail. Just one hour before, she had sat in shock and listened to her parents tell her that she was adopted. She did the math in her head. Just thirty six hundred seconds ago her life had been altered forever. Time was her new enemy. If she hadn't gone downstairs for a snack, her heart wouldn't have been shred by the two people she trusted most in the world. She wanted to slam the clock against her bedroom wall. Her hand shook as their words echoed through her head. She buried her face in her pillow and tried to drown out the sound of their voices. But the voices were real and so was the story that they told her. She lay on her back and closed her eyes. She couldn't breathe. It felt like an elephant was sitting on her chest. She sat up. Grabbing the paper, she stared at her mother's shaky handwriting. She wanted to tear the paper to shreds, but her curiosity got the best of her. She settled into her bed and read her story.

Dear Grace, We wrote this down so you would know some of your history before we get too old to remember it. Some of what we wrote is our own interpretation, but at least it tells you a little bit about your blood kinfolk. You are our adopted daughter. We adopted you when you were almost two years old.

Your birth mother's name was Lydia Moore. She was the daughter of Amelia and Michael Moore, a prominent family from Wilmette, Illinois. The Moore family owned a large estate on the East Side of Sheridan Road with Lake Michigan as their backyard. They were wealthy, and they were white. Now, I know you're probably shocked to learn that your mother was white, but please keep reading. Your father and I worked for the Moore family until Lydia became a teenager. Your dad was their chauffeur, and I was Lydia's nanny and the family's cook. We grew to love the Moore family and they treated us like their family.

We were all like one big happy family. We're writing this to help you, not to disrespect that family in anyway.

Lydia was their only child and led a privileged lifestyle. Watching her grow up, she sometimes rebelled against her parent's conservative values and longed to experience life beyond the walls of her gated home on Lake Michigan. All of her friends were white and rich like she was. We were the only black people that she ever saw except on the news. She was driven to and from school by your dad and the places where the family shopped and socialized didn't have any black people. In the early sixties, we often heard her parents talk about moving because the city of Evanston near their home had started to become home to many bi-racial couples because of Northwestern University.

After Lydia finished her studies at the North Shore Country Day School and Roycemore, she was accepted to Wellesley College, but she deferred her admission for one year and decided to take courses at Northwestern University.

The year was nineteen sixty five, and the Civil Rights Movement was in full swing. The Civil Rights Act had been passed the year before and Lydia watched with interest the brief news clips highlighting the prejudice and Jim Crow segregation that was prevalent in the South. She spent more time with me in the kitchen than she did with her parents so she watched a lot of the Civil Rights coverage on television and heard our opinions about the unfairness of the segregation in the South and the way black people were treated in America. Lydia was moved by the eloquence of Rev. Dr. Martin Luther King, Jr. and believed in her heart that segregation was wrong. She deeply wanted to get involved in the Civil Rights Movement.

I remember when Lydia's parents learned that she wasn't ready to go to Wellesley. They believed her hesitation in heading east for college was good old fashioned homesickness. But we knew the truth. She wanted to experience life, and she knew that if she went to Wellesley where her parents had connections, her life there would be as sheltered as her life in Wilmette. They agreed to her request to enroll at Northwestern University for one year with the expectation that she transfer to Wellesley College the following fall. They allowed her to live on campus in Allison Hall, the all-girls dorm located just south of the Northwestern University sorority quads.

We stopped working for the Moore family when Lydia was a senior in high school, and we moved to Newberry East. While attending classes at Northwestern University, your mother fell in love with her drama professor. He was half white and half black. He was also married. Now we know that your mother was a girl of high moral principles but she must have convinced herself that a brief fling with her professor would not prove harmful since she believed herself to be in love with him. Lydia shared with us that she and the professor had only had two brief encounters in his office when she realized that she was pregnant.

An unwed pregnant daughter created quite a scandal for a prominent North Shore family. The fact that their only daughter had become pregnant by a married, black professor was more than the Moore family could handle. In an effort to hide the family's shame, her parents arranged for her to live with us. This is what families did when a daughter was in the family way, but wasn't married. The girl was just sent to "care for a sick aunt" for one year. White families and black families did this all the time. Good families just couldn't have their family name marred by having an unmarried pregnant daughter parading around the house. It just wasn't done back in the day, and especially in a white family as rich and connected as the Moore family.

Anyway, they used their influence at Northwestern University and had the drama professor terminated. Since he wasn't a tenured professor it was easy for the university to let him go. Your daddy learned that from a custodial friend of his at the university. Lydia was devastated, but there was nothing that she could do. The university refused to release any forwarding information on where he'd moved. She sent letters to the university hoping that they would be forwarded, but a friend of Lydia's later told her that her parents had arranged for a colleague in the university office to open and read all mail directed to the drama teacher and to screen out any letters from their daughter, Lydia. The Moores were generous contributors to the University, and so the University complied with this special request. People with money can do almost anything that they want.

The Moores expectation was that Lydia would deliver the baby and place the baby up for adoption immediately. She would then be free to return to her North shore lifestyle and enroll in Wellesley the following fall as planned.

Lydia agreed to live with us during her pregnancy and pretended to go along with the adoption idea; however, she had no intention of giving up her baby. I knew that the first time I saw her rubbing her belly with pride. I knew she was keeping you. She named you when she started to show. She knew you were going to be a girl. I don't know how she knew it, but she said she just knew that you were a girl. She said you were her "Grace from God."   But I didn't say a word to her mama. It wasn't my place. She was a grown woman. She was nineteen years old, and she knew that her parents couldn't force her to place her baby up for adoption.

Until you came into our lives, your father and I had never been blessed with children. We tried, but it wasn't the good Lord's will for us. But I raised Lydia so that counts for something. We were more than happy to have your mother move in with us. We couldn't have loved her more had she been our own daughter. And when you came, it was like heaven opened the flood gates and poured out another bountiful blessing to us. We were so excited to have you in our lives. It was a miracle. We felt like Sarah and Abraham in the book of Genesis, two old people finally blessed with the child that we'd prayed about for so long.   I *always thought that once Lydia gave birth, her parents would fall in love with you and welcome Lydia home. But once you were born, and the Moores learned of Lydia's refusal to place you up for adoption, they refused to speak with her. Whenever she talked to them they would ask her if she'd changed her mind. And when she said no, they hung up the phone. It was sad. After two months they sent a check for $5,000 and asked that they never be contacted again. Lydia was devastated but we assured her that she was part of our family. The only thing that kept her going was your sweet smiling face.*

This part is really hard for me to write, but you need to know it. When you were almost two years old, your mother died of a stroke. She was perfectly healthy, and then one day she just collapsed and died. The doctor said she had an aneurysm. It was the saddest time of our life. Here you were this little bitty thing, and we had to bury your momma. We tried to notify Lydia's parents, but their phone had been disconnected. Your daddy sent a certified letter that was returned unopened. It appeared that the Moores had completely disowned their daughter, just like they said they would when she refused to put you up for adoption.

Your mother was a smart woman and had left behind a will listing your daddy and me as your legal guardians in case anything happened to her. So we used the money that your grandparents had sent your momma, hired an attorney and legally adopted you like your momma wanted.

We didn't even try to reach your birth father because after watching your mother try to find him through the university for all those months, we figured there was no use. We didn't even have a name to go by because we never pressured your mother for any information about him. We just never thought to ask his name. When she died, we went through her things, but we couldn't find any of the letters that had been returned. All we know is that he was a drama professor at Northwestern University in 1965. The janitor that your daddy knew who worked at the university died the year before your momma died, so we couldn't contact him for any information.

The photo in the living room over the television that I always told you was my distant cousin was really your mother. She was a beautiful girl inside and out. And she loved you more than anything in this world. There was no way that she was going to give you up. She wanted to be your mother more than anything. She gave up her own family to make a family with you. We decided to tell you this near your fourteenth birthday in case something happened to us even though we wrote this down so you could read it again and again. We knew your mother when she was little and have some photographs that we took when she was a girl. We'll share those with you too when you're ready. They're just in a shoe box in the attic. Here's your mother's high school graduation picture that she sent us. Please don't be mad at us. We love you more than you know. Love, Mom and Dad

৯৵

Grace studied the small wallet sized photo in her hand. Her mother's long hair caressed her bare shoulders. A single strand of pearls hung gracefully around her thin neck. Her lips were serious, but her eyes smiled. Lydia Moore was pretty. Grace resembled her mother a great deal except for the skin tone. Grace's skin was an olive complexion while her mother's skin was porcelain white, almost pink. Grace sighed slowly. When people saw Grace they assumed that she was a light skinned African American, which is how she saw herself. But what was she now? Was she white? If her mother was white and her father was half white, that made her more white than black.

She studied her hand closely. Mrs. Dudley was a very light skinned African American woman with straight black hair. She had grown up in the Jim Crow South and would often pass for white if necessary. Mr. Dudley was very dark skinned, and Grace had always believed that her complexion was a cross between both of theirs. Until now, it had never occurred to Grace that her parents had been too old to have a child born in nineteen sixty six. She had never given it any thought. "Now I know where I get this blonde hair from," she sighed.

Grace loved her parents, but she was angry. She was angry with Lydia for not leaving her a letter telling her more about herself. She was also angry with her mother for dying and for not trying harder to contact her biological father. She was furious with her grandparents for abandoning her mother and abandoning her as well. A few days before learning that she was adopted, she learned that Justine would be moving to Evanston. Grace wanted to die. It was too much information for a fourteen year old to handle. I'm adopted, I'm more white than black, my grandparents were wealthy bigots who disowned my mother, and my best friend is moving seventy miles away! I hate life!

Grace was hurting deeply inside and didn't know how to channel it. She was ashamed that her life was not as it seemed and her thoughts raced. How will my friends handle the news that I'm adopted? What will they think when they find out that my mother was white and my father was half white? Will they think that I should be hanging around the white girls at school and not them? Grace wanted desperately to contact the Moores but she was afraid. If the Moores had not even gone to their own daughter's funeral, then efforts to contact them would be futile. They would probably slam the door in my black face!

Grace didn't know what to do. She was losing control. She had to re-group and get her thoughts in order. Her stomach growled loudly. She remembered that she'd gone downstairs for a snack before her world was turned upside down. It was now almost ten o'clock. She tiptoed down to the pantry. She could hear her parents watching television in the basement. She pulled out a bag of Chips Ahoy Chocolate Chip Cookies. She quickly ate four cookies and chugged a glass of orange juice. She shoved three more cookies in her mouth and chewed furiously. She poured more orange juice. Before she knew it, she had consumed the entire sleeve of cookies and washed it down with a pint of orange juice. She grabbed her stomach. She felt sick. You make me sick. You're a sicko. That's why your grandparents didn't want you, you're sick.

Grace walked over to the kitchen drawer, pulled out a spoon and went into the powder room. She shut the door quietly and turned on the ceiling fan. She dropped to her knees and assumed a prayer position before slowly pressing the bowl portion of the spoon against the back of her throat and triggering the gag reflex. As she threw up the contents of her stomach into the toilet, Grace felt as though she were punishing her maternal grandparents with every heave. She inserted the spoon six more times until she was convinced that she'd thrown up all of the cookies. She rinsed out her mouth with water and wiped her face with a towel. She smiled. Grace felt like she was re-gaining control.

Since learning that she was adopted weeks before, Grace had made throwing up a daily ritual. Her weight had dropped to one hundred and eleven pounds, down from one hundred and twenty three pounds. She made sure to leave herself at least ten minutes after she ate breakfast in the morning so that she had time to heave the contents of her stomach. She'd purchased her own box of white plastic spoons and hid them under the bathroom sink. Her parents never looked on her side of the sink. After every meal, Grace retired to the bathroom to make herself throw up. She'd gotten amazingly good at vomiting. She routinely brushed her teeth and gargled to erase the bitter taste from her tongue. The whir of the bathroom fan drowned out the telltale regurgitation sound. Throwing up had become as routine to her as brushing her teeth.

Grace wasn't able to vomit after lunch, because the girls' bathroom was usually too crowded. She'd tried it one day and another student in the next stall had heard the heaves and summoned a teacher for assistance. Grace faked stomach flu and had to rest in the nurse's office for the remainder of the day. Lunch was the only meal that stayed on her stomach.

Grace had never been a thin girl and had always been comfortable with her size. She was not throwing up to become thin. She didn't like being thin. She loved her tall muscular athletic frame. But when she threw up, she felt a sense of power and control. The life she'd known for the past fourteen years had all been a lie. A big fat, white lie! Every time she thought about her muddled past she wanted to throw up again and again. If she threw up enough, maybe she would disappear and she wouldn't feel the pain she felt in her heart.

Her friends at Battle Creek Junior High were the first to notice her weight loss.

"Grace, you look like you're losing weight." Lori said one day at lunch. Grace munched on her cheeseburger and dipped her French fries in ketchup.

"I think I'm just going through another growth spurt. Plus, my metabolism has increased since I joined the track team." Grace took a sip from her chocolate milk. "I eat like a horse, so I don't know why I'm losing weight," Grace lied.

Tanisha shook her head from side to side and took a bite of her cheeseburger. "You're lucky. I have a high metabolism too. It's good when you're active because you can eat almost anything you want and not gain a pound."

Her parents had grown accustomed to Grace's sullenness. Several weeks had passed since the Dudleys shared the adoption story, and Grace had not talked about her biological mother until one Sunday evening at dinner.

"I think I want to meet my grandparents," Grace announced. She pushed the peas around on her plate, and lined her mashed potatoes with them.

Mrs. Dudley's jaw fell and she dropped her fork. Mr. Dudley spoke, "Grace, we tried to reach them, but the letter was sent back unopened."

Grace slammed her fork into her plate. "But that was a long time ago," she said. "I'm sure they've probably changed now that the world is a lot different than it was back then. I want to try to reach them."

Mr. Dudley took a deep breath. The grandfather clock in the living room chimed six o'clock. "All right then, I'll help you. I know the phone number that we had is disconnected, so we'll send them another letter."

"Thanks, Daddy." Grace finished her meal and excused herself. "I'll write the letter tonight."

The letter read:

Dear Mr. & Mrs. Moore: I don't know where to start so here goes. My name is Grace Dudley and I am fourteen years old. I was born on March 13, 1966. My parents are Ethel and Greg Dudley. They recently told me that they are my adoptive parents, and that my birth

mother was Lydia Moore, your daughter. My mother died when I was very young so I didn't get a chance to know her. I would like to meet you to learn about my mother. Please call me at 555-1036. Thank you.
Grace Dudley

❧

That night Grace gave the letter to Mr. Dudley. He mailed it the following morning. Three days later, Mr. Dudley retrieved Grace's letter from the mailbox. It had been returned unopened with the word "Deceased" stamped across the letter. Mr. Dudley furrowed his brow and scratched his bald head. He went to his desk and pulled out a worn address book. He finally decided to call Willie, the landscaper that had cared for the Moore's estate for many years. He had never reached out to Willie before because he respected the Moore's privacy and didn't want to spread their family business in the street. As far as he knew, Willie didn't even know that Lydia had been pregnant, and he didn't believe it was his business to share that information. But enough time had passed, and now Mr. Dudley needed some answers. Grace deserved some answers.

Mr. Dudley dialed the rotary dial phone carefully studying the numbers over the plastic frame of his glasses. "Hello, Willie? This is Greg Dudley! (pause) Oh I can't complain. I'm fair to middlin, I presume. Fair to middlin. How you doin'? (pause) Sho' nuff. If the good Lord's willing and the creek don't rise that's fo' sho! (pause) I know it's been a long time. Too long. Listen buddy! I was wondering if you knew how to reach Mr. and Mrs. Moore. I sent something to their house, and it came back unopened with "deceased" stamped across the top. You know anything 'bout that?" Mr. Dudley paused. "I see. Um, Um, Um. Goodness gracious. That family done seen its share a troubles for sure." (pause) "Naw, we didn't know nothing 'bout it or we show would have paid our respects. You know they was nothing but good to us for all those years. Um, um, um! Well you tell the Missus hello from us. (pause) "Oh, Miss Ethel is fine, just as hornery as ever, but she's my heart. (pause) Okay. Will do."

Mr. Dudley was hanging up the extension as Grace walked into the kitchen.

"Hey, Dad! Was that for me? Did I get anything in the mail today?" Grace asked confidently. She was certain that after thirteen years they would want to meet their granddaughter even if they hadn't gone to their daughter's funeral.

Mr. Dudley sighed deeply and showed Grace the envelope. Grace was puzzled. As she studied the envelope, Mr. Dudley told her that Mr. and Mrs. Moore had died in a car accident in nineteen sixty six, just three months after she was born. Grace was devastated. Her last hope to understanding what her mother was like was gone. But at least the pieces were coming together. "That's why they hadn't gone to my mother's funeral," she said softly. "They were already dead."

Grace studied the letter in her hand and smiled at her dad. She hugged her father and spoke into his chest. "Thanks for calling your friend, Daddy. At least now I have some answers. Maybe they weren't monsters after all," she whispered.

Mr. Dudley squeezed Grace's shoulders and tilted her chin up with his hand. Grace was almost as tall as Mr. Dudley. He stared into her eyes and spoke carefully and deliberately.

"Grace, Mr. and Mrs. Moore were lovely people. I don't for a second agree with how they decided to treat their only child, but they were decent white folks. Coming up in the forties and fifties the way I did, I met some white folks who were mean as the devil.

They would just as soon lynch you as help you, but Mr. and Mrs. Moore were good and kind. I believe in my heart that they would have eventually come around and forgiven your mother and they would have loved you. And now that I know they died shortly after you were born, I'm certain they would have come around. They was just angry and ashamed about your mother getting pregnant by a colored man. They was upstanding people in their community, and they just couldn't accept that their daughter had been with a black man. But I know that in due time, they would have come around. I know they would, and I'm going to carry that belief to my grave." Mr. Dudley rubbed Grace's back. "We never know the cards the good Lord is going to deal us, but we play what we're dealt. God gave us you to love and cherish, and we're grateful for it. You are our Grace from God, and we love you."

Grace squeezed her father's waist tighter. For the first time in a long time, Grace did not have the desire to throw up.

"And don't forget. Your mother raised Lydia Moore. She can tell you all about what your mother was like as a child. She probably has more stories than Mrs. Moore did anyway, since Lydia spent more time with Ethel than with her own mama. So when you're ready, we can share some stories about your birth mama." Mr. Dudley patted Grace's head.

She kissed the photo of her mother that she'd framed and placed on her dresser. *My grandparents weren't monsters. I wonder what they looked like?* Grace stared at her ceiling. She hadn't made herself throw up all day. She climbed out of bed and walked into the bathroom. She pulled out the small box of plastic spoons that she'd hidden under the bathroom sink. There were eleven spoons remaining. She slowly broke each spoon in half and smiled at her reflection. *I think it's time to stop hurting myself.*

Eight days later, Grace hadn't made herself throw up once. She had also gained two pounds back.

A few weeks later, Grace decided to share her story with her friends. She was tired of keeping this news to herself and wanted to share her feelings with her friends. She invited the girls over for a Friday night pizza party. The girls were munching on pizza and sipping lemonade when Grace tapped on her glass with a fork to get everyone's attention.

"Can I have everyone's attention? I have something that I want to tell you," Grace said as she nervously twirled a straw in between her fingers.

The girls quieted down and continued to eat their pizza. They stared at Grace with puzzled expressions.

"I don't know how to say this, so I'll just go for it," she whispered. "A few weeks ago, I found out that I'm adopted, and my birth mother was white." Grace blurted out quickly.

The girls were stunned silent. Grace looked from face to face and decided to just keep talking. She told her friends the adoption story that her parents had shared with her. She continued uninterrupted for several minutes. She was glad that she had rehearsed what she would say. When she was finished, she stared at her friends, and braced herself for their reaction. Tanisha spoke first.

"Wow! Grace, that's a lot of information to digest," Tanisha said softly. "How do you feel?"

"Teenie, that's a good question," Grace exhaled. "Honestly, I was angry at first. But now that I understand that my grandparents died before my mother died, I'm not angry with them anymore. My dad helped me understand that they really were good people. They just didn't know how to react to my mom getting pregnant by a black man," Grace explained. "I really feel in my heart that if they'd lived they would have forgiven my mother and wanted to meet me. I really believe that," Grace shared.

"That's a good positive Christian attitude, Grace. You should hold on to that thought," Lori said.

"I have to admit. I was scared to tell you guys about this because I didn't know how you would react," Grace confessed. She bit her lip and lowered her head.

"Why were you scared to tell us that you were adopted, Grace? Most of us have white blood flowing through our veins, that's why we're all different shades of brown," Tanisha said.

"She's right, Grace. It doesn't bother me that you're adopted or that you're half white. Your parents are the ones who raised you. It's too bad you never knew your mom or your grandparents, but the mom and dad that you know as your parents are cool parents to have," Rashanda said.

"I know. But I just wasn't sure. I always wondered where I got this reddish blonde hair from, and now I know. My mother had blonde hair. This is a picture of my mother." Grace pointed to the photo in the living room.

"She was pretty. You look just like your mom." Rashanda took another bite of her pizza. "I think it's cool that they told you now. That way, if you want to try and do some research to find your father, you have some information. I don't want to sound cruel or morbid, but your parents are getting older and won't be around forever."

"That's a good point," Maria agreed. "If you develop a medical condition and you need blood from your mom and dad, at least you'll understand if the blood types don't match," Maria finished.

"Good point, Maria. You might want to think about doing some research to try and find your biological father just for that reason alone, Grace. It sounds like he didn't have a choice but to disappear," Tanisha offered. She shook her head and puffed out her cheeks, slowly blowing the air out of her lungs like a deflating balloon before continuing. "That's a deep story how your grandparents had the clout to make your father just disappear like that," she snapped her fingers. "People with money can do all kinds of things."

Tanisha smacked her hand against her forehead. "I just had an idea. My Aunt Helen is the associate provost at Northwestern University. I bet she can dig around and find out something about your biological father. Even though we don't have his name, how many black drama professors could there have been at Northwestern in 1965? If you want me to, I can ask her to help you, Grace," Tanisha finished.

"Is that your aunt who's a Delta?" Lori asked.

"Uh huh. Aunt Helen is my dad's youngest sister, but all three of his sisters are Deltas," Tanisha explained.

"I need to get her information from you because my dad wants to talk to her about something. I'll call you later tonight," Lori said.

Grace took another bite of her now cold sausage pizza, careful to pick off the mushrooms. "Thanks you guys, but to be perfectly honest, I'm not sure if I'm ready to try to find my birth father yet. I need to let this information settle a little longer," she explained between chews. "I'll let you know if I change my mind and need your aunt's help, Tanisha." Grace smiled at her friends. She noticed that Justine had sat silent while the other girls asked questions. Of all the girls, Grace was closest to Justine. "You're awfully quiet, Justine. What are you thinking?" Grace asked tentatively.

"Wow! I was just taking all of this in. I had no idea. Why didn't you tell me right away, Grace? You've been carrying this around by yourself for three weeks?" Justine asked. "I'm your best friend, I can't believe you didn't tell me sooner," Justine said. Her tone was soft and hurtful.

"Actually, I've carried it around for almost four weeks. I wanted to tell you first, Justine, I really did. But after everything that happened with your family, I didn't want to bother you with my personal drama. I felt like you'd been through enough. I found out the weekend all that stuff went down with your parents, and it took me a week to digest it," Grace shrugged. "I was hurt, angry, depressed. I didn't want to talk to anybody," she paused. "I dealt with it in my own way," she whispered. Should I tell them about my bulimia too? Go for it, what do you have to lose. Grace took a deep breath and continued. "Since I'm telling you all of this, I might as well tell you everything," she said. "Right after I found out that I was adopted, I started making myself throw up. It made me feel better in a weird way. Every time I threw up I felt like I was in control of something in my life. I know it sounds stupid, but it gave me power," Grace whispered softly. She took a deep breath and prepared herself once again for her friends' reaction.

Maria spoke first. "Grace, please tell me that you've stopped making yourself throw up! It's not healthy. You could become bulimic." Maria grabbed her throat with both of her hands. "I know what I'm talking about," she shared softly. "Last year I used to make myself throw up. I was trying to lose weight to please Todd, but my mother caught me and took me to see a psychiatrist. It really helped. Do your parents know?"

"No. I made myself throw up for about three weeks, but as far as I know my parents were clueless. That's why I was losing weight. I wasn't trying to lose weight, but when you throw up your breakfast and dinner, you lose weight." Grace shifted her weight in her chair.

"I felt a lot better after talking to my mom about my birth mother. She told me a lot of stories about what she was like as a young girl." Grace self consciously twirled her hair. "Like I said, once I learned that my grandparents died right after I was born, it made me feel better, and I haven't thrown up since."

"You should still think about going to talk to a psychiatrist. It couldn't hurt," Maria coaxed. "You've been through a lot. It made me feel better. I could get you my doctor's information if you want to schedule an appointment," Maria offered.

Lori shook her head. "My God!" Lori exclaimed. "Maria, I didn't know you were making yourself throw up too," she sighed. "You guys, we need to tell each other when we're going through tough situations like this. That's what friends are for, to support each other through tough times." Lori looked directly at Maria. "Maria, if you were feeling that bad about yourself, you should have talked to us too. We could have helped. I knew you were getting too skinny too fast." Lori lowered her head. From past experience, the other girls knew that Lori was saying a silent prayer. They sat quietly and waited for her to finish. Seconds later, she raised her head and continued. "Let's make a pact that we'll be there for each other no matter what, okay? And we won't be afraid to tell each other anything!" Lori made eye contact with each of the girls one by one. The girls nodded their heads in agreement. The room was silent as they stared at each other in a bond of friendship.

Tanisha broke the silence. "I agree with Lori. We need to be there for each other no matter what. That's why Lori and I said something to you about your weight last spring, Maria. We were just worried about you. If I had suspected that you were making yourself throw up, I would have told your mother," Tanisha shared. "You would have just been mad at me, but I wouldn't have kept that secret. Real friends help friends when they're being harmful to themselves, and I would have let Mama Liz know what was going on," she paused and looked at Grace. "I'm glad you told us about your adoption and your bulimia, Grace. I think you're blessed to have such wonderful parents. The Dudleys are angels on earth," Tanisha paused. "And that also explains why you are so rhythmically challenged. You're half white, and you know white people can't dance. That's why you don't see any white people on Soul Train!" Tanisha fell on the floor laughing. The other girls all laughed heartily. The familiar tune of the Good Humor truck could be heard in the distance.

Grace laughed so hard that tears streamed down her cheeks. "It feels good to laugh again," she said. "This has been a heavy night. I think we need to lighten the mood with some ice cream."

"I'll second that!" Maria offered.

"And if we see anyone take a spoon into the bathroom, it's on!" Lori laughed.

The girls broke out in giggles and grabbed their purses to get money. Grace grinned with pride at the support that she received from her friends. She had shared her worst secrets with them, and they hadn't rejected her or made her feel ashamed of herself. She took a deep breath and smiled. "Leave your purses, ladies," Grace said. She waved a twenty dollar bill in the air. "This ice cream treat is on me!"

⚬✦⚬

Grace stared at Lori who seemed deep in her own thoughts. She squeezed Lori's hand as the car pulled into the mall parking lot. She knew that her friend had meant no harm when she said that she had hair like a white girl. She did have white girl hair. Her mother was a white girl, and she wasn't ashamed of it.

Chapter 9

Jefferson Mall

Mrs. Jordan steered the car into the parking lot and headed to Sears.

"Mom, can't you just drop us off at Carson Pirie Scott?" Rashanda whined as she rolled her eyes into the back of her head. She knows I hate Sears. She's just doing this to annoy me because I asked my dad if we could drive the Lincoln! She's being so evil today!

"Rashanda, I have to run into Sears to return something. You girls can just walk to Carson Pirie Scott from here." She parked the car, and the girls quickly scrambled out. They mumbled thank you as Mrs. Jordan gathered her purse. She turned around and shook her head slowly. The girls were inside the vestibule before she reached the trunk to retrieve her return item.

"I have to go to the bathroom, so let's stop in the restroom first," Maria suggested.

"Groovy!" Teenie and Lori offered simultaneously. "Jinks you owe me a Snickers, TC."

"Are we still doing initials or last names?" Lori fumbled in her small purse in search of a mint.

Maria powdered her nose in the air conditioned vestibule. "Let's just do first names in case we meet some boys at the arcade.

We may not want them to know our last names or else it will be too easy for them to just look up our phone numbers in the Newberry East phone book."

"Good point, Maria. Some of our last names are pretty unique and there are only a few other Newberry East families with the same last name. Let's not make it easy for any knuckleheads that we meet to do some basic detective work to track us down," Grace confirmed. She borrowed Maria's compact and powdered her nose too.

The girls walked swiftly through Sears and headed to the restroom. More a hang out spot for teens than a shopping destination, the mall had once been the premier shopping haven in the south suburbs boasting Marshall Fields, Lord & Taylor, Carson Pirie Scott, and Sears as its anchor department stores. But as the demographics of the south suburbs changed, with more African American families moving to the surrounding neighborhoods, the stores gradually closed.

"This mall is turning into a ghost town," Rashanda noticed.

"It's a product of the white flight happening in the area," Tanisha stated flatly.

"What's white flight, Teenie?" Lori asked.

"My dad told me that it's when the white people sell their houses as more African American families move into a neighborhood. He said that a lot of white people believe that their property values will decline if too many blacks live in their community," Tanisha explained.

Maria shook her head in disgust. "My dad was talking about that too. There are two for sale signs on our street right now," she agreed. The stores must think that black people don't shop because they're moving to Finley Park and Trunkford where the white people are moving."

"You're right, Maria. The retailers follow white flight patterns. It's sad that it still happens when too many blacks move into a neighborhood. My dad said that a lot of people still don't think that the races should mix socially. A lot of white families flock away like birds heading south for the winter. That's why it's called white flight," she continued. The girls huddled in a small semi circle and listened. "When we lived in Chicago, we were the first African American family on our block. I was so little that I didn't know any different. My brother Jack and I played with a little white boy named Ricky who lived at the end of our block. I remember we cried when he moved away, because he was the only friend we had on the block. We were four and five when he moved. I don't remember playing with any other white children on the block, though. I remember seeing them, but we never played with them. I never asked why. My brother and I had each other, and we had Ricky to play with, so we didn't think about the other white kids on the block. But I remember that as other black families moved in, the white people started moving out. All of a sudden the block changed, and it was all black. It must have happened over the course of one or two years, because by the time my brother started school, there were a lot of black kids in the school. I was just glad that some kids moved in that liked to play outside. There was only one white family that didn't move away, but they didn't have any kids. It was two old white ladies, a mother and a daughter. It was weird. They never talked to anyone on the block, they just stayed in their house with the shades pulled," Tanisha paused. "My dad called the daughter a spinster."

"What's a spinster?" Grace asked.

"It's a woman who's over a certain age but has never gotten married," Lori explained. Tanisha nodded her head in agreement.

"I remember they drove an old blue Studebaker car. The

daughter would drive around the front of the house and blow the horn as she passed her house. It was crazy. My dad said that she did that so her mother would know that she was on her way to the garage and could look out for her. I think they were scared being the only white people on the block. My parents told us to stay away from their house, so we did. When we went trick or treating on the block, we never rang their bell. It was like their house was invisible. Nobody ever bothered them. They never came to any block club meetings or parties, they just stayed to themselves. They were still living there when we moved to Newberry East. I wonder if they're still living there now," she wondered aloud.

"Probably not, Teenie. You moved here when you were nine and now you're almost sixteen. If they were old when you lived there, they're probably dead as doorknobs by now," Maria offered.

"Maria! That's not nice to say," Lori scolded.

"But she's probably right. I'm sure they're dead," Tanisha agreed.

"Why did you guys move away, Teenie?" Rashanda asked.

"My dad wanted to be closer to his new job in Indiana," Tanisha shared. "Too bad McDonald's is closed. I wanted a vanilla shake," Tanisha finished.

As the whites moved west to new subdivisions that were being developed in what was once farmland, the retailers followed them. Lord & Taylor and Marshall Fields shuttered their stores and opened in Finley Park Square. Slowly the nicer boutique stores were closing at Jefferson mall. The Gap had been replaced by a small independent gold jewelry specialty store owned by a Pakistani family. Stride Rite shoe store was replaced by a music store and the Gloria Jeans coffee shop was replaced by a currency exchange. Even the McDonald's restaurant closed its Jefferson mall store. A small hot dog cart was stationed near the now boarded up entrance to Marshall Fields and remained the only food choice other than the Karmelkorn popcorn store and the Cookie Factory.

"I completely forgot that McDonald's closed last week, and I'm starving," Rashanda groaned. "Let's swing by the Karmelkorn store so I can at least grab some popcorn," she suggested.

"That works for me. I want to get a karmelkorn-cheesecorn mix," Grace said.

"I just painted my nails, and I don't want my finger tips to look orange. Besides, I want to go to the arcade and see who's here." Teenie wiggled her fingertips at her friends to emphasize her point. "So let's just split up."

Maria chimed in. "I have to pick up these jeans that they're holding for me. And don't forget we came to get a gift for Justine. Let's pool our money together for Justine's present," she suggested. "Lori and Teenie can get the stationery and a card, and I'll run and get my jeans. Grace and Rashanda can get their popcorn and we'll all meet at the arcade in fifteen minutes."

The girls contributed three dollars apiece for Justine's gift. Lori and Teenie headed to the Hallmark store. A sign in the window read Store Closing – Most Merchandise 50% off! They quickly chose a box of stationery with a border of white daisies, since daisies were Justine's favorite flower. They selected a card and walked to the cashier to pay for their items.

"Why is this store going out of business?" Tanisha asked.

The clerk responded without raising her head. "We're not really going out of business. We're just moving to Finley Park Square next month to be closer to our customer base. All of the merchandise that we don't want to pay the movers to pack and move is being discounted," she explained. "Thanks for coming in." She smiled as she handed Tanisha her change.

Lori and Tanisha exchanged a knowing glance and shook

their heads as they left the store. They bumped into Maria carrying her Levi Strauss bag and walked to the arcade.

"Everything in the Hallmark store was 50% off, so we have over nine dollars left," Tanisha explained. "We should get Justine a tee-shirt or something at Boston Shirt Yard," she suggested. "We could all get matching shirts." Teenie stuffed the change into her purse.

"If we wait a few weeks, Boston Shirt Yard will probably be having a going out of business sale too," Lori sighed. "It's so sad that we won't have any good stores here to shop in. It makes me so mad! I'm glad we'll all be getting our driver's licenses in a few months so we can drive to Finley Park Square for some decent shopping."

The girls walked quietly to the arcade. The Speedway Arcade remained the last hangout spot at the mall. Teens from all neighborhoods gathered at the Speedway to race bumper cars and play arcade games on Saturday afternoons. The movie theatre arcade had tightened its policy after a recent fight between rival basketball teams. Teenagers were now only allowed into the movie theatre arcade with a movie ticket stub. At the end of each movie, the ushers stood at the outside of the movie theatre and offered theatre goers a piece of chewing gum or a mint in exchange for their movie ticket stub to discourage people from giving their ticket stub to teens loitering in the parking lot.

The girls passed the Cookie Factory and inhaled the sweet smell of chocolate chip cookies. Tanisha noticed two high school boys grinning at the girls as they walked by.

"Don't look! But those two boys at the Cookie Factory are checking us out," she giggled. Maria and Lori stopped walking. They turned around and stared boldly at the two boys in question.

"They're so NOT my type," Maria stated flatly. She flipped her long hair and kept walking.

"They could be my type. They're totally cute," Lori whispered.

"Well, that was obvious!" Teenie blushed from embarrassment. She carefully looked back over her shoulder as they walked away. The taller of the two boys smiled at her before turning around to pay for his cookie purchase. She nervously smiled back and kept walking.

The girls spotted Grace and Rashanda enjoying their popcorn on a bench in front of the arcade. Tanisha showed the girls Justine's stationery and card.

Grace fingered the stationery. "That's really cute! Justine loves daisies! This is perfect, Teenie," Grace gushed.

Rashanda shoved a handful of popcorn into her mouth, savoring the treat that her braces had forbidden for two years. "And since it was on clearance, we definitely have enough money left to get her a tee-shirt as part of her going away gift," Rashanda explained.

"Don't get popcorn stains on the card!" Tanisha cautioned. She put the gift back in the bag. "I'm sad that Justine is moving. But it will be fun having a pen pal, and we can always meet her downtown on the weekend. We can shop like maniacs at Marshall Field's on State Street and hoof it up to Water Tower Place on Michigan Avenue."

"I can't believe that she's moving next weekend," Grace said sadly.

Maria counted her money. "We're all sad that Justine is moving, but let's go back to our happy place, people. We don't need to lose it in the mall," she stamped her foot and groaned. "Shoot! I've got to go back to Levi Strauss. I totally forgot that

I have enough money to get this shirt that matches my jeans. I'll meet you ladies in the arcade in ten minutes," Maria explained.

Rashanda and Grace finished their popcorn and scooted off to the restroom to wash their orange hued fingertips.

Teenie and Lori gathered their packages and walked slowly into the crowded arcade. Their eyes adjusted to the darkness as their ears captured the rhythm of the arcade melody. They walked confidently through the arcade like teen royalty surveying their subjects.

"Should we get some tokens?" Lori shouted.

"Not yet. Let's just do a once around and scout out who's here," Teenie suggested. The arcade was crowded. The empty parking lot notwithstanding, the Jefferson mall was a popular spot with the teen crowd too young to drive to the Finley Park mall.

"Do you see anyone interesting?" Tanisha had to repeat her question twice as they walked deeper into the arcade.

"Not yet. Let's keep walking," Lori replied. "I'm sure we'll spot some D.I.D. candidates."

Damsel in Distress or D.I.D. was their tried and true strategy for meeting boys. The girls would casually stand next to cute boys playing the arcade games and admire their technique. When it was their turn to play the game, the girls would ask the boy to give them tips to help improve their score thereby breaking the ice. There were usually more boys than girls in the Speedway Arcade and today was no exception. The ratio was four to one in favor of the girls. Sometimes the damsel in distress strategy didn't result in a phone number request, but sometimes it did.

"Teenie, there are three cute boys huddled at the NASCAR booth. Look!" Lori pointed. "Let's get tokens and do D.I.D."

The girls inserted singles in the token machine and casually walked over to the NASCAR booth. Their presence went unnoticed by the boys who watched intently as the driver maneuvered the steering wheel and shifted the manual transmission gear like an expert.

Teenie whispered to Lori. "It is so tricky meeting guys in the summer because they don't have on their school letterman jackets so we can see their graduation year. How old do you think these guys are?"

"I'm not sure, but they're pretty tall. I'm guessing they're at least freshman. I just hope they don't go to Pillcrest and know Doug."

Lori and Doug had broken up in May. He'd lasted almost a year before Lori tired of him and suggested that they take some time off. He'd taken the break up hard, and had only recently stopped calling every day just to hear her voice. He sometimes drove to her family's church on Sunday just to see her.

"You get first dibs, Lori," Tanisha whispered.

"I like the guy with the rugby shirt," Lori replied.

"He's cute." Teenie ran her tongue across her lips. "I like the driver. He's handling that stick shift!"

The driver put his initials into the number one spot. Teenie tapped him on the shoulder. "Hi. Can my friend and I drive when you guys are done?" Teenie smiled coyly.

"Sure. We were finished anyway," he offered.

"Don't let us scare you away. In fact, why don't you stick around and give me some pointers since you just got the top spot. I don't know how to drive a stick, but watching you makes me want to learn. Can you show me the basics?" Teenie bit the side of her lower lip and batted her eyelashes several times crossing her hands in a plea. "Please?" She pleaded.

"No problem. It's really not that hard. It's a standard H gear shift. We'll get you started on the basic track so you can get the hang of it." The driver slid out of the seat and stood next to Teenie. He towered at least six feet two inches tall. Teenie tilted her head back and stared up into his face.

"I'm Teenie by the way. Teenie Carlson and this is my friend Lori Perkins."

"Hi. I'm George Randall, and these are my friends Leroy, Hakim and Will," George said.

"How did you learn how to drive so well, George?" Teenie asked.

"I've hung out at the arcade since I was in middle school, and this is my favorite game, so I got pretty good at it," George explained. "Have a seat, Teenie. You'll need to adjust the seat forward so your feet can reach the pedals," he instructed.

Teenie settled into the driver's seat and adjusted the seat closer to the steering wheel. "Where do you go to school, George?" she flirted.

"I'm a freshman at Morgan Park Academy. I live in Beverly, but I'm out here visiting my boy Hakim for the weekend. He used to live across the street from me until his parents moved to Glen a few months ago." Teenie dropped two tokens into the slot. "Now to choose your car you click the steering wheel and press start when you find the car that you want to drive," George coached.

Strike one. George was an underclassman which means that I will be driving before he is. Strike two. He's a city boy which means that his trips to the south suburbs will be infrequent.

Teenie selected a red Ferrari as George explained the basic steps in manual stick shift operation. She glanced over her shoulder and noticed that Lori was getting a lesson in Asteroids from Will in the

Rugby shirt.

At first Teenie struggled with the concept of shifting, but caught on quickly.

"I've never driven a stick shift before, but isn't there a clutch involved?" Teenie asked.

"Yeah, normally, but in this game there's no clutch pedal, just the brake and accelerator," George explained. "So just relax your left foot."

Teenie squealed as her car sped off into the giant Redwood forest and crashed into several trees. "I can't believe I chose the hardest course!" She exhaled as her car finished in tenth place.

"You were getting the hang of it, Teenie. You just have to practice," George said. He reached down and helped Teenie out of her seat.

His compliment was interrupted by a deep male voice. "Hey man, what are you doing talking to my girlfriend?"

Startled, George turned slowly and stared nervously toward the voice. Teenie recognized him. It was the boy that smiled at her at the Cookie Factory.

"I'm sorry, Glen. I didn't know this was your girl." George backed away from Teenie. "I was just giving her some driving tips, man. No harm no foul," George explained with his hands in the surrender posture.

Glen punched George in the shoulder. "I'm kidding, man. She's not my girl. I was just messing with you, freshman."

Teenie self consciously smoothed out her denim shorts. Glen stood at least two inches taller than George. He hadn't looked quite that tall at the Cookie Factory. George looked from Glen to Teenie. "Do you two know each other?"

Teenie blushed and shook her head. "No, we don't." She was careful to conceal her decayed front fang as she spoke.

"I'm Glen Horton. I noticed you earlier. You walked by with your friends when I was at the Cookie Factory. I was trying to get your attention, but you walked away. What's your name?" Glen had a deep baritone voice and articulated each word slowly. His hazel eyes locked into Teenie's eyes like a hypnotist.

"I'm Teenie. Teenie Carlson." Teenie studied Glen's face. His skin was a rich caramel color that reminded her of a Snickers candy bar. His hair was cut in a short fade. She noticed a small gold stud in his left ear lobe. He smiled widely showing white teeth with a large gap. His left eyebrow arched provocatively as his eyes admired Teenie's figure. She shifted her feet self consciously under his careful gaze, and nervously switched her purse from her right shoulder to her left. Glen wore a black tee-shirt with a photo of Malcolm X standing in the window parting a curtain with one hand, a rifle held casually in his other hand. The words By Any Means Necessary were printed across the bottom of the shirt.

George spoke. "Glen is Hakim's older brother, Teenie. He gave us a ride to the mall," George explained. He gave Glen a light punch in the chest. "He's always giving us a hard time." George directed his next comment to Glen. "Man, the way you rolled up on us, I thought she was your girl," George shared. "I thought you were going to flatten me!"

"Watch and learn, freshman. Watch and learn," Glen coached as he stared at Teenie.

Teenie titled her head back and studied Glen's face. She noticed a deep dimple in his left cheek. She blushed slightly as his eyes locked into hers again. He's tall. He drives. He's adorable, and he's flirting with me! Breathe, Teenie. Breathe!

Chapter 10

Cover Girl Tears

The contents of her purse emptied, she reached for a tissue, her carefully applied make-up smudged by the tears that streamed down her face like a waterfall.

"So let me get this straight," he growled. "You were going to pay for the mascara but you reached into your purse for a mint and accidentally dropped the mascara into your purse?" he questioned. "And then you forgot about it and left the store. Is that your story?" he asked sarcastically.

She nervously folded the make-up stained tissue into a triangle. "It's the truth. I swear," she pleaded. "I have the money right here," she explained, pulling a twenty dollar bill from her purse and waving it in his face. "Why would I need to steal a three dollar tube of mascara, sir? Do I look like a shoplifter?" she pleaded.

The security guard stared directly into Maria's face. "Do you look like a shoplifter? Do you look like a shoplifter?" he repeated. "I get that question all the time. But the thing is this, pretty lady. Shoplifters never look like shoplifters," he paused. "I've caught eighty year old grandmothers who look like they sing in the church choir shoplifting. I've caught men in suits shoplifting. I've caught ladies carrying expensive designer purses and wearing big diamond rings shoplifting. I've seen it all," he boasted. "I've been doing this job for a very long time, and every time someone gets caught, they always offer a version of the same story."

He laid his pen on the desk and used his fingers as quotation marks. "I was going to pay for it, sir," he chided in a sing song falsetto. "I just put it in my purse so my hands could be free and then I forgot it was in there," he mocked. He waved his hand across her face. "Save the drama. I've heard all of the stories. Now let me ask you something. Do I look stupid to you?" he growled. "Huh? Do I?" The guard shoved another stick of chewing gum in his mouth and casually tossed the wrapper on the floor.

Maria knew better than to respond to that question. She gulped. To her, he looked like a slightly younger version of Barney Fife from the Andy Griffith show. He was short, thin, goofy, and extremely unattractive. But he was the only thing standing between her and a humiliating ride in a police car and a call to her parents. She took a deep breath.

"Sir, I swear I'm telling the truth. I am an honors student at River North High School, and I'm a cheerleader," she listed. "And I've never been in trouble before. I swear to you that I was going to pay for the mascara. I got distracted at the magazine rack and then realized that it was time to meet my friends. I'll give you the money for it right now." Maria pushed the twenty dollar bill toward the security guard whose name badge read Officer J. Barber. Ignoring her plea, Officer Barber continued writing the theft report.

"Officer Barber, I came to the mall with my girlfriends to buy a going away present for our friend who's moving away next weekend. You may have heard the story. Her mother was confronted with a blowtorch by her dad's girlfriend, and the police shot the girlfriend dead in their doorway," Maria explained.

Officer Barber looked up from his paperwork. His eyes grew wide. "That was your friend?" he asked slowly. "I saw that on the news. That story was unbelievable. This area never gets that type of excitement. Was your friend really in the house when it happened?" Officer Barber asked excitedly. He laid the pen on the desk and stared at Maria like she was a celebrity.

Maria's eyes grew more serious as she continued. "Yes she was, sir. She ran out the back door when Angela waved a blow torch at her mother and stated that she had a gun. My friend's name is Justine Wellington, and she is the one who called the police from a neighbor's house," Maria continued. "She's my best friend," she sniffled. "Mrs. Wellington was so distraught that she's moving the family away to start a new life. They're both still haunted by what happened. Of course, Justine's parents are getting divorced now, so not only is Justine moving, but she won't see her dad every day," Maria sniffled.

"Wow! Did the police actually shoot the woman in the doorway of your friend's house?" Officer Barber leaned in closer and stared into Maria's eyes.

"Yes, it was really scary. My friend Justine was outside giving information to a police officer when the shots were fired. Her mother didn't even know that her father had been having an affair," she continued. "And to make matters worse, Angela babysat for Justine's family a few times when she was in high school. It was really sad," Maria finished. Officer Barber's jaw was ajar as he listened.

It's working. He feels sorry for me. Don't blow it, Maria. She reached for another tissue. "Justine was my best friend, and now she's moving to Rogers Park. Her mother can barely stand to sleep in that house any longer," Maria shared. "I don't blame her though. I helped them clean up some of the blood in their foyer. The crime scene investigation team cleaned most of it," she added. "But they didn't get it all. Blood splattered everywhere, I've never seen so much blood," Maria groaned. "We used Pepsi and Coke to clean the tile so it wouldn't stain. Justine's mom is a nurse, so she got some solutions from the hospital to help clean up the blood." Maria grabbed a tissue and dabbed her eyes. "I didn't know that soda would clean up blood, did you?" she asked.

"I've heard that police officers will pour cola sodas onto the pavement after an accident to break up the blood molecules so it doesn't leave a big stain," he offered.

"Anyway, I stopped in the magazine and card aisle to buy her a going away card. I put the mascara on top of my purse so I could read a magazine," she continued. "It must have just slipped in when I reached for a peppermint in my purse," Maria explained. "I am not a thief, Officer Barber," she whined, as a fresh batch of tears spilled from her eyes. "I was just so distraught thinking about my best friend's move that I got upset and couldn't pick out a going away card. I felt like I was about to cry so I left the store to meet my friends and completely forgot about the mascara," she defended. "In fact, my friends are at the arcade. If you'd like, you can come with me to meet them, and they'll verify my story about Justine and confirm that I was charged with picking out the card."

Officer Barber's eyes had softened. "I'm really sorry about your friend," he shared softly. "Listen. Since you don't have any prior incidents with this store, and the mascara was less than five dollars in value, I'm going to let you go with just a warning," he winked. "You've been through enough with your friend. Pay for the mascara at the register and you're free to go," he explained as he ripped the report in half and tore it into pieces.

"Thank you, Officer Barber," Maria beamed, her hand resting over her heart. "I really appreciate that. I don't even want the mascara now," Maria sniffled. "I just want to meet my friends."

"Don't cry. This won't be on your record, young lady. Just be more careful when you're in a store. Security watches teenagers very closely for shoplifting," he offered. "You can't be distracted and let something slip into your purse. That's the lamest excuse of all."

Maria tossed the items back into her purse, grabbed her Levi Strauss shopping bags and left the store. She sniffled and dabbed at her eyes until she was back in the mall area. She quickly darted into the bathroom to reapply her smeared make-up. She smiled at her reflection. She was pleased with her performance as she sauntered casually to the arcade.

"Where've you been, Maria?" Grace asked. "You've been gone for a long time. We've been looking all over for you. Rashanda and I went to Levi Strauss to try and find you, but you weren't there." Grace sat at the Ms. Pac Man table with a line of tokens.

"We thought maybe you'd been kidnapped or something," Rashanda teased.

"Oh, I had to get something from another store, and then I lost track of the time," Maria lied. "I see Lori found a cutie in here. Where is Teenie?"

Rashanda tilted her head over her shoulder. "She's over there. She's been talking to that tall guy since we came back from looking for you."

Maria turned and scowled. "Him? He looks like a thug," Maria frowned. "Is that an earring in his ear? Why is Teenie talking to him?"

"Yup, it's a gold earring stud," Rashanda confirmed.

"Personally, I think it's cute, and Teenie must think so too. Look at the way she's flirting with him," Rashanda pointed.

Rolling her eyes, Maria walked over to Teenie and coughed. "Uh uhm!" she stated loudly. Glen turned around slowly. "Hi. I'm Maria," she introduced.

Glen smiled curiously at Maria. "Hello, Maria. I'm Glen, and this is Teenie," he shrugged. "Is there something that I can do for you?"

"I need to talk to Teenie, genius," she blurted. "Teenie, can I talk to you for a minute?" Maria tugged at Teenie's elbow and led her out of earshot of Glen.

"What's up, girl? Why are you being so rude, and why'd you pull me away like that?" Teenie asked.

"What are you doing, Teenie? He's so not your type. He looks like a wannabe thug with that earring in his ear. And you could kick a football through that gap in his teeth. He needs braces. Why are you wasting your time talking to him?" Maria demanded.

Self consciously, Teenie's tongue traced the concealed tooth decay in her front fang. *If she saw my raggedy teeth, what would she think of me?* Tanisha took a deep breath. "Lower your voice, Maria. He might hear you. First of all, I don't think he looks like a thug. I like the earring, and I think he's cute," she said confidently. "And what's wrong with someone having a gap? Not everyone has perfect teeth, Maria! You shouldn't judge someone by their teeth," she scolded quietly.

"I'm not judging him based on that, Teenie," she defended. "But overall, he looks kind of edgy and hard. Plus, he just looks like he's too old for you if you ask me," Maria whispered.

Teenie giggled. "You're kidding, right? You're not lecturing me about a boy being too old when you've been dating Todd for the last two years, and Todd is three years older than you!"

"That's different. At least Todd doesn't look like a thug," Maria explained.

Teenie held her tongue, but her mind drifted to David Barton's birthday party where Todd flirted with every girl in sight. Todd may not look like a thug, but he acts like one. "There you go judging someone that you don't even know. I'm curious. What exactly does a thug look like, Maria?" Tanisha asked.

"Well, this guy has an earring and he just looks like he's from around the way," Maria whispered. "He looks edgy like he's from the wrong side of the tracks."

Tanisha placed her hands on her hips and stared at Maria. "From around the way? I can't believe that you just said that," she whispered, scowling at Maria disapprovingly. First of all, he lives in Glen and he's a junior at Morgan Park Academy. He just moved here from Beverly, and his parents are going to let him finish his senior year at MPA. I have a cousin who goes to MPA, and the tuition is twelve thousand dollars a year. So it doesn't sound like he's from 'around the way' to me," Tanisha retorted. She turned to walk away and changed her mind, her index finger pointed at Maria's face. "And even if he was from around the way, he's cute, smart and interesting," she finished.

"Well, what's with that Malcolm X tee-shirt?" Maria asked.

"It's a tee-shirt, Maria. In fact, I think it's cool. He's a very interesting guy. He's interested in the Black Panthers, and he was telling me about a book that he read on Huey Newton. I'm just impressed that he reads. Most of the guys we meet only read what they have to read for school." Teenie checked her watch. Mrs. Perkins would be picking them up soon. "Listen, Maria. We've got to get going soon, so I'm going to go back and talk to him some more. He hasn't asked for my number yet, so if you don't mind." Teenie walked backwards and rejoined Glen.

"Is everything okay?" Glen asked. "It looked like you and your friend were having a heated discussion."

"Everything's fine. Just fine. My friend Maria wanted to ask my opinion about something that she bought," Teenie shrugged. "She's a professional shopper and has an opinion about everything," Tanisha groaned. She waved her hand across her face and shrugged.

"What were we talking about? I remember," she answered quickly. "I was asking you how you were going to get to MPA every day now that you live in the suburbs."

"My old man will drop me off on his way to work, and my mom will pick me up in the afternoon. She's a teacher at Percy Julian High School which is just a few blocks away from MPA," Glen explained. "They're going to let me drive myself my senior year."

"My cousin Nathan goes to MPA. He's a freshman. Do you know Nathan Thomas?" Teenie asked.

Glen stroked his temple. "No. I don't know too many underclassmen. I probably know his face since MPA is so small and there aren't too many blacks there, but I'm sure my brother knows him."

Teenie giggled. "Yeah, I know how that is. Once you become an upperclassman, you don't pay too much attention to the grades below you."

Glen checked his watch. "Listen, I've got to get going," he said. "My dad needs the car back by five thirty. Do you think I could call you some time, Teenie?"

"Sure. Do you have a pen?" Teenie asked. Yeah! He wants my phone number!

"I don't. But I have a great memory, Teenie Carlson. Just tell me your number, and I'll remember it."

Teenie rattled off her phone number as Lori walked up with Will.

"You have impeccable timing, Will." Glen patted Will's shoulder. "Round up the rest of the gang so we can hit the road," Glen ordered.

"We've got to get going, too." Teenie played with the strap of her purse.

Glen reached for Teenie's hand. "You have soft hands. I knew your hands would be soft," he said. He raised her hand to his mouth and air kissed it. "It was a pleasure meeting you, Teenie. Or should I call you 474-5589?" His hands felt warm and soft. Teenie's face flushed as Glen winked and sauntered away. Her body quivered as she watched his swagger.

"That was smooth. How old is he?" Lori asked.

"He's a junior, and he just turned seventeen," Teenie said. "He is too fine."

"Agreed," Lori offered. "At least one of us met someone interesting today. Will was a little too immature for me. He was goofy and annoying and kept asking me trivia questions about Star Trek," she groaned. "Fortunately, he didn't ask for my phone number or I would have been forced to give him a fake number," she finished. "Maybe I'll give Doug another chance. At least he's not a Star Trek geek."

"Watch out there now, I love Star Trek," Teenie replied.

"I like Star Trek too," Lori added. "But I don't watch it every waking hour."

"Do we have time to go to Boston Shirt Yard to pick out tee-shirts?" Rashanda interrupted. "I also want to get a cookie from the Cookie Factory before we hit the road."

Grace giggled. "Rashanda, you just ate popcorn! I can't believe that you're still hungry!"

"You know I have to eat something every thirty minutes or I turn into a crabby pumpkin," Rashanda joked.

"When you get older and your metabolism slows, you're going to look like a big, round, pumpkin if you continue to eat something every thirty minutes," Maria laughed. "In fact, you should start training your body to operate on less fuel," she suggested. "I try to only eat when I'm feeling light headed."

Teenie scowled at Maria. "That's the dumbest thing that I've ever heard, Maria. When you starve your body, your metabolism shuts down because it goes into starvation mode," Teenie explained.

"It does?" Maria asked.

"Yes, silly. It thinks that you're starving it, so it shuts down to preserve energy, and you burn fewer calories, duh! It's counter productive. You have to feed your body fuel in order for it to operate efficiently. You should eat small portions throughout the day and only indulge in bad stuff in moderation," Teenie stated. "Rashanda, you keep doing you. You're so thin you're still able to dodge raindrops, so enjoy your metabolism while you can and eat until your heart's content! Life is short. Eat a cookie and when you need to beef up your workouts, ratchet them up," Teenie encouraged. "I have a taste for a cookie myself," she added. "So if we hurry, we can swing by the Cookie Factory and grab some cookies and hoof it to Boston Shirt Yard to pick out matching tee-shirts," Teenie suggested. "Let's go, ladies. Lori's mom will be here in twenty minutes, and I don't want to be late for work. Besides, I want to see if they have a Malcolm X tee- shirt," Teenie giggled.

"Why do you want a Malcolm X tee-shirt, Teenie? I thought we were getting matching tee-shirts to match Justine?" Grace asked.

"We are. But I might also treat myself and get a Malcolm X tee-shirt too if they have one," Teenie shrugged.

"Teenie has a boyfriend. Teenie has a boyfriend," Lori sang. "Teenie wants to get a Malcolm X tee-shirt to match her new boyfriend," Lori teased.

"He was a cutie, Teenie," Rashanda offered. "Tall, dark and handsome are a winning combination in my book," she giggled.

"I thought he was cute too, Teenie," Grace agreed. "And he couldn't take his eyes off of you. I thought he was going to kiss you in the arcade the way he was staring into your eyes!"

Maria rolled her eyes into the top of her head and glared at Teenie. She shook her head from side to side.

Tanisha pointed her finger in Maria's face and made her eyes tiny slits. "I don't want to hear a word from you, Maria Wesley! Not with your yo-yo dieting to please Todd," she smiled.

Maria grabbed Teenie's arm and spun her around. "That is totally different, and you know it, Teenie. Todd is my boyfriend. Sometimes, girls do special things to please their boyfriend," she argued. "But you just met this guy, Teenie. At least let him call you first before you start altering your wardrobe to please him," Maria suggested.

"I'm not altering my wardrobe. It's just a silly tee-shirt, Maria. Don't make a federal case out of it." Teenie brushed Maria's arm from her shoulder and playfully stuck her tongue out at her friend. She quickened her pace to catch up to the other girls. Teenie has a boyfriend. Teenie has a boyfriend. I like the sound of that.

Chapter 11

Just One More Day

The heat hung in the air like a heavy, wet, wool poncho. It was only eleven o'clock in the morning, and the temperature had already climbed to ninety six degrees. The weatherman predicted a record breaking high of ninety nine degrees Fahrenheit. It was going to be a scorcher.

A good rain was needed to cool off the day. Justine stared at her packing-weary hands and wished that it would rain. And not just a light drizzle, but a heavy downpour complete with thunder and lightning. That's what she wanted, a good old fashioned thunderstorm warning. They couldn't move in the middle of a thunderstorm! Maybe if it rained, her mother would postpone the move just one more day.

Justine wanted just one more day with her friends. On the hottest day of the year, with the sun shining bright in the sky, Justine was blue. She rubbed the bright yellow tee-shirt that her friends had given her as a going away present. In the center of the tee-shirt were the letters: T.W.F.A.F. Each letter was a different color. The girls pledged to wear the tee-shirt on the first Friday of every month. Justine traced the letters on her tee-shirt and smiled. "That's What Friends Are For," she sighed.

It wasn't fair. How did it get to this point? She couldn't believe that over the course of one year, her life had been turned upside down.   Now that their move date was finally here, Justine was filled with despair. She didn't want to move to the Rogers Park neighborhood. She wanted to live in Newberry East and attend River North High School with her friends.

The week leading up to the move, she had begged her mom to reconsider, but her mother insisted that a fresh start would do them all some good. Besides, she had already signed the lease and put down the security deposit on their new apartment. They were moving today. Justine peered out the window to check for the moving van. The sun stood center stage like a one woman show mocking Justine's plea for rain. There wasn't a cloud in the sky. Justine's melodrama was interrupted by her mother's cheery voice.

"I can't wait to get out of here," Mrs. Wellington stated. "This has been the longest and most horrific year of my life." Mrs. Wellington instinctively unplugged the kitchen phone from the wall and disconnected the answering machine. She had filed a temporary restraining order against her husband, but the police had informed her that he could phone the house between nine o'clock a.m. and nine o'clock p.m. to speak with their children. So whenever she was home, she unplugged the phones. She wanted to make sure that she didn't inadvertently answer one of his calls. The sound of her ex-husband's voice made her sick to her stomach.

She loathed him with a hatred that caused her to destroy every one of their wedding photos. Her best friend had convinced her that the children deserved to have some pictures of their father, so she stopped short of destroying every photo in which he appeared. She was grateful that none of her children bore a significant resemblance to her estranged ex-husband so she wouldn't be reminded of him whenever she looked at them. She had filed for a divorce less than one week after the incident and planned to use her maiden name to further distance herself from her ex-husband.

Justine and her brothers had attended all of the divorce court proceedings. Her mother had insisted on that. In court, the judge was sympathetic to Mrs. Wellington's recent encounter, granting sole custody of the three children to her with one year of supervised visitation for her dad on the weekends.

The court appointed supervisor was Mrs. Jones. Justine hated Mrs. Jones. She'd grown to detest her black wire rimmed glasses, stern expression, and the kitchen cleanser aroma that hung to her clothes. The liaison's presence made the visits with their dad sterile and uncomfortable. But Justine was polite and cordial because she knew that if Mrs. Jones gave a good report to the judge, the supervised visitation restriction could be lifted sooner. Justine thought it unfair that her father was treated like a criminal. He hadn't pulled the trigger.

The final court proceedings happened so fast that it was almost like a blur to Justine. Her mother had insisted that they wear their Sunday best for the final divorce hearing. As they entered the court room, Justine spotted her father at a rectangular conference table. His head was hung low as he sat on the opposite side of the small court room. He smiled weakly and waved at the children. He was afraid to walk over and hug them, since it would mean that he would come within one hundred feet of his wife, which was a violation of the restraining order.

Staring at her dad, Justine thought that he looked different. His hair was grayer. Leading up to the final court date, her father had missed three weeks of supervised visits with Justine and her brothers. He looked older. His face was unshaven, and Justine could tell that he hadn't had a haircut in a few weeks. She wiped a tear from her eye as she remembered the lengthy statement that the judge made in court before ruling on the divorce proceedings.

❧❦

"Mrs. Wellington, I know that you have been through a great deal over the past year. The trauma that you suffered at the hands of your husband's girlfriend is so surreal that when I read your attorney's divorce documents I thought that I was reading a well written piece of fiction," Judge Core paused.

"It says here that your husband's girlfriend came to your home with a blow torch and bleach," he read. "Based on the statement that you gave to the police, her intent was to create an explosive and burn down your home unless you agreed to leave your husband. Am I reading this correctly, Mrs. Wellington?" he asked.

"Yes, your honor. That is what she said to me," Justine's mother stated. "I feared for my life."

The judge studied the papers in his hand and wiped his brow with a white handkerchief. He shook his head in disbelief. "The fact that she came to your home and tried to carry out her psychotic pursuit of passionate justice is unimaginable," he continued. "It is by the grace of God that you and your children were not physically harmed by this deranged woman," he offered softly. His eyes shifted to Mr. Wellington's table. Mr. Wellington sat with his head slumped low. His eyes were downcast.

"As a Christian man, I find it deplorable that your husband committed adultery. But I also find it sad that your husband's mistress had to die at the hands of that police officer. But if taking one life saved four lives, then I believe in my heart that it was justifiable homicide. I know that the good Lord will forgive the officer who fired that shot just as I hope you can find it in your heart to one day grant forgiveness to your husband for his brazen infidelity, stupidity, and the danger he placed your family in," he offered. "He will have to live with himself every day which is sufficient punishment for his sexual misconduct," Judge Core glared at Mr. Wellington. Justine's brothers played hangman at the table, seemingly oblivious to the life altering event taking place right before their eyes. Justine sat on the edge of her seat and listened intently to the judge's every word.

"But I do trust that you will behave civilly toward him, since he is the father of your three children." The judge paused again and took a long sip of water. He pounded on his chest a few times and coughed again before continuing. "After careful consideration, this court will not honor Mr. Wellington's request for a geographic restriction limiting where you may move with the children. You are free to move wherever your heart desires within the continental United States, and you do not need the court's permission or Mr. Wellington's permission to do so." Justine watched as Judge Core directed his gaze back to her father's table. His eyes bore holes through her dad, who continued to sit with his head slumped low, his eyes downcast. Justine felt sorry for him. Her father sat like a beaten man.

"I'm sure that Mr. Wellington will make whatever financial arrangements he needs to make in order to visit his children if you decide to relocate to another state," Judge Core said. He turned his attention back to Mrs. Wellington and smiled. "May God bless you and keep you. And may your new start in life be filled with God's continued grace and mercy." Judge Core slammed the gavel as the bailiff ordered everyone to rise. The judge left the courtroom, and Mrs. Wellington reluctantly allowed the children to hug their father before ushering them into the hallway.

෨෪

Justine's daydream was interrupted by the sound of her mother's voice. "Justine, I know you're sad now, but you'll meet new friends in no time," Mrs. Wellington said. "Sweetie, did you hear what I said?"

"Yes, I heard you. But Mom, I have really good friends here, and now I have to start over and make new friends as a sophomore in high school. Do you know how hard that's going to be?" she whined. "Why can't I just stay here with Dad so I can finish high school with my friends?" Justine pleaded.

Mrs. Wellington gently set down the cookbooks that she was packing and stared at Justine with soft eyes. "Justine, your father's poor judgment almost got me killed and could have gotten you killed or your brothers killed. I know he's your father, and he will always be your father. I don't expect you to stop loving him, but I can't allow you to live with someone who was that thoughtless. If you hadn't run next door and called the police, who knows what may have happened. His crazy, deranged girlfriend could have started a fire and killed us all. You heard what the judge ruled," she reminded. "The court doesn't even believe that your dad is responsible enough to spend time with you guys without a court appointed babysitter right now. He can't be trusted. Do you really think that your dad is responsible enough to care for you properly?"

Justine hadn't considered that point. "I'm sorry, mom. I guess you're right. It's just that it's hard to start over at a new school. Girls can be so mean and catty," she whined.

"I know, sweetheart, but you'll be fine." Mrs. Wellington continued to pack the cookbooks. "You made friends when we moved here," she reminded. "And you'll meet new friends when we move."

Justine rolled her eyes and shook her head "But mom, the girls I met at Battle Creek Junior High are very special. I don't know if I'll meet girls like that again. We look out for each other, and we've promised to tell each other when we're going through tough times. We've bonded," Justine explained.

Mrs. Wellington nodded her head and placed tape across the box. "That's nice, honey. Now hand me that packing tape. The movers will be here any minute. Let's finish these last few boxes quickly." Mrs. Wellington resumed her packing. "Justine, drink some water, baby. I don't want you to dehydrate in this heat."

Chapter 12

Home Town Honey

"Pretend the steering wheel is a clock, Teenie," David coached. "The top of the steering wheel is the number twelve. The bottom is the number six. The left and right sides are nine and three on the clock face," he paused. "Your hands should always be in the three and nine position or the ten and two position," he coached. "Actually, you just have to practice driving like this until you pass your driving test and get your license, and then you can drive with one hand like the rest of the world does," he shrugged. "Only old ladies drive with their hands in the proper position," he laughed. "When you get to be a good driver like me, you can drive with your knees while changing your pants."

Giggling, she rested her left hand firmly in the number ten position and her right hand in the number two position. She rubbed the steering wheel gently. She missed David's driving lessons.

"What's so funny," Jack asked.

"Oh, nothing," she replied. "I was just thinking about something funny that a friend of mine said."

"Well, focus now, Sis. Learning to drive is serious," Jack insisted. "You should slow down through here because the Steiffer police have a speed trap for the next mile," Jack explained. "They'll pull you over for just going five miles over the speed limit." Jack carefully looked out the large windshield of the car. "And technically, you're not supposed to be driving with me since you only have your permit, and I'm not over twenty-one," he continued. Tanisha lifted her foot from the accelerator and slowed down her speed.

"Maybe I'll speed so we can get arrested! Wouldn't that be funny?" she teased. Tanisha lowered her head over the steering wheel. "Let's see how fast this baby can really go!" She smiled at her big brother. He stared back at her somberly. "Relax. I was just teasing, Jack. But thanks for letting me get some driving practice in Bruce the Blue Goose. I really appreciate it," Tanisha grinned.

"Don't mention it. Driving once a week with Dad isn't enough practice. Besides, you've got to get accustomed to driving Bruce since you'll more than likely drive this car for your driving test," Jack said. "You're driving really well, Tanisha. You seem really comfortable behind the wheel."

Tanisha smiled warmly at Jack. David's driving tips had paid off. She turned into the Save Mart parking lot and carefully parallel parked the car along the curb. She opened the door and grabbed her backpack. Jack slid across the large bench seat of the car and sat behind the steering wheel. "Tanisha, sit back down and help me push the seat back," Jack ordered. Tanisha plopped down and pulled the lever under her seat and pushed back as Jack pushed his side.

"I always forget that your lanky legs need more room," Tanisha laughed. "This car is such a dinosaur! She groaned. "It's probably the only car that doesn't have automatic seat adjusters now!"

"At least it gets us from point A to point B, so stop complaining. I'll pick you up at 9:15 tonight, Tanisha," Jack said. "Have fun at work."

"Yeah right. Work is always big fun with prizes. Woo Hoo!" Tanisha laughed. Her family had not caught on to her nickname and refused to call her Teenie. Billie Mae didn't believe in nicknames.

Tanisha tossed her backpack across her shoulder and walked into the store. Now every time she came to work, she thought about David Barton. Before David left for Georgetown, he had driven to Save Mart every day that she was scheduled to work. If she worked an eight hour shift, David treated her to lunch or dinner. He usually took her to Dudz and Sudz or anyplace that she wanted to go. Once she tried to pay for their meal, and she recalled David's reaction.

David grabbed her hand as she pulled her wallet from her purse. "Teenie, what are you doing?" he asked.

"You're always treating me so I thought I'd treat you this time," she replied.

"Absolutely not! How would I look letting you pay? Put your wallet away!" David ordered.

Tanisha was taken aback by the seriousness of his tone. She stared at him in stunned silence. Reacting to her expression, David continued softly. "Teenie, my parents are wealthy, and I can well afford to buy you lunch a few times a week," David whispered. "I appreciate the thought of you trying to treat me to lunch, it's sweet, it really is, but I got this," he repeated softly. He smiled at Tanisha. "I enjoy treating you to lunch, I really do," he smiled again. "It makes me feel like you need me for something," he finished. Tanisha exhaled and smiled back.

As soon as Tanisha received her driving permit, David tried to teach her how to drive his car. He was more excited than she was by the yellow slip of paper. At his insistence, she climbed into the driver's seat of the sleek Corvette in the parking lot. She listened intently as David explained the basic handling of a standard H gear shift. Although focused on his words, she was nervous and confused by the clutch and gear shift. She heard the gears grinding as she tried to coordinate her left foot to push in the clutch while changing the gears with her right hand. The car lurched forward, sputtered and stalled as she hit the accelerator instead of the clutch. Frustrated, she put the car in neutral and unfastened her seatbelt. She stepped out of the car and pouted as David laughed. "Teenie, you'll get the hang of it. It'll just take practice," he explained. "I've been driving a stick for so long that I forgot that there are too many fundamentals for a novice driver to master." David vowed to teach her how to drive a stick shift once she got more comfortable driving an automatic transmission.

At least once or twice each week, David drove his parent's BMW or Mercedes to Save Mart so that he could give Tanisha pointers on her driving. The first time she drove one of his parent's luxury cars, she was a nervous wreck and feared that she would have an accident. But David calmly assured her that it would be fine. And it was. After a few weeks of practice, she loved driving the expensive cars and no longer felt nervous. Although both cars were far nicer than the cars her parents drove, and certainly much nicer than the Caprice Classic that Jack drove, she preferred driving the BMW. She would sometimes boldly ask David to drive the BMW to Save Mart for her driving lesson; a request he usually honored if his mom was home.

True to the agreement that they'd made at his seventeenth

birthday party, Tanisha and David Barton had remained just friends. Now that she was fifteen and could officially date, David asked Tanisha to his senior prom, but she politely turned him down. He knew she would. So he escorted Patty to the Homer Glen prom as expected.

Tanisha also refused his many requests to meet his parents. She knew that if he introduced her to his parents then he would want to meet her parents. She didn't mind introducing David to her dad, Jackie. But she couldn't bear the thought of introducing him to Billie Mae. There was no telling which Billie Mae he would meet. Would he meet the nice Billie Mae? Or would he meet the Billie Mae who hadn't taken her bipolar medication? Billie's behavior was still erratic and unpredictable.

It had been over a year since Tanisha and her brother learned about Billie Mae's mental illness from their dad. Billie Mae still hadn't broached the subject with her teenage children. The closest she came to acknowledging her condition happened once when she yawned and spoke aloud.

"I hate these pills. They make me so tired. I don't feel like myself," Billie Mae mumbled in between yawns.

Tanisha seized the opportunity. "What pills are you taking, Mom?"

Billie Mae shook her head and frowned. She'd forgotten that Tanisha was sitting in the room. "Don't worry about it. I was talking to myself. It's none of your business," her mother replied.

And the matter was dropped. Billie Mae knew that Tanisha and Jack had spoken with her psychiatrist, Dr. Dudley, but she never followed up with either of them on their chats with the doctor. Billie continued to act as though the visits to the doctor had been a routine part of her job like a training seminar that everyone was required to attend. Her mandatory psychological evaluation was now complete, and she had celebrated her one year anniversary at the cable company.

There was no way that Tanisha was ready for David to meet Billie Mae, so she simply told him that she didn't want to do the meet the parent thing.

"David, you know that I'm not allowed to go on solo dates yet, and if my parents meet you, they'll get suspicious and start tracking my every move," she explained. "Besides, you're leaving for college in a few months, so your parents don't need to meet me. They won't like me anyway, since they want you to date Patty."

"My parents will like you, Teenie. And they just want me to be happy. They like Patty and her family, but if I stopped hanging out with Patty tomorrow, my parents wouldn't care one way or the other," he explained. "As long as I'm happy, that's all they care about."

Once again, he reluctantly agreed to Tanisha's request and she hadn't met his parents. They only saw each other at Save Mart or on carefully coordinated visits to the mall. Now he was gone, and she missed him terribly.

Tanisha tossed her backpack in her locker and placed the key in her smock pocket. She tugged at the lock to ensure that it was securely attached before walking to the front of the store to begin her shift at the service desk.

She really missed David Barton. She missed the late night marathon telephone conversations that they had. She'd bought a small black and white television for her bedroom and most nights they talked on the telephone and watched the same program. She logged more phone time with David than she did with her girlfriends. David had become a really close friend, and Tanisha knew almost everything about him including his relationship with

Patty. Maria and Lori thought Tanisha was crazy not to claim him as her boyfriend, but Tanisha stood her ground. She didn't want to get romantically involved with him knowing that he was leaving for college in the fall so she made sure that they were never alone for long periods of time. When he picked her up for her lunch or dinner break, she had to be back within one hour. Their friendship was comfortable, innocent and platonic. She knew that he was physically attracted to her and she was attracted to him, but they were just friends. They had grown really close and talked openly about everything.

☙❧

"If you and Patty went on a trip together, would you sleep in separate beds like Rob and Laura Petrie?" Tanisha asked one night as they chatted on the phone watching late night reruns of the Dick Van Dyke show.

"Are you trying to find out if Patty and I have done the deed?"

"Uh huh," Teenie giggled.

"Whoa! Where did that come from, Teenie?" David asked.

"I was just wondering. Whenever I watch the Dick Van Dyke Show I always wonder how Laura and Rob do the deed," she giggled. "I know it's none of my business so you don't have to answer that question if you don't want to," Tanisha said.

There was a long silence before he responded. "Yeah. I'm not going to lie to you. We've done the deed," David said softly. "Does that bother you?"

"No big deal. I figured as much," Tanisha confessed.

"Have you?" David asked.

"What do you think?" Tanisha replied.

"I think you haven't, but you might surprise me," David stated.

"No surprises tonight. I haven't," Tanisha finished. "Not even close. I'm waiting for marriage. Can we change the subject?"

"You brought it up. But let me just say one thing. If you decide not to wait for marriage, your first time should be with someone very special. Or at least someone that you think is very special," David said confidently.

"So is Patty special to you?" Tanisha asked quietly.

"Patty wasn't my first time," David replied.

"This is really way too much information for me," Tanisha blushed. "Let's change the subject."

"Okay, we'll change the subject, but let me just say this. It's different with guys. We barely remember our first time," David explained. "Most guys will do it with the first girl who says yes, and then he won't remember her name six months later. I'm glad you're saving yourself for marriage. It should be with someone really special that you care about and love," he finished. "That's what God intended."

"Is that how you feel about Patty?" Teenie challenged.

"This isn't about me. This is about you," he advised. "In a perfect world, we'd all wait until marriage," David offered.

"You didn't," she reminded.

"I'm not perfect," David replied.

"Neither am I," she replied.

"To me you're perfect," David said softly. "Now we can change the subject."

"You didn't answer my question, David. Is Patty special to you?" Tanisha asked.

David took a deep breath. "Patty is Patty. And you're you," David replied. "Next subject, please."

❧

That was the first and last time that they talked about anything intimate or personal. David was always a perfect gentleman when they hung out and had not even tried to kiss her. He was like a big brother figure to her and she felt safe and comfortable in his presence.

Between her school work, writing for the student newspaper, participating on the track team, her part-time job at Save Mart and time spent with her girlfriends, Tanisha was busy. She hadn't met anyone interesting at the Jefferson Mall in over a year and David was openly glad about that. But Tanisha wasn't. She really wanted to meet a boy that she could call her boyfriend. David was her friend, but she wanted a boyfriend, someone who could take her to the homecoming dance. Plus, she secretly wanted to test her friendship with David Barton to see how he would handle her discussing a boy that she liked.

David had been gone for three weeks and Tanisha had already written him two letters. He'd called her the first week he was at college and they'd talked for forty-five minutes. She didn't want him to have a high telephone bill on her account so she suggested that they become pen pals. She'd written him another letter detailing the highlights of the last few weeks. She told him about Justine's move to Rogers Park and detailed her first week of school. It was a long letter. She spritzed the envelope flap with Lauren cologne so he would smell her perfume when he opened it. She hoped the scent lasted through the mail delivery.

She dropped the letter in the mailbox, confident that she'd brought David up to speed on everything in her life. Everything that is, except the boy that she'd met the week before at the mall.

133

The tall, dark, handsome boy that she'd met, with a gold stud earring and a gap between his teeth.

Glen Horton called her the night they met. Tanisha had just stepped out of the shower after finishing her shift at Save Mart. She picked up the phone after one ring.

"Hello." A deep male voice said. "May I speak to Teenie, please?"

"This is Teenie." The deep voice caught her off guard. She expected the caller to be one of her girlfriends. Her heart raced as she dried off with her towel.

"Hi, Teenie. This is Glen Horton. I met you at the arcade this afternoon," he explained.

Tanisha self consciously gripped the towel around her body. "Oh. Hi, Glen!"

"Did I catch you at a bad time? I hope I haven't called too late," he offered quickly. "I was trying to call before ten o'clock. I called you a few times earlier but no one picked up so I thought I'd try you one more time before it got too late," Glen explained.

Tanisha smiled into the receiver. "No, this is fine. I just got home from work, and I literally just stepped out of the shower."

"Do you want me to call you back?" he asked.

"I can talk now," she replied.

"What color towel are you wearing so I can get the visual?" Glen asked.

"Excuse me!" Teenie replied.

"I'm just kidding," Glen said quickly. "I didn't mean to offend you, but if I did I'm sorry. I was just playing around. I'm really sorry about that. Where do you work?" Glen stammered nervously.

Tanisha sat on her bed and rubbed lotion on her legs. "It's

okay. Thanks for the apology. I work at the Save Mart in Steiffer. I usually work at the service desk, but sometimes I supervise the checkouts."

Tanisha hadn't talked to a boy on the phone since David Barton. It felt weird to hear a male voice that wasn't David's. She slipped on her new pink pajamas.

Glen coughed lightly into the phone. "Oh. That's cool. I work too. My dad owns a few parking garages downtown, and I work in the exit booth sometimes. I usually work on Saturday if there's a big event downtown, but there was nothing going on today, so I didn't have to work," he explained. "That's why I agreed to take my brother Hakim and his friends to the mall since they don't have their driver's licenses yet. Are you taking driver's education now, Teenie?" Glen asked.

"I'm taking it this semester. I'll be sixteen in December, and I can get my license in a few months," Tanisha explained. She propped her pillows against her headboard and leaned back.

"Once you get your license your freedom really increases," Glen continued. "My parents promised to buy me a used car this year, but I have to make sure that I don't get any grade lower than a C+ on my next report card," he paused. "But even if I mess up and get a C they'll probably still buy me a car so that I can pick my brother Hakim up and tote him to his activities while they're at work. Do you have any brothers and sisters, Teenie?"

"I have three brothers. Jack is a senior and Byron and Allen are thirteen and ten," Tanisha said.

"So you're the only girl. You must be spoiled rotten!" Glen laughed.

"Not exactly," Tanisha said. "I wish. My parents are divorced, but I'm still a daddy's girl. I'm the responsible other mother to my younger brothers."

"I know how that works. Usually the only girl in the family is either spoiled rotten or she's ultra responsible," Glen paused. "I'm glad you answered the phone. I was beginning to think that you'd given me the wrong number."

"Why would I do that?" Tanisha asked.

"You know how you pretty girls are," Glen paused.

He thinks I'm pretty? Well, duh, stupid! He asked for your number didn't he?

"You don't want to let a guy know that you're not interested so you give him a fake name and a fake number," he continued. "By the way, is Teenie your real name?"

Teenie laughed heartily. "Actually, my real name is Tanisha, but my nickname is Teenie."

"Tanisha," he repeated. "I like that name. What's your middle name?" Glen asked.

"It's Denise," Tanisha said.

"Tanisha Denise," Glen repeated. "Tanisha Denise Horton. That has a nice ring to it, don't you think?"

Tanisha shook her head. "It's Tanisha Denise Carlson, thank you very much!" Tanisha stated firmly. Her tone softened and she giggled. "You're cracking me up. I've talked to you for a total of maybe thirty minutes, including at the arcade, and you're giving me your last name?"

"I didn't say I was giving it to you. But I think you have what it takes to earn it," Glen teased playfully.

"Is that right? And what if I'm not interested in earning it?" Tanisha asked.

Glen coughed into the receiver. "Excuse me. I have a tickle in my throat," Glen explained. He cleared his throat and continued.

"You will be. Once you get to know me, you'll like me," he coughed again. "Teenie, I need to grab a drink of water, and I prefer to talk face to face. Can you go on dates? I'd love to take you on a date so we can get to know each other. What are you doing tomorrow?"

Tanisha twirled the pink phone cord in between her fingers. "Technically, I'm only supposed to go on double dates until I turn sixteen, but I have to work tomorrow, so you could pick me up from work. I work until one thirty," she explained.

"I don't want you to get in trouble," Glen cautioned.

"It's fine. I'll just have you drop me off at my friend's house and walk home from there," she explained. "It'll be fine."

"Great!" Glen said. "We get home from church at about one o'clock so I could meet you at the store. I know where the Save Mart is. We can grab a bite to eat and maybe catch a matinee. Does that work for you?" Glen spoke rapidly.

He goes to church! David never went to church, or at least if he did he never talked about church. I wonder why David's family never went to church. Tanisha started to place her curlers in her hair. "Sure. That works," she replied. "If you're coming right from church, should I bring something dressy to change into after work?" Tanisha asked.

"No. I'll change into shorts and a tee-shirt after church since it's so hot." There was a slight pause before Glen continued. "Teenie, before we hang up, can I ask you something?"

His tone sounded serious. Tanisha put down the pink sponge curler before responding. "Sure. Go ahead," she said cautiously.

"Why don't you have a boyfriend, Teenie?" Glen asked.

She took a deep breath, caught off guard by the boldness of his question. "Why don't I have a boyfriend?" she repeated. "I have no idea," she shrugged. "I just don't."

Glen exhaled. "Okay, good. I just wanted to get that out in the open. I wanted to make sure that I wasn't treading on someone else's turf. I don't have a girlfriend right now either. I did have a girlfriend, but we broke up. But I'll tell you all about that tomorrow," Glen paused. "Actually, when I saw you at the mall I almost didn't say anything to you because I assumed you had a boyfriend. But when I saw my brother's friend George talking to you in the arcade I had to step in. I hope you don't mind," Glen said nervously.

Tanisha smiled. "No. I don't mind at all." The smile carried in her voice.

"Good. Very good," Glen continued. "But even if you had a boyfriend, that's a fence that I'd be willing to climb. I'd climb the fence and compete for your attention like they did in the old days. I would court you, because he would have no more right to you than I do," Glen offered.

"Is that right?" Tanisha blushed. "You would court me? You and my grandmother are the only people who still use the word court," she giggled.

"Even if you had a boyfriend, I would insist that you let me get to know you so you could decide if you like me better than him. That's only fair," he explained. "Here's my theory. That's what's wrong with relationships these days, people don't date anymore. They just claim someone as their boyfriend or girlfriend before they really even know the person, and then if they date someone else, they're accused of cheating," he finished.

"I see you have this all figured out, huh?" Tanisha teased. "And what if I didn't let you court me? What if I had a boyfriend and I told him about you and he got mad?"

"Well, I'd have to deal with that," Glen laughed. "I'd have to challenge him to a duel."

"You don't even know if we have anything in common, and you're willing to duel for my attention? You're hysterical," Tanisha laughed.

"That's right. I would duel your boyfriend and then court you because I want to get to know you, Tanisha Denise Carlson," he teased. "But seriously, I'll pick you up tomorrow at one thirty," Glen said. "And if something comes up on my end, I'll just call you at the store, but otherwise I'll be there," Glen explained. "Take my number in case something comes up on your end," Glen suggested.

"Good idea," Tanisha agreed. "I have a pen, so go ahead. She quickly scribbled Glen's number in her notebook.

"Goodnight, pretty girl," Glen whispered slowly.

Tanisha was taken aback by his soft tone. It sent shivers down her arms. She found her voice and managed to mumble. "Goodnight, Glen."

Placing the receiver back in the cradle, she squeezed her pillow tightly and tried to remember every detail of his handsome face. She flapped her arms and legs making a snow angel in her sheets. I have a date with a handsome boy who wants to court me. He would climb a fence for me and duel for my affection? I like this.

Chapter 13

The Chemistry Lesson

Rashanda loved her new look. She tossed her head in the mirror and smiled. Surprisingly, Grace's dad had agreed to let her get her hair cut short, agreeing that a fresh look might give her a fresh perspective. Motivated by Grace's boldness, Rashanda also decided to start her sophomore year in high school with a fresh new look. She accompanied Grace to the stylist and also got her hair restyled into a fresh, short style. Grace's transformation was far more dramatic than Rashanda's, but Rashanda's new look was a big change too. Where Grace lost almost eighteen inches of hair, Rashanda lost two inches from her short bob. The new pixie cut was spiky and sassy, and she loved it.

She walked the halls of River North High School with confidence. Rashanda's locker was in sophomore row, down the hallway from the automotive classroom in the basement of the school building. The class was all male, and the boys always huddled in the doorway in order to ogle the new girls as they struggled to open their lockers.

Rashanda watched as a group of boys whistled at two girls who walked ahead of her headed to their lockers. The girls blushed and giggled. Rashanda slowed her pace. She stuck out her chest and walked tall. She was glad that she'd worn a tight pink tank top with a white shirt tied at the waist. Her white cuffed shorts still held a crisp crease. She shifted her backpack on her shoulder and smoothed her shorts with her free hand.

"Who's that?" A tall boy whispered in the automotive doorway.

"I have no idea," another boy said.

"I don't remember seeing her at Battle Creek Junior High when I was there last year," the tall boy said louder. "She's cute."

Rashanda blushed and smiled as she approached, showing off her newly straightened teeth.

"Maybe she just transferred here this year, genius."

They didn't recognize her. She recognized Charles and Mike from her neighborhood pool. She'd known both boys for over four years, but they didn't recognize her. As she got closer, she stopped at the automotive door and smiled widely.

"Hi, Charles. Hi Mike," Rashanda smiled.

Charles and Mike stared at each other.

"It's me, Rashanda," she explained.

Charles spoke first. "Rashanda Jordan? You look so, so different," Charles stammered. His mouth hung open.

Rashanda smiled widely. "Is that a compliment?"

"Of course it's a compliment. We didn't recognize you. You got your braces off, and your hair looks different. You look great," Mike offered.

"You guys look the same," Rashanda said. "I'd better hurry. I have to get to chemistry. I'll see you around."

Rashanda slowly shifted her hips in a seductive rhythm down the hallway. She grabbed her chemistry book from her locker and stepped inside the classroom just as the second bell rang.

She looked around and saw an empty seat near the front row. Mr. Field didn't believe in assigned seats. He was the only teacher at River North who allowed the students to sit wherever they wanted to sit on a daily basis. Rashanda preferred assigned seats. At least you didn't have to worry about being told that the seat was taken or being held for a friend as you walked foolishly around the classroom looking for another available seat. Rashanda was the only sophomore in the class, and the upper class students hazed her mercilessly. They developed a special dislike for her when they learned that she outscored everyone else on the chemistry assessment exam. Rashanda was glad that the boy sitting next to her was reading. He didn't even look up when she took her seat.

Maria and Tanisha had chemistry first period and Algebra II seventh period. This would be the first year that Rashanda had not had her math and science classes with her friends. They had the same teachers for chemistry and Algebra II, so they were still able to do their homework together on the telephone.

Rashanda loved chemistry. She had memorized the Periodic Chart over the summer and often doodled the chemical abbreviations in her notebook. She still giggled when she wrote the chemical symbols for gold (Au) and potassium (K). The other students in the class struggled to memorize the Periodic Chart and performed miserably on the weekly quizzes. Rashanda was outperforming all of the other students in the classroom and needed to be challenged. Her chemistry teacher had suggested that she receive advanced placement tutoring from the college student who was completing a summer internship in the chemistry department. Rashanda stared out the window casually scribbling the formula for hydrogen peroxide in her notebook.

"Rashanda, I'd like to introduce you to someone." She looked up quickly and closed her notebook. "This is Ian. He's doing his student teaching and has agreed to provide advanced placement tutoring to you," Mr. Field said.

Startled, she dropped her pencil on the floor. Ian bent down to pick it up and handed it to her.

"I'm Ian Hall," he said. Ian stood six feet three inches tall. Rashanda tilted her head back and introduced herself.

"Hello. I'm Rashanda Jordan," she stammered taking the pencil from Ian's outstretched hand. "Thanks."

"So, I hear that you're a chemistry super star," Ian offered. "Mr. Field tells me that you've gotten perfect scores on all of his pop quizzes."

"Well, so far I guess I'm doing okay," Rashanda blushed. She studied Ian's attire. He wore a pair of Levi jeans and a white tennis shirt. The shirt didn't have an alligator or a polo emblem. It was just a white tennis shirt. She hadn't seen a tennis shirt without a designer logo in a long time. He wore tattered Converse All Star sneakers. Rashanda frowned at his appearance.

Mr. Field clapped his hands together. "Rashanda, Ian is majoring in chemistry at Northwestern University. He doesn't start school again until the end of September, so he's going to work with me for a few weeks for class credit. He's pre-med," Mr. Field explained. "I've already outlined the material that I'd like him to cover with you since you are so much further along than the other students right now. You can work with Ian, and he can get you ready for the advanced placement test. You guys can pull a couple of desks into the hallway, and I'll work with the other students," Mr. Field explained. "Rashanda, if you do well on the AP test, you can skip into Chemistry II next semester."

Rashanda and Ian quickly moved two of the small desks into the hallway.

"I detect a slight accent. Where are you from, Ian?" Rashanda asked curiously.

Ian laughed softly. "Try as I might to cover up my accent, every now and then it slips out. Let's see if you can guess where I'm from. Go ahead and try." Ian lined the desks side by side against the wall of lockers in the hallway.

Rashanda rubbed her chin. "My parents are from Alabama, so I'm familiar with the Bama drawl, and that's not it. Are you from Mississippi?"

"Nope," Ian said firmly. "I'm not from Mis-si-pi, but if I were, I'd scold you for pronouncing all of those syllables. True Mississippians pronounce it with three syllables and not four. Try again."

"Georgia? I give up." Rashanda shrugged her shoulders and sat in the desk nearest the lockers.

Ian sat in the desk next to her and pulled out his notebook and stacked his papers neatly. He lined two pencils parallel to the paper. "I'm from Springhill, Tennessee which is not far from Nashville. My folks are still in Springhill. It's beautiful down there. It's God's country," Ian paused. "Actually, my parents really wanted me to go to Vanderbilt University in Nashville. I got accepted there, but I wanted to spread my wings and get out of the nest so I was ecstatic when I got accepted to Northwestern." Ian rapped his pencil on the desk and put on a pair of glasses that he held in his hand. "Fortunately, I got an academic scholarship too, so my parents had no reason not to let me attend," he continued. "I got accepted at Harvard and Stanford too, but I didn't want to go that far away from home," he added. "Now, I only have a few weeks to work with you to get you ready for the advanced placement test, so let's get started."

Rashanda smiled as she saw Ian writing with his left hand. "You're a lefty?" she asked. "I'm a lefty too. That's why I sat in the desk near the wall so my hand wouldn't bump into you."

Ian chuckled. "What do you know? We're both left handed chemistry whizzes. Go figure. I'll move my desk to face yours so we don't bump elbows."

Rashanda smiled as Ian quickly rearranged his desk and began her lesson. She listened intently as Ian reviewed the material that would be on the advanced placement test. After twenty-five minutes of reviewing material, Ian gave Rashanda an assessment test that he'd prepared to determine where he should focus. Rashanda got everything correct except the volume section.

Ian stretched his arms over his head and yawned. "You're really smart. I also tutor some of the freshman at Northwestern, and when I give them the chemistry assessment test that I just gave you, you did as well as they usually do. You should really do well on the AP test; especially with one on one tutoring for an hour each day for three weeks. You're going to blow that test out of the water," Ian assured.

Rashanda smiled and glanced at the clock. There were eight minutes left in the class period. She didn't want to go back in the classroom and hear Mr. Field review material that she had already mastered. "Are you a junior at Northwestern?" Rashanda asked.

Ian stacked his papers on his desk. "I'm a sophomore, but I placed out of the chemistry requirement at NU," he said. "Actually, I should be a freshman, but I skipped fourth grade so I'm a school year ahead of my age."

"How old are you?" Rashanda asked.

"I just turned eighteen in July," Ian said. "But I don't tell my students that. I don't want them to realize that most of them are older than I am. They might feel bad," Ian laughed. "So I just let them think that I'm twenty like most college sophomores. What they don't know won't hurt them," he winked.

Rashanda smiled. "I know what you mean," she agreed. "I was offered a chance to skip second grade, but my parents didn't want me to be the youngest person in my class. I don't think it matters, and now I wish I had skipped a grade so I'd be a junior now."

Ian grinned at Rashanda. "My parents almost didn't let me skip a grade either for the very same reason. But I begged them so they agreed. And I was still way ahead of the students in fifth grade even though I was a year younger. I don't think age matters. It's just a number."

"So how did you get interested in chemistry?" Rashanda asked.

Ian giggled. "I'm on to you, Rashanda. I know you keep asking me questions so that you don't have to go back to class. But I don't blame you. You're way ahead of where the other students are. You must be bored silly in there every day," he continued. "I've always liked chemistry. My parents bought me a chemistry set when I was five years old, and I used to mix different things together and make concoctions," Ian laughed. "Once I mixed bleach with ammonia and almost passed out. That's when my dad started explaining the chemical make-up of different products so that I could understand that if you mix certain things together it could be lethal. I was hooked after that," Ian finished. He glanced at his watch quickly. "There's only three minutes left in the class period, so let's go ahead and slip these desks back into the classroom before the bell rings and we're stampeded by students."

Rashanda smiled and opened the classroom door as Ian neatly lined the desks back in their row.

"How did it go?" Mr. Field asked.

"Rashanda is really smart. I'll have her ready for the AP test in no time, Mr. Field," Ian whispered. "See you tomorrow, Rashanda," Ian winked.

"Thanks, Ian," Rashanda said.

The bell rang and Rashanda gathered her books and walked quickly to her locker. Chemistry had just become her favorite subject.

Chapter 14

Helping Out

Nervous, Lori reviewed her notes to make sure that she was ready for the call. She inhaled. On the exhale, she slowly stretched her arms over her head. She didn't have much time. One of her family members could walk in the door at any moment and ruin this rare moment of privacy.

For good measure, Lori mentally reviewed her agenda items. First, she would ask Teenie's Aunt Helen to send her the information on the Delta Sigma Theta Literacy Program. She decided that she wouldn't tell Aunt Helen that she needed it for her father. Instead, she would tell her that she needed it for a research project. Once the brochures arrived, she would review them and research a literacy center near their house that her father could visit to complete his General Equivalency Degree studies. If she gave him all of the information and made it easy for him to participate, Lori was confident that he would agree to take the G.E.D. Even though he seldom talked about it, deep down, Lori believed that he longed to be able to say that he had a high school diploma. And it would mean a lot for him to receive his G.E.D. before his daughter, Charlotte, graduated from high school. Lori had also rehearsed how she would ask Aunt Helen for information on Grace's biological father. She was ready to make the call.

Lori was not accustomed to her house being quiet. It felt eerie. Her parents were at work, and her siblings were participating in their summer activities. She smoothed the crinkled slip of paper with Aunt Helen's number on it and dialed.

A woman answered on the third ring.

"Helloooo." The woman sang into the phone. She answers the phone like Teenie does! How cute is that? Or I guess I should say that Teenie answers the phone like her Aunt Helen does since Teenie probably imitates her Aunt's phone mannerisms. She sounds pretty. I wonder if she's pretty.

"Helloooo," Aunt Helen repeated.

"Uh, hello?" Lori stammered. "May I speak to Helen Carlson, please?" Lori asked.

"This is Helen Carlson," Aunt Helen replied. "How may I help you?"

"Hi. Dr. Carlson, my name is Lori Perkins, and I'm a friend of your niece, Teenie," Lori stammered nervously.

"You're a friend of whom?" Aunt Helen asked softly.

"Teenie Carlson. I mean your niece, Tanisha Carlson," Lori corrected.

"Oh, that's right. Tanisha told me that she gave my number to a friend. I've been expecting your call," Aunt Helen said. "Teenie, huh? I didn't know that Tanisha's nickname was Teenie. That's cute. Tell me your name again, sweetie?"

Lori spoke louder. "My name is Lori Perkins. I go to high school with Tanisha, Dr. Carlson."

"Well, if you're a friend of Tanisha's you can feel free to call me Aunt Helen," she said. "Calling me Dr. Carlson makes me feel like I'm at work," she giggled. "What can I do for you, sweetie pie?"

"I understand that your sorority has an adult literacy program, and I'm doing a project on adult literacy. My specific focus is the general equivalency degree program for adults or the G.E.D. I was hoping that you could send me any information that you have on your sorority's G.E.D. process," Lori paused.

"Absolutely! I'll send you a brochure. I'm on the adult literacy committee," Aunt Helen said. "In fact, I used to be one of the G.E.D. tutors, but I got busy with my new job so I couldn't tutor anymore," she paused. "But I'm still on the committee. I'll also give you the number to my good friend who is in the South Suburban Chapter of Delta, and she can give you information on their literacy program and forward some additional research materials to you. Better yet, she can set it up so that you can take a tour of their literacy center and meet with some of the tutors. It's only a few miles from where you live," Aunt Helen finished.

Lori smiled widely. "That would be great, Aunt Helen."

"Hold on, and I'll get my phone book and give you my friend's number right now," Aunt Helen said.

A few seconds passed, and Aunt Helen recited the number for Lori. Lori repeated the phone number to make sure that she'd written it correctly.

"That's it. She's my very good friend. We pledged Delta together years ago and completed our Ph.D. studies together. She's a professor, so she loves to help students with research projects," Aunt Helen offered. "She's a sweetie pie, but I'm going to warn you, she's a talker. You need to be prepared that she may ask you a lot of questions about your project," Aunt Helen chided. "She may keep you on the phone longer than you expected. So be prepared to share your thesis and your other research plans. Make sure you mention my name, and she'll be glad to help you, baby doll," Aunt Helen explained.

Lori giggled at the terms of endearment that were peppered

into Aunt Helen's speech. I see why Tanisha looks up to Aunt Helen; she seems like a really nice lady. "I really appreciate your help, Aunt Helen," Lori offered. "There's one more thing that I'm hoping you can help me with," Lori continued. "If you have a few more minutes," she added.

"Absolutely. What else do you need?"

She took a deep breath. "I'm also doing a report on African American college professors who were in the Big Ten Conference during the Civil Rights movement. I know there weren't that many during that time, but in my research, I saw that there was an African American drama professor at Northwestern University back in the nineteen sixties," she paused. "But I haven't been able to find any information about him. I don't even know his name. My friend's grandfather used to be part of the grounds keeping crew at Northwestern and mentioned that he saw one African American professor on campus in the sixties," Lori continued. "When I called the Northwestern library for some research assistance they weren't able to locate any information on him," she lied. "Tanisha mentioned that you're the Associate Provost at Northwestern, and she suggested that you might be able to help me find out his name and where he's teaching now. I'd like to interview him for my report." Lori bit her lip and prayed.

The silence in Lori's house transferred through the phone. In the distance, Lori could hear the chimes of a grandfather clock. "Hello," Lori said. "Are you still there, Aunt Helen?"

Lori could hear a deep sigh through the receiver. "I'm still here," Aunt Helen said. "I hesitated because until now I thought that the story that I'd been told was an urban legend. It sounded like a fictional tale, but now I'm beginning to think that perhaps it's true. I think I may know the person to whom you are referencing."

Lori's face lit up. "You do? Do you know his name, and

know how I can reach him?" she asked. *This is too good to be true!*

Aunt Helen spoke softly. "The name that I've heard is Charles Lovett. There aren't any personnel records left of him, but a few of the old cleaning staff members told me the story about a Professor Charles Lovett. Lovett is spelled with two T's."

Lori scribbled the name on her piece of paper. "Do you know where he's teaching now, Aunt Helen?"

"I don't know anything else about him except his name," Aunt Helen said. "I don't know if there's any truth to this, and I probably shouldn't be repeating this, but the cleaning staff gossip is that he got a rich white student pregnant back in the late sixties, and her parents got him fired," Aunt Helen paused. "As the story goes, they were big contributors to the university and threatened to withdraw their financial support unless his record of service at the university was destroyed as though he never existed," she paused. "When I first heard the story, I had one of my research students pour through the Northwestern archives at the original library in Deering Meadow looking for any information on a Professor Charles Lovett. The only thing my student found was a yearbook that had a picture of a Charles Lovett. He was so fair, that he almost looks white in the photo," she offered. "The administration must have forgotten to destroy the yearbook photo when they were destroying his personnel records. But at least we know that he was in fact on staff here," she finished. "Makes you wonder if the other part of the story is true," she said. "How odd that you are asking about him," Aunt Helen finished. A hint of suspicion registered in her tone.

Lori remembered that her mother had said that he was from a small town in Arkansas. She'd laughed when she told her the name of the town. She rapped her pencil on the kitchen table to jog her memory. And then it hit her. Strong! The name of the town that he was from was Strong, Arkansas.

"Aunt Helen, I don't know if this is helpful. But the person who told me about him said that his family was from Strong, Arkansas," Lori offered. "Lovett isn't a common last name, so I bet if I started searching for the Lovett family in Strong, Arkansas I might find someone who is related to him or at least knows the family."

"Strong, Arkansas? Is that so?" Aunt Helen said. "That's very helpful. I'll do you one better, Lori. I'll have my research intern see what he can turn up on a Professor Charles Lovett in Strong, Arkansas. If he's still teaching, we should be able to find him," Aunt Helen continued. "My intern loves to do investigative reporting. He's a student in the Medill School of Journalism. I'll see what I can dig up on my end. Once I find out something, I'll call you or I'll have my intern call you. What's your number, Lori?" Aunt Helen asked. "I have a pen and paper ready."

Lori smiled widely and shared her number. "Thanks, Aunt Helen. You've been so helpful."

The screen door slammed as Lori finished her call. It was Lori's sister Charlotte. She marched into the kitchen and hovered over Lori's shoulder. "Lori, I know you've been on the phone all afternoon, since no one was home, so hand it over," Charlotte said loudly. "I need to call my boyfriend right now."

Lori covered the mouthpiece on the phone and glared at Charlotte. She waved Charlotte away with her free hand before continuing. "Thanks again, Aunt Helen. I really appreciate your help. I'll tell Tanisha that you said hello."

Lori hung up the phone and pursed her lips to scream at Charlotte. As the words were preparing to leave her tongue, Lori remembered that she needed a favor from her older sister. She bit her tongue to stop the words from coming out. She literally bit her tongue. "Ouch!" Lori winced.

"What's wrong with you?" Charlotte asked.

Lori took a sip from her glass and swirled water around in her mouth. "I bit my tongue. I'll be fine." Lori swallowed the water. She tasted blood. *I can't believe that I bit my tongue hard enough to make it bleed.* She took another sip of water. "Charlotte, remember you have to take Justine and me to the mall. Ma told me that you would give us a ride," Lori said softly.

Charlotte cut her eyes at Lori and yawned. "Aaargh! I completely forgot," Charlotte groaned loudly. "I thought Justine moved already." She pulled a jar of peanut butter and a loaf of bread from the pantry and grabbed a small spoon from the drawer.

Lori placed her empty water glass in the dishwasher. "She did. But she's in town visiting her dad for the weekend," she explained.

Charlotte dipped a spoon in the peanut butter jar and shoved the spoon in her mouth. Her words were slurred as she chewed on the peanut butter. "I was going to take a nap before my date tonight. What time do you need to leave?" Charlotte spread peanut butter on her bread.

Lori checked her watch. "Well, we can go now if you're ready," Lori said. "I can call Justine and make sure she's ready."

Dipping the spoon again, Charlotte shoveled another large heaping of peanut butter into her mouth. "Give me five minutes," she mumbled. "I'll be so glad when you get your license. I'm so tired of chauffeuring you and your silly friends around," Charlotte groaned.

She reached to dip her spoon again but Lori snatched the jar. "Charlotte, that's gross! Don't dip that spoon from your mouth back into the jar! That's double dipping, and other people have to eat this peanut butter too! Put some peanut butter in a bowl," Lori ordered.

Charlotte grabbed the jar from Lori and dipped again. "Get over it! Hurry up and get ready because I have a date tonight, and I'm really tired," Charlotte snapped. "I need to drop you off so I can get back and take a quick nap," she yawned. "By the way, who was on the phone? We don't have an aunt named Helen." Charlotte's voice trailed away as Lori raced up the stairs two at a time to change for the mall.

Quite pleased with herself, she closed the bathroom door and leaned against it.   Lori was well on her way to helping her dad get his high school equivalency diploma, and she'd learned the name of Grace's biological father. Operation Helping Out was now in full swing!

Chapter 15

Ragtime

Cupid's arrow pierced the center of his carefully printed name. She wrote her name below his and outlined each letter carefully. Ian loves Rashanda. Shading the letters, she drew a heart around her artwork. It was now official. Rashanda had a crush on her chemistry tutor.

"Maria, may I ask you a question?" Rashanda asked nervously. She twirled the long squiggly phone cord between her fingers and whispered into the mouthpiece.

Maria sat on the floor in her bedroom and painted her toenails. She had three different colors on her toes trying to decide which color she liked best.

"Sure. What's up?" Maria asked.

"How did you know that Todd was the one for you?" Rashanda asked.

Maria wiped off the bubblegum pink and strawberry red color with a cotton ball soaked in nail polish remover. She repainted those toes a frosted mauve. "Well, I just knew," she said. "When we met, I just knew that he was the one for me." Maria perched the phone under her chin. "Why do you ask?"

"Hold on for a second," Rashanda said. Closing her bedroom door, Rashanda sat cross legged on her bed. She turned on her radio and continued. "Remember the chemistry intern that's helping me get ready for the AP exam? His name is Ian Hall. Anyway, I told you about him last week." She continued before Maria could respond. "I know you don't ever get to see him because he only helps Mr. Field during my class. I really like him, and I think he likes me," she whispered.

Neal opened Maria's bedroom door to spy on his sister. "Neal! Close my door! I told you to knock before you come into my room. Beat it you bum, or I'm telling Mom!" Maria screamed. She walked over to her door and locked it. "Sorry about that, Rashanda. My little brother is such a creep sometimes. So why do you think he likes you? What happened?" Maria asked.

"Well, he asked me out on a date," Rashanda said shyly.

"Get outta here!" Maria giggled. "Then he definitely likes you, girlfriend! Why didn't you say anything at school?"

"Ian asked me not to talk about it," Rashanda said. "His contract states that he's not supposed to date the students or he could get in trouble," she continued. "But I had to tell somebody."

"Are your parents going to let you go out with him?" Maria asked.

"No way! He's only eighteen, but he's still a college boy," Rashanda explained. "My parents would hit the roof. I was hoping that I could just walk over to your house and have him pick me up over there so I don't have to tell my parents," Rashanda whispered.

Maria finished painting her toenails and waved her Teen magazine across her feet. "Girl, you know I'll cover for you. Don't even worry about it," Maria offered. "That's what friends are for. When are you going out with him?"

Rashanda listened at her bedroom door to make sure that she didn't hear anyone. "Tonight. He wants to take me to his friend's party in the city," she whispered.

"No problem. Just come over and bring your clothes in a backpack. You can change here. I can help you do your hair and make-up," Maria offered. "My mom and dad are going to some party so they'll be gone. I have to watch my obnoxious brother, so I can't go anywhere. If Todd was here I'd have him sneak over, but he's away at college," she sighed.

Rashanda rummaged through her closet and inspected her wardrobe. "Maria, what should I wear?" she asked. "I've never been to a college party before."

"You should wear that pink halter top with the white oxford shirt tied at your waist. That'll be cute. And wear your white shorts with your sandals," Maria said. "And don't forget to paint your toenails. Boys like girls with freshly painted toes."

Rashanda shook her head and stared at her bare toenails. She reached on her dresser and pulled down a bottle of pink nail polish and struggled with the tight top. She was amazed at how quickly Maria could coordinate the perfect outfit. The pink halter top was the outfit that she'd worn the first time she met Ian. It was the perfect choice for their first date. She wondered if he would remember.

"Clip and file your toenails before painting them," Maria suggested. "You want it to look like you just got a pedicure. Boys like girls who take care of their feet. My father said that a woman who takes the time to groom and pamper her feet even in the winter, takes care of herself. And use a pumice stone on your heel," she continued.

"I don't have a pumice stone," Rashanda groaned as she grabbed her manicure set and began to clip her already short toenails.

The sigh was exaggerated and loud. "I told you to get a pumice stone to scrape the dead skin from your feet," Maria groaned. "The last time you wore sandals you had enough crust on your heel to bake a pie! Nobody wants to look at your dry, crusty feet so just use an SOS pad and smooth them out!" she ordered.

"I am not using an SOS pad on my feet!" Rashanda replied.

"It's just steel wool," Maria assured. "Just use it to scrape your heel and smooth it out and then apply a mixture of Vaseline and lotion to moisten them up."

"Won't that make my feet bleed?" she asked.

"Of course they won't bleed, silly. Besides, trust me when I tell you that you have enough dead skin on the bottom of your heel that you won't even feel it. You're going to be at least a half inch shorter after you smooth out your rough feet," Maria giggled. "But seriously, work the SOS pad while sitting on the edge of the tub because you need water, and the blue dye in the SOS pad will run and make a mess," she cautioned.

Rashanda reached for the emery board and filed her toes. "Maria, have you and Todd done it?" Rashanda whispered.

"Done what?" Maria asked.

"You know. Done the deed," Rashanda repeated.

"You mean have we gone all the way around the bases?" Maria asked.

"Yeah. I know it's none of my business. But since Todd's in college now, I want to know what I can expect from a college boy," Rashanda continued. "I haven't been on that many dates, and I'm nervous."

"Todd and I have gone to second base, but we haven't hit a homerun," Maria giggled. "I told him that we have to wait," she said. "He knows that I'm saving myself for marriage. I suspect that he might be doing it with someone else, but he denies it. Before he left for college, I saw a hickey on his neck that he tried to hide,"

Maria laughed. "It was too funny," she giggled. "At first, I was really upset. Pissed, actually. But now that he's away at college, I don't even worry about it anymore," she shrugged. "My mother always says that you shouldn't worry about something that you can't control, and Lord knows you can't control a teenage boy away at college with raging hormones," she stated confidently. "Did I tell you that when he graduated from Homer Glen High School, he tried to convince me that my virginity should be his graduation present?" she asked without awaiting a reply. "But I just laughed at him. Sometimes I think he forgets that I'm a straight A, high honor student and I didn't just fall off the lemon truck last week," she continued. "He doesn't pressure me about it anymore," she finished. "I honestly believe that he thinks that I'm saving myself for him and that we'll eventually get married. He's so vain," she paused. "I really love him, but I know that I'll meet someone else when I go off to college, and Todd will probably become a thing of the past."

"Wow! I know you were planning to save yourself for marriage, but because Todd is so much older, I just assumed that you guys were doing it, Maria," Rashanda admitted.

"Nope," Maria said. "We make out, but that's it. He would do it if I agreed, but I really want to be a virgin on my wedding night. I know it sounds like a fairy tale, but I want my husband to be my first sexual experience," she continued. "Since Todd and I started making out when I was in eighth grade he just assumed that by now we would be going all the way. But he understands my values. He was mad at first, and tried to break up with me thinking that I would give in and give it up. But when I didn't, he kept calling me like a love struck puppy. He's wrapped around my little finger," Maria boasted.

Rashanda laid out her clothes for her date and folded them neatly into her backpack. She listened intently as Maria continued.

"Todd and I have a special relationship. We really love each other, but he respects my boundaries. He thinks I'm young and naïve. I honestly don't think he realizes that I know that he's seeing other girls. But I'm not stupid. Of course he's seeing other girls. He drives a sports car, he's fine, and he's in college. I'm not sure who he's seeing, but I know he's seeing somebody on the side." Maria took a deep breath. "That's why I flirt with guys at the mall. I really love Todd, but if another bus comes along, I'm jumping on it!" Maria laughed. "Please tell me that Ian hasn't brought up doing the deed already, my friend?"

Rashanda blushed. "No. We haven't talked about anything like that," she paused. "But whenever he's tutoring me he makes sure that his knee touches mine. The first time I moved my knee thinking he bumped me on accident, but he just moved his knee so our knees could touch. And then he smiled at me," she shared. "So I knew he'd done it on purpose."

"Aww, that sounds so sweet," Maria giggled. "It sounds like he really likes you. How did he ask you out? And speak up, I can barely hear you. Why are you whispering?" Maria asked.

Rashanda sat on her bedroom floor, her head practically underneath her bed. "I don't want my mother to hear me. Is that better?" Rashanda said louder.

"I can hear you much better now. Go ahead," Maria said.

"He asked me if I wanted to go to his friend's party, so I said sure."

"You've kissed a boy before right?" Maria asked.

"Uh huh. I've kissed one boy," Rashanda admitted.

"Good," she continued. "At least you have a little experience. Just remember, don't let Ian pressure you into doing anything that you're not ready to do." Maria's voice was serious. "Even though he's only eighteen, college boys have more experience than high school boys," Maria coached. "If he tries to kiss you, and you're not feeling it, just pull your head away. It's your body, and you control it, Rashanda. Remember that, okay."

Rashanda heard her mother walking up the stairs calling her name. "Maria, my mom is calling me. I'll be at your house at six o'clock," Rashanda said quickly. She hung up the phone and walked into the hallway. "Yes, Mom? Did you call me?"

Mrs. Jordan stopped at the top of the stairs. "Why was your door closed, honey? I called your name three times."

"I was just talking to Maria, and I thought that you were taking a nap. I didn't want to wake you," Rashanda said.

"How is Maria? I'm glad you guys are still friends. She's a sweet girl," Mrs. Jordan said.

Rashanda smiled. "Maria's fine. She invited me over tonight for pizza and a movie. I'm going over at six o'clock. Teenie's brother Jack will bring me home tonight."

"Oh, that's nice. Well, come on downstairs so you can practice your piano. Your grandmother is on the phone, and she wants to hear you play."

"I'll be right there." Rashanda was glad that she hadn't painted her finger nails. Rashanda picked up the kitchen receiver.

"Hi, Big Momma!" Rashanda said cheerily. "Yes. I know you're calling long distance, and I'm sorry that you had to hold on so long. I didn't hear mom calling me," Rashanda explained. "School is fine. What song do you want to hear today, Big Momma? You got it. Just let me get set-up." Rashanda stretched the phone cord to the upright piano in the living room. She laid the receiver on top of the piano and played Ragtime from memory.

Rashanda smiled, imagining her aging grandmother playing

along on her kitchen table as her arthritic fingers strummed the imaginary keyboard along with Rashanda's melody.

When Rashanda started taking lessons, her grandmother had given Rashanda the piano that she played as a young girl; the same piano that her mother, Rashanda's great grandmother, had played. So pleased was she that her granddaughter played the piano, each month Big Momma sent Rashanda a crisp twenty dollar bill to defray the cost of her piano lessons, lessons Rashanda hadn't taken in over three years, a fact that Big Momma had been told repeatedly, but her dementia prevented her from remembering. The only song she ever asked Rashanda to play was Joplin's Ragtime. Rashanda knew that this was the only song that her ailing grandmother still remembered how to play, but she enjoyed giving her grandmother the courtesy of requesting the song when she called. Rashanda smiled as she played the piece perfectly and picked up the phone.

"Thanks, Big Momma! I'm glad you enjoyed it," she smiled. "Yes Ma'am, I got your twenty dollar bill. But you don't have to keep sending me money for lessons. I haven't taken piano lessons in a long time, remember?" Rashanda paused. "Yes, Ma'am. I'm still your little girl." Rashanda smiled as she hung up the receiver.

She could smell dinner cooking in the kitchen. Her mother stood over the sink shucking fresh corn.

"Mom, my nail polish cap is stuck, can you twist this off?" she asked as she handed her mother the small bottle. Rashanda watched as her mother grabbed a rubber glove and wrapped it around the top of the bottle before effortlessly twisting the cap off and handing her daughter the pink polish.

"Thanks, Mom," she stated. "By the way, do we have any fresh SOS pads under the sink?" she asked.

Chapter 16

Pine Lake

The Save Mart service desk was unusually slow for a Sunday morning. The sky was cloudy, but the sun was beginning to peek through the clouds. A severe thunderstorm watch had been in effect for most of the morning holding the shoppers hostage in their homes. Tanisha yawned, stretched and looked out the window. The sun was drying up the small puddles in the near empty parking lot. It was easy for Tanisha to notice the navy blue Buick that pulled into the parking lot. Tanisha watched closely, but no one got out of the car. She glanced at the clock above the door. It was now 1:25, and her replacement had just raced to the back of the store to punch in on time. Tanisha wiped the service desk counter again and waited. Moments later, Kathy walked behind her and popped a stick of gum in her mouth. Tanisha quickly reviewed the service desk activity with Kathy and raced to the back of the store to freshen up and change for her date with Glen.

She quickly unlocked her locker and grabbed her things. She locked the small employee bathroom door and pulled a washcloth from her backpack. Splashing water on her face, she applied soap to the washcloth. She hastily washed her private area and her armpits in the small sink. Crap! I forgot to bring a towel to dry myself. She considered using her smock as a towel, but thought better of it and grabbed a fist full of paper towels instead. She slipped into her white shirt and pulled on her khaki shorts. Next, she applied deodorant and sprayed perfume on her neck and wrists. Tanisha checked her watch. It was 1:36. She remembered to use the bathroom and washed her hands again before placing the washcloth in a plastic bag inside her backpack. Almost finished, she brushed her teeth and applied lipstick before running her fingers through her hair. She stared at her reflection in the mirror. Not bad for a five minute makeover. Not bad at all. She stuffed her work clothes into her backpack and headed to the front of the store. As she approached the service desk, she saw Glen speaking with Kathy. She watched as Kathy turned and pointed in her direction. Glen glanced over his shoulder and smiled widely.

Leaned casually against the service desk counter, Glen stared at her as she walked. Tanisha smiled back and waved. Under his intense gaze, she became very self conscious. God, please don't let me trip while I'm walking toward him! I'll be mortified.

"Hi, Glen," she smiled. "Did you meet Kathy?" Tanisha asked.

"Hey, Teenie. I did meet Kathy. She told me that you were in the back getting your things," Glen said. "You look cute. Here, let me take that." Glen took her backpack from her shoulder and placed it on his. "You smell good too," Glen complimented. "I love that perfume you're wearing."

"Thanks," Teenie blushed. I'm so glad I thought to freshen up for him.

"So where are you guys going?" Kathy quizzed. "I hope it's some place fun."

Tanisha twisted the small purse strap that hung at her hip and shrugged her shoulders. "I think we're going to a movie?" she replied. Her response phrased in the form of a question.

"Nope. I've changed my mind about the movie," Glen smiled. "It's a surprise. You'll find out soon enough. Are you all set?" Glen asked. "Are you hungry?"

"Yup. I'm good to go," Tanisha said. "I'm not hungry, but if you are I could nibble on something."

"Kathy, it was nice to meet you," Glen said as he led Tanisha toward the door.

Tanisha waved at Kathy who winked and gave Tanisha the thumbs up sign.

Glen walked across the parking lot to the blue car that Tanisha noticed earlier. She chuckled slightly.

"What's so funny?" Glen asked.

Tanisha nodded her head from side to side. "I knew this was your car. I saw this car in the parking lot earlier and didn't see anyone get out of it, so I guessed that it might be you," Tanisha smiled at Glen. "And I was right." He opened her door and tossed her backpack on the floor in the back seat. He waited for Tanisha to get settled before closing her door.

He whistled as he walked quickly to the driver's side of the car and climbed in. "I wanted to make sure that you didn't have to wait for me, so I got here fifteen minutes early. I saw you through the window, so I thought I'd just chill until it was time for you to finish your shift," he smiled. "You should be a detective." Glen stared at Tanisha's profile. "Maybe I should call you Sherlock instead of Teenie." He playfully pinched Tanisha's thigh.

Tanisha smiled as she settled into her seat.

"How long has your tooth been decayed like that?" Glen asked.

Tanisha's smile faded. "What did you say?" Tanisha asked.

"Your tooth. How long has it been decayed like that?" Glen repeated.

Tanisha was at a loss for words. No one had ever asked her about her tooth before. As far as she knew, her best friends hadn't noticed her decayed tooth. Or if they had, they were too polite to ask her about it. She swallowed hard. "It grew in like that," Tanisha said softly. Her heart sank into her stomach.

"That's what I thought. You probably sucked on a bottle too long as a child and the sugar from the milk created tooth decay. It's quite common," he explained. "It's a primary or baby tooth, right?" Glen asked as he pushed the buttons on the car stereo.

"Yeah. My dad took me to the dentist, and the dentist said that the permanent tooth will eventually push the primary tooth out," she said quietly. "They don't want to pull it yet, but if it hasn't fallen out in a few months, they'll pull it." Tanisha couldn't believe that she was talking openly about her tooth. She'd been ashamed of that rotten tooth for as long as she could remember. She thought she'd perfected her demure smile. How had he noticed it?

As though reading her mind, Glen placed his hand over the back of Tanisha's seat and slowly backed the car out of the parking space. "I noticed it at the arcade when I met you, but I could tell that you were trying to hide it so I didn't say anything then. I didn't want to make you feel uncomfortable about it," he offered.

Tanisha lowered her head. He must think that I'm a hillbilly. She wanted to melt away or at least jump out of his car and run as far away as she could.

"Don't worry, you're still gorgeous," he assured. "You'll get that tooth straightened out soon," he comforted. "Besides, nobody's perfect. If you haven't noticed, you could kick a field goal through the gap in my teeth," Glen smiled widely and stuck his tongue between his large gap. Tanisha smiled at Glen's efforts to comfort her. "I want to be a dentist so I always notice people's teeth," he said.

"Thanks," she whispered. She smiled at him and settled into her seat. "Where are we going, Glen?" Tanisha asked.

"You just can't wait can you?" Glen teased. "Okay, we're going on a picnic. If we go to a movie we won't be able to talk and get to know each other. So I packed us a picnic lunch, and we're going to this place called Pine Lake by my house. Does that work for you, Miss I must know everything now?"

Tanisha nodded her head. "That sounds fine."

"When I was at church, I said a prayer to the big guy in the sky and asked him to make it stop raining. And since I always get whatever I ask of the universe, the rain has stopped and the sun is peeking through the clouds," he teased. "I wasn't sure what you might like to eat so I packed a little bit of everything," Glen said. "We can sit on the blanket, eat, talk and you can feed me grapes like the king that I am. In fact, call me King Glen."

Tanisha swatted Glen on his arm. "You think way too highly of yourself," she giggled.

"Hey, if I don't treat myself like a king how can I expect you to treat me like royalty?" Glen continued. He stared at Tanisha with a serious expression. "You know I'm kidding, right? You don't have to feed me grapes, but you can wipe my mouth with a napkin after I eat." Glen smacked the steering wheel and patted Tanisha's thigh lightly. The gesture sent a chill down her spine.

He drove through the Homer community and turned into a small empty parking lot hidden from the street by a grove of mature trees. Glen parked the car and Tanisha studied her surroundings. The gray rain clouds had been replaced by fluffy white clouds that nestled in the sky like pillows.

Tanisha opened her door and met Glen at the trunk. He pulled out a small picnic basket and a large blanket. Glen led her toward a narrow gravel pathway that opened to a beautiful man made lake. The sun peeked behind the clouds casting a glow on the lake and drying the damp grass. The lake was the length of a football field with a grassy area the size of another football field. In the center of the grassy area was a small red pavilion with six brown picnic benches.

"I'm glad the sun finally came out," Glen said. "When I heard the weather forecast I was concerned that it might ruin my picnic plans, but I figured we could sit under the pavilion at the picnic table if the grass was too wet," he explained. Glen bent down and felt the grass. "It's actually pretty dry. Do you want to sit on the blanket or at the table?" Glen asked.

Tanisha stared intently at a family of ducks that waddled to the small lake. She watched closely as the mother duck expertly guided the ducklings into the water. She was amazed at how the ducks stayed in a straight line and followed the mother duck so effortlessly. She wondered if the ducks were lined up in birth order.

"Teenie, did you hear me?" Glen repeated.

"I'm sorry. I was watching those ducks in the water. What did you say?" she asked.

"I think the grass is dry enough for us to sit on the blanket, but if you'd rather sit at the picnic bench under the pavilion we can sit there," Glen said.

"Let's sit on the grass," Tanisha replied. "I've never seen ducks following their mother in a perfect line like that," Tanisha explained.

"I know, it's cool isn't it? When I saw those ducklings with their mother the first time, I wondered if they were walking in birth order," he said.

Tanisha stared at him in amazement. Can he read my mind? "I was wondering the same thing," she admitted. Tanisha grabbed one end of the blanket and helped spread it across the grass. She kicked off her shoes and sat down. Glen placed the picnic basket on the grass and pulled out the food. He'd packed sandwiches from the deli, chips, carrot sticks, grapes and two small bottles of lemonade.

"I hope you're not disappointed about not going to a movie," Glen said. "I just don't like to go to a movie on a first date, because you don't get a chance to talk." Glen handed Tanisha a sandwich. "I hope you're not a vegetarian, because the sandwiches have meat on them," Glen said. He pulled out paper plates and napkins.

"Actually, I don't eat animal flesh," Tanisha said. "I think it's inhumane to slaughter an animal to eat it. I don't eat anything that had parents," she explained.

Glen paused and stared at Tanisha. He took the sandwich from Tanisha. "I'm so sorry, Teenie. I should have asked you if you ate meat." Glen stood up and pulled his car keys from his pocket. "I can drive to the deli and pick up a salad or something for you. I can be back here in ten minutes," he advised. "Just relax on the blanket and nibble these carrot sticks, and I'll be right back."

Tanisha laughed. "Gotcha! Glen, I am so not a vegetarian," she giggled.

Glen balled up a napkin and tossed it at her. He missed. She scooped it up and tossed it squarely at his chest. He kicked off his loafers and stretched his long legs along the blanket. "You really had me going there. But seriously, isn't this place perfect?" he asked. "Sometimes I come here with a book and just read or just watch the water," he explained. "It's a catch and release lake, so it's well stocked with fish."

"What's catch and release?" Teenie asked.

"If you catch a fish, you have to release it back into the water," Glen explained. "You can't take it home and eat it, so people who are fishing here are just fishing for the sport of it. Have you ever been fishing?" he asked.

"I haven't," Teenie said. "My dad takes my brothers fishing sometimes, but I've never gone. Fishing is my dad's way of bonding with my brothers, so I don't get invited," she explained. "My dad is a bit old fashioned and believes that men should catch the fish and women should cook them," she laughed.

"Actually, my dad is the same way," Glen agreed. "He says that women talk too much and wouldn't be able to sit quiet long enough to catch any fish," he laughed. "My mom never goes fishing with us. I'll have to take you fishing then," he offered. "As long as you promise not to talk me to death," he teased.

He's already planning a second date with me? "That would be fun," Tanisha smiled. "But you will have to bait the hook. I don't do worms!"

"Now you definitely sound like a girl," he smiled. "I'll bait your hook, princess!" Glen unwrapped his sandwich and placed two lemonade bottles on the blanket. Tanisha played with a blade of grass and studied his profile. He is so cute!

"There's a big crane that hangs out at the lake pretty regularly. Whenever I see him he usually catches a frog or a fish," Glen continued.

"It's really pretty here," she agreed. "The different colored wild flowers are amazing. How did you find this place?" Tanisha asked.

"When we moved here last year I rode my bike around the neighborhood a lot. I was really missing my old friends in Chicago and just needed to get away. Anyway, one day I saw the road leading to the lake and I rode my bike down it. I almost turned around because the road wasn't paved, and I didn't want to get a flat tire, but I was curious. When I got to the parking lot, I saw this lake," Glen paused. "Look! The crane is flying into the water now." He pointed over the lake.

Tanisha watched as a large bird with pole legs landed in the water. He walked into the lake with his head bowed. He slowed his pace and froze. Tanisha held her breath. He lowered his head and bobbed it into the water. When he lifted his head, the hind leg of a frog wiggled in his beak. The crane sucked in the limb and kept walking.

"Did you see that?" Glen asked. "That was pretty cool, huh?"

"Actually, it was. It was like something from an Animal Kingdom public television special," Tanisha said. "My brothers and I always watch those programs where the lion hunts its prey. Our favorite one is where the snakes follow mice in the desert and eat them whole."

"I watch those too. I could watch nature all day. I'm just fascinated by all of the different species and how everything just flows," Glen stared at Tanisha. "It's amazing."

Tanisha bit into a carrot. Glen took a bite from his sandwich and opened the lemonades. He handed one of the bottles to Tanisha and tilted his bottle to clink hers. "Cheers to us," he said.

Tanisha smiled and tapped her lemonade bottle against his. She took another bite of her carrot and unwrapped her turkey sandwich. Glen stared at her intently. She felt slightly nervous under his intense gaze. *I hope he doesn't want to talk about my tooth anymore.*

"So tell me, Tanisha Denise Carlson," he said. "Why don't you have a boyfriend? I'm really curious, and take your time, we've got all day." Glen crossed his legs and took another bite of his sandwich.

She blushed nervously. "I just don't," she shrugged. "Does that make me a rare species?" she asked.

Sitting up on the blanket, Glen re-crossed his legs at the knee. "Sort of," he paused. "Because you're almost too good to be true," he said. "You're pretty, you seem very kind," he paused. "And I was asking Kathy about you and she told me that you're a straight A high honors student," he continued.

"You were asking Kathy about me?" Teenie repeated.

"I was just fact gathering," he confessed, his hands in the surrender pose. "You smell good. You're funny. And did I mention that you're pretty?" he repeated.

"Yes, you said that already," Teenie giggled.

"I just don't understand why you haven't been snatched up yet," he said. "So tell me Tanisha Denise Carlson, why don't you have a boyfriend?"

Stalling for time, she bit into her sandwich and chewed slowly, a wee bit uncomfortable under his penetrating gaze. This boy saw my rotten tooth and still asked for my phone number. He reads for pleasure. He studies nature. He works. He goes to church. He has a romantic side. He's funny and polite. He has a nice sense of humor, and he's cute! Can he be too good to be true?

Tanisha swallowed her food and shrugged her shoulders. "Why don't I have a boyfriend?" she repeated. What about David? Should I tell him about David? But David is not my boyfriend. He's dating Patty. Don't tell him about David, yet.

"Why don't I have a boyfriend? I really have no idea, but after you get to know me, maybe you can tell me, because I wouldn't know where to begin."

Chapter 17

Sleeping Beauties

Her wooden heeled sandals made a rhythmic click clack sound on the linoleum tile. She stopped at the elevator and pressed the call button, nervously glancing at the numbers and watching as the elevator descended from the eighth floor to the lobby. She prayed that no one else was in the elevator, especially not a sick person. She hated sick people. She hated hospitals. She tried to hold her breath as she walked through the hallway, but she knew she couldn't hold her breath all the way to the room. It was a large hospital with long winding corridors. She took a quick breath. The hospital smelled like alcohol and urine. Why do all hospitals smell like alcohol and urine?

The smell reminded Mrs. Wesley of the twice weekly visits to see her mother in the oncology ward. The sight of the mostly bald and always frail cancer patients with tubes inserted in their weakened bodies made her want to cry. Her stomach would churn as she entered the hospital with her dad holding her younger brother's hand. The nurses were always friendly and they usually had candy for them. But the sweets weren't enough to dull the pain in her heart. Emmett was easily distracted by the candy, but Liz knew that she would be sad as soon as she saw her dying mother. She was old enough to know that her mother was dying a little bit more each time they saw her. And there was nothing that could be done.

But this was different. Mrs. Wesley knew that she had to get over her hospital issues and be strong for Maria. She had never seen Maria so upset. Maria had almost hyperventilated trying to explain what happened when she hung up the phone.

The only thing she understood from Maria's tearful explanation was that two of her closest friends were in the hospital, and she had to get to the hospital immediately. Maria grabbed Mrs. Wesley's car keys and ran to the garage. Mrs. Wesley raced after her, afraid that Maria might actually take the car in her excited state. She coaxed the keys from her daughter after agreeing to take her to the hospital immediately. Maria sobbed the entire way, gripping her stomach and rocking back and forth in her seat. Each time Maria tried to talk, she was overcome with emotion.

Five minutes later, when Mrs. Wesley pulled the car into the hospital parking lot, Maria jumped out of the car before her mother could learn any additional information. Mrs. Wesley parked the car and speed walked into the emergency room waiting area. She approached the registration desk.

"Hello. This may sound silly, but my daughter just raced in here to see one of her friends but she didn't tell me the name of her friend," Mrs. Wesley said.

"Oh. The patient that she asked about was Justine Wellington. I sent her up to the Surgical Intensive Care Unit," the clerk offered.

"Thank you," Mrs. Wesley said.

"She's not supposed to have more than two visitors at a time, and her father is already up there with her, but under the circumstances, I'll let you go on up," the clerk winked somberly.

"Under the circumstances? Do you know anything about what happened?" Mrs. Wesley asked. "My daughter was so upset that she couldn't talk."

"It was a terrible car accident," the clerk explained. "I'm not sure, but I don't think that the driver made it. But the Wellington girl came out of surgery a couple of hours ago."

"Oh my God!" Mrs. Wesley grabbed her throat and walked quickly down the corridor. Afraid of what she would see, she quickened her pace.

Mrs. Wesley peered in the window and saw Maria's friend. Justine was unconscious. Tubes dangled from her wrists and nose. Maria hugged Mr. Wellington quickly and peered at her friend through the glass surgical intensive care unit window. The SICU Nurse Coordinator continued to explain Justine's condition to her father.

"Sir, your daughter came through surgery fine," she said. "It's a good thing that she was wearing her seatbelt or she may have been tossed from the car. A lot of kids don't believe that you need to wear your seatbelt while riding in the back seat, but I think it saved your daughter's life," she continued. "In fact, I'm certain that it saved her life. The impact of the crash, and the seatbelt around her midsection caused a small rupture in her spleen, which created some nasty internal bleeding. Fortunately, an emergency medical technician was on the scene quickly and stabilized your daughter, and the surgeons worked on her immediately."

"Will she live?" Mr. Wellington whispered. "Please tell me that she'll live."

"Sir, you know that I can't promise you that, because with any surgery there are always complications. But she did come through the surgery fine. She's young and healthy, so her prognosis looks good," the nurse stated. "She will be asleep for at least twelve hours, so you may want to get some rest." The nurse patted Mr. Wellington's hand and walked away.

Mrs. Wesley walked up and hugged Maria tightly. She closed her eyes and said a prayer for Justine. She hugged Mr. Wellington too.

"If there's anything I can do for you, just let me know," Mrs. Wesley offered.

"Thank you," he mumbled. "I've called her mother, and she's on her way from the city. I hope she doesn't blame me for this accident," Mr. Wellington said softly.

Mrs. Wesley grabbed Mr. Wellington's hands in her hands. "This was not your fault. You were not driving the car. It's no one's fault. It was an accident," she comforted. "Who was driving the car?" she whispered.

"Mom, do you know which room Lori is in?" Maria asked softly. "I really want to see her."

Mrs. Wesley turned slowly and faced Maria as the blood drained from her face. She smoothed her daughter's hair and studied her face.

"Sweetie, was Lori the one driving?" she asked. "Who called you and what did they say?" Mrs. Wesley asked.

She handed Maria a tissue. Maria blew her nose loudly and handed her mother the soiled tissue. Mrs. Wesley's gaze shifted between Maria and Mr. Wellington.

Mr. Wellington slumped in the chair and covered his face with his hands.

Maria tucked her hair behind her ears. "Grace called me," she explained. "Mr. Wellington called Grace's parents when the police called him because his car is in the shop and he needed a ride to the hospital. All she said was that Justine and Lori had been in an accident and they were at St. Mary's Hospital," Maria explained. "She was rushing because she was riding with her parents to bring

Mr. Wellington to the hospital."

Mrs. Wesley looked at Mr. Wellington for a sign. He made eye contact with her and shook his head from side to side. He bit his lip, lowered his chin to his chest, and closed his eyes as tears slowly streamed down his face.

"Does Lori have her license yet, Maria?" Mrs. Wesley asked.

Maria scowled at her mother's question. "Not yet. But what difference does that make now, Mom?" Maria groaned.

Mrs. Wesley gently guided Maria into the hallway. "Let's go sit in the waiting area, sweetie."

"Don't be silly, Mom. I don't want to sit down. I want to see Lori," Maria said. She pulled away from her mother and walked to the receptionist's desk near the elevator.

"Excuse me," she said. "Can you tell me which room Lori Perkins is in?"

The receptionist typed into her computer. She shook her head. "I don't show a Lori Perkins in the computer. Are you sure that she was taken to this hospital?"

"That's what my friend told me," Maria said. "But Grace was really upset, so she might have gotten the hospital name wrong."

"Well, I'm new," the receptionist explained. "This is only my second day on the job. I'll do a hospital wide search and keep looking," she offered.

The elevator bell dinged and Grace walked out of the elevator. Her face was wet with tears.

"Hey, Grace." Maria hugged her tightly. "I'm glad you're here. Have you seen Lori yet? The receptionist can't find her in the computer, but she's still searching."

Grace's eyes were swollen, and a new flood of tears gushed forth like a waterfall.

"Grace, you're scaring me. What's the matter?" Maria asked.

"I found your friend's name," the receptionist interrupted. "She was in a different system."

Maria turned to face the receptionist. "Thanks for checking. Can you tell me where she is? I'd like to see her."

Mrs. Wesley walked to Maria's side. She gently laid her arm across her daughter's shoulder. "Sweetie, I need to tell you something," she whispered.

The receptionist continued. "Lori Perkins is in M103 and there's a Charlotte Perkins in M104."

"Can you tell me how to get to that room?' Maria asked.

"It's in the basement of the hospital. You just take this elevator all the way down to the basement," she replied softly. "But it's not a room. It's the morgue. Only immediate family can go to the morgue. Are you her immediate family?"

The receptionist's voice was interrupted by a loud thud as Maria fell to the floor.

"Oh, my God! I thought she knew," the receptionist said. "I thought she knew!"

Mrs. Wesley kneeled down and cradled Maria's head in her hands. Her eyes bore holes through the receptionist. "She did not know that!" Mrs. Wesley screamed. "Someone help us! My daughter needs medical assistance!" she yelled sternly.

Chapter 18

Jamaican Paradise

Ian arrived at exactly seven o'clock. Rashanda smiled to herself. *He's punctual. I like punctual people.* She met him on the driveway before he reached Maria's front door.

"Your timing is perfect," Rashanda gushed. "I saw you pull into the driveway."

"I'm glad you're ready. I appreciate promptness," Ian said. "Do I need to meet your parents?"

Rashanda chuckled. *We have so much in common, that it's scary!* "Actually, this is my friend Maria's house. It's a long story," Rashanda said. She walked to the passenger side and climbed into the car.

"My friend Maria is on the phone with her boyfriend or else I would introduce you to her," Rashanda explained. "Her boyfriend called about two minutes before you drove up. She doesn't talk to him that often so I didn't want to interrupt her."

"You look nice by the way," Ian said. "I like your hair tucked behind your ear like that."

As Ian drove through the Newberry East neighborhood, the couple chatted effortlessly about Rashanda's upcoming chemistry advanced placement exam. A cool September breeze blew through the partially open windows. Twenty minutes later, Ian exited the highway and drove through the Morgan Park neighborhood on Chicago's far south side.

She grinned at Ian as he drove. Rashanda Jordan was on a date in the city. She suddenly felt more mature than her fifteen and a half years.

Ian parallel parked and met Rashanda at her door just as she was stepping out of the car. He reached for Rashanda's hand as they walked up the sidewalk leading to the large bungalow house. He rubbed his fingers along her hand. "I knew your hands would be soft," he said. "Every time I tutor you, I've wanted to touch your hands," he admitted. "But I was always scared Mr. Field would see me."

Rashanda smiled widely, glad that her braces had been removed before starting sophomore year. Her teeth had turned out beautifully and she was proud of her new smile.

Ian stopped walking and turned to face Rashanda. He squeezed both of her hands in his. "Rashanda, I told my friends that I was bringing my new girlfriend to the party," Ian said. "I know I haven't asked you to be my girlfriend but I really like you."

Rashanda blushed. No boy had ever told her that he liked her. She'd pecked a few boys playing truth or dare and had kissed a boy while slow dancing at a John & Judy party recently, but she had never had a boyfriend. "I really like you too," she confessed. "I don't mind if you tell people that I'm your girlfriend."

"I don't want to just tell people that you're my girlfriend. I want you to be my girlfriend. Is that okay?" Ian asked nervously.

Rashanda shook her head. "That's fine, Ian."

They walked up the stairs and rang the doorbell.

A short boy wearing a Cubs tee-shirt answered the door. "Ian, welcome to me Island paradise, Mon," the boy said.

"Hey Roger, what's up, man?" Ian said. "Roger, this is my girlfriend Rashanda that I told you about," Ian introduced.

"Hello, my queen. Welcome to my home. You are free to make yourself at home. Mi casa es su casa." Roger bowed at the waist and tipped his imaginary hat.

Ian led Rashanda into the house and introduced her to all of the guests. All were college friends who'd come home for the long weekend. Rashanda smiled as she met the eight couples at the party. Some of the couples played bid whist and others played charades. Two couples sat on the floor playing Scrabble.

Ian led her to the kitchen where a table was covered with platters of jerk chicken, curry goat, peas and rice, plantains, sautéed spinach and Jamaican cabbage. A coconut cake sat next to a caramel cake on the kitchen counter. Bottles of soda and lemonade chilled in the sink which was filled with ice like a cooler.

"I'm starving," Ian said. "I hope you like Jamaican food. My boy Roger is from the south side of Chicago, but he loves to throw Jamaican parties. His mom has a friend who's Jamaican, so she hooks up the food." Ian grabbed two plates and handed one to Rashanda. He piled his plate high with food and Rashanda did the same.

"I love any kind of food," Rashanda said. Her stomach growled as she inhaled the delicious aromas. She'd been so busy prepping for her date with Ian that she hadn't eaten since lunch.

"Help yourself to something to drink," Ian said. "I'm going to have lemonade."

He led her to the dining room where they settled in and watched the charades game as they ate. Rashanda licked her fingers and savored the jerk sauce.

"I'm impressed," Ian said. "I didn't think you would eat all of the food on your plate because you're so tiny. Did you leave room for dessert?"

Rashanda smiled. "I may look tiny, but I eat like a man. I have a super high metabolism. And I always leave room for dessert," she said.

"I like that in you," Ian said. "I like a woman who can eat like a man and maintain her girlish figure. What kind of cake would you like? I'll get it for you."

"Can I have a small slice of both?" Rashanda asked.

"Of course you can," Ian chuckled. "I was going to try both of them myself."

He returned moments later with four sizable slices of cake on one plate and two forks. They shared the cake and talked. Ian's knee leaned comfortably into Rashanda's knee, as Bob Marley and the Melody Makers played in the background.

Rashanda felt comfortable with Ian. They'd spent three weeks together and had become friends. He was a great tutor, and her chemistry comprehension had improved under his tutelage. She felt ready for her advanced placement examination.

She knew that he would be leaving to go back to Northwestern in two weeks to facilitate freshman new student week as a resident hall assistant. She liked Ian a lot. And now she was his girlfriend. She smiled at the sound of that. I have a boyfriend! I have a boyfriend!

Ian gently rested his right hand on her thigh as they ate. His fingers slowly traced the outline of her short cuff. Roger walked into the dining room as they ate their cake. "You two are both lefties?" he squealed. "That's too cute. You're both chemistry experts, and lefties." Ian and Rashanda smiled at each other and shrugged.

She placed her right hand on top of his hand on her thigh. He squeezed her hand under the table and smiled at her. They finished their cake and tossed their paper plates into the trash in the kitchen.

They held hands as they walked through the house. "Let's go sit on the porch in the back," Rashanda suggested. They walked through the kitchen and sat on the enclosed porch. Rashanda noticed a door at the end of the porch. "What does that door lead to, Ian?" Rashanda asked.

"Oh, that's Roger's room. It used to be his parents' room, but they remodeled the second floor of the house and put in a new master bedroom and bathroom upstairs so he got the old master bedroom," Ian explained.

"Are his parents here tonight?" Rashanda asked.

"His folks went to Indianapolis for the Grambling State vs. Mississippi State game. His parents graduated from college at Mississippi State in Jackson, Mississippi," Ian said. "His dad used to play snare drum in the marching band, so they always go to the Indianapolis Classic to hear the bands," he explained. "I don't think anyone really cares about the football game. It's all about the halftime band competition," he finished. Ian stood up and stared into the back yard. "I can see the Big Dipper. Come over and take a look," Ian said.

Rashanda walked over to the window as he pointed out the constellation. She placed her arms around his waist and leaned her head into his chest. Her head rested snugly under his armpit as she squeezed his waist gently and sighed. She listened as he pointed out Asia Minor. "Ian, since I'm your girlfriend now, we should seal it with a kiss don't you think?" She asked softly, somewhat surprised by her boldness.

Ian looked down into her eyes and pulled her into his body. He kissed her softly on the lips. He ran his tongue along her teeth slowly before gently parting her lips with his tongue. She leaned her head back and pressed her small frame tighter into his embrace. Her heart felt like it would beat out of her chest.

Suddenly embarrassed, she pulled away and wiped her mouth with the back of her hand.

"What's the matter?" Ian asked. "Are you okay?"

Rashanda wiped her mouth and smiled. "I'm fine," she explained. "I've just never been kissed like that before," she admitted.

Ian rubbed her hands in his. "I'm so sorry," he said. "We're going way too fast."

"No, it's not that," she explained. "I enjoyed the kiss. It was really nice. But I don't want your friends to come out here and see us making out," she flushed. "Especially since they just met me," she explained.

"I understand," Ian said. Rubbing her hands in his, he walked her toward the door that led to the backyard. "Watch your step," he cautioned as he guided her down the small wooden steps leading to the patio. The light from the moon cast a glow on a small pond adjacent to the garage.

"How's this?" he asked. "May I dance with you by the light of the moon?"

As a firefly fluttered around their heads, Rashanda nodded and smiled.

Chapter 19

A September to Forget

Maria dialed the numbers again. Busy. She called Grace.

"Hey, Grace," she said. "Have you talked to Teenie or Rashanda? Every time I call them, their lines are busy," she sniffled.

Grace exhaled loudly. "They're probably on the phone together. They both had dates, and they're probably comparing notes," she deduced.

"You're probably right," Maria agreed. "But if they don't hang up soon, I'm going to have the phone company interrupt the line," Maria said. "I'll say that it's an emergency. It is an emergency. One of our best friends is now dead. If that's not an emergency I don't know what is," Maria sighed. "I'll try them again," she said. She hung up the phone and wiped her face.

She glared at her desk calendar. She would hate this day for the rest of her life. Lifting her head slowly, Maria stared at her reflection. Her eyes were puffy, and her hair was a mess. But she didn't care. Nothing else mattered. Her friend was dead. She still couldn't believe it. Her mind drifted back to the terrible turn of events that clouded her thoughts.

After awaking from her fainting spell, an attendant wheeled her down to the lobby where she saw Lori's parents. Mr. Perkins spoke with the hospital administrator as Mrs. Perkins prayed.

"Lord, Jesus, I know you know better and you do not make mistakes, but Lord you have to send healing to us right now," Mrs. Perkins prayed loudly. "Father, God we need your strength and grace to get through this," she sobbed. Her words were directed to no one in particular as she paced the corridor waiting for the funeral director to pick up her daughters. The hospital staff ignored Mrs. Perkins' prayer. They'd seen all forms of grief and were numb to it. "You must have needed my angels in heaven more than we needed them on Earth. Jehovah, please watch over my babies," she continued. She threw her arms into the air and waved her hands as she paced back and forth with her eyes closed.

Mr. Perkins walked over to Maria and Mrs. Wesley. "How is Justine?" he asked softly. His eyes, though vacant, carried the weight of genuine concern.

"Her father is with her, and her mother is on her way," Mrs. Wesley explained. "The nurse said that she pulled out of surgery fine. She'll need extensive physical therapy, but she should make a full recovery," Mrs. Wesley said. "I'm so sad about your loss." She gripped his arm firmly. "I-I don't know what to say," she stammered.

His large hand covered Mrs. Wesley's petite wrist, his strong fingers gripped around her hand firmly. "Thank you," he managed. "It's horrible, but we gonna be alright," he said confidently. "We gonna be alright," he repeated, as though trying to convince himself. He slowly shoved his hands into his overall pockets and inhaled deeply before continuing. "Life won't be the same without Charlotte and Lori in the house going at it over that telephone. That's fo' sure," he chuckled softly. "But I know that God knows what's best. And our good Lord is going to carry us through this difficult time," he paused. "He has to," he finished, his voice but a whisper as his eyes studied Maria. "Why is she in a wheelchair, Liz?" he asked.

"She fainted," Mrs. Wesley whispered softly. "But she's fine. She just bumped her head, when she heard the news about Lori," her voice trailed and the tears flowed freely.

"This is a lot for these girls to experience. They're still so young," Mr. Perkins offered. "I didn't lose a friend until I was a grown man."

"Do they know what happened? Were they hit by a drunk driver?" Mrs. Wesley asked.

"No. The police said that they think that Charlotte fell asleep at the wheel and lost control of the car. The officer said that it appears that Lori unfastened her seatbelt to grab the steering wheel and stop the car," he sniffled. "But it was too late, and the car crashed into a telephone pole," he paused. He shook his head from side to side. "I know that Lori must have unfastened her seatbelt, because she always wore it. Always. She would not let you start the car if her seatbelt wasn't fastened," he said. His voice cracked slightly as he spoke. "But Charlotte never wore her seatbelt. She said that it wrinkled her clothes. They were both thrown through the windshield," he continued. "They died instantly," he gasped. "But thank God that Justine was wearing her seatbelt. That is the blessing in this tragedy."

Mrs. Wesley squeezed his arm again. "I am so sorry. If there is anything that I can do, anything at all, just let me know," Mrs. Wesley offered.

Maria sobbed again. Mr. Perkins walked over to her and leaned his large frame over the wheelchair. He squeezed both of her hands in his large mitts. "Everything is gonna be okay, Maria. We're going to get through this bad patch together," he patted Maria's hand. "Now don't you go getting upset all over again. Lori would want you to be strong for her," he comforted.

Mrs. Wesley and the attendant wheeled Maria to the car.

∽◌∼

Maria had been trying to reach Teenie and Rashanda since she got home from the hospital. She wiped her eyes with a tissue and applied Vaseline to her chapped lips. Lips whose only moisture had been her salty tears. *I can't believe that I haven't moisturized my lips all afternoon. I guess in the face of tragedy, personal hygiene isn't so important.*

Maria called Tanisha's number again. Busy. "What could they possibly be talking about for this long?" she groaned aloud. "If they don't hang up in five minutes, I'm breaking into the line!"

∽◌∼

"Hey, Rashanda!" Tanisha said. "I just walked in the door."

Rashanda smiled, glad that she'd been able to reach one of her friends on the phone. "I did too," she whispered. "I had a date with Ian."

"I know. I talked to Maria before Glen picked me up, and she told me that you were going out with him. How was it?" Tanisha asked.

"You go first. How was your date with Glen?"

Tanisha told Rashanda about their picnic at Pine Lake.

"It was really cool. He's so laid back. We just ate, chilled and talked. It was really romantic," Tanisha said. "It started getting dark, and the mosquitoes were biting so we went to this ice cream parlor near his house and split a sundae and talked some more. He's a really soulful dude," Tanisha said.

"Did you kiss him?" Rashanda asked.

"I wanted to, but he didn't try. I was kind of disappointed actually. We didn't even hold hands," she paused. "He opened my car door and was a perfect gentleman, but he didn't try to kiss me," Tanisha groaned. "When he dropped me off, he walked around to my side of the car, gave me a hug and told me that he'd call me tomorrow," Tanisha finished. "We had a great time, and I felt the chemistry between us, but there was no lip action," she sighed.

As she placed her jewelry on her dresser, she noticed a letter. She picked it up and read the return address. The letter was from David Barton. She smiled and decided to read it after she hung up with Rashanda. "Speaking of chemistry, that's enough about me. It's your turn now," Tanisha said. "How was your date with the chemistry tutor?" she asked.

"My date was unbelievable," Rashanda said softly. "Ian and I made out!"

"You did what?" Tanisha asked.

"We made out," Rashanda repeated softly.

"Yeah! Your first make out session! How was it?" Tanisha squealed.

"It was great! But let's call it something else in case one of my parents or my sister picks up the phone. Let's call it bowling," Rashanda said.

"I want to hear all of the details. Talk, girlfriend!" Tanisha was glad that she hadn't tried to read David's letter while talking on the phone with Rashanda.

Rashanda gave the long version of the date.

"So it was your idea?" Tanisha asked. "You led him to the bowling alley? Were you planning to bowl with him?"

"Not really. He asked me to be his girlfriend before the party, and then we were studying the constellations, and it was so romantic, so I told him that he should kiss me to make us an official couple," Rashanda giggled. "I didn't want anyone to see us, so we went outside and bowled by the light of the moon," she giggled. "It was soooo romantic," she purred.

"Was he a good kisser?" Tanisha asked.

"Teenie!" Rashanda yelled. "Don't say that word," she whispered. "It's bowling, remember?"

"I'm sorry, I forgot. Was he a good bowler?" she corrected. "I've heard that a lot of cute guys aren't good bowlers," Tanisha explained. "Think Darryl Hunter for instance. Not that I have that much experience bowling myself since I haven't bowled with anyone since my camp experience with that white guy, Brian Kraft," she paused. "And he was a great bowler!" Tanisha shared. "Did you bowl like they do in France?" Tanisha asked.

"Yup! We French bowled the whole time. He's a great bowler," Rashanda shared. "This was the first time that I bowled like they do in France, but it was awesome," she continued. "It was really nice."

"Did he know that you'd never been French bowling?" Tanisha giggled.

"He did," Rashanda said. "I was nervous at first, and he asked me if I was sure that I wanted to keep bowling, and I told him that I was positive. And I must say I'm glad that my first French bowling experience was with him. He was so sweet," she smiled. "By the way, if my parents should ask, French bowling is where you bowl and only speak French while you're bowling, got it?"

"Got it. Girl, you have the world's most descriptive imagination," Tanisha laughed. "How long did the bowling last?"

"I think it was about fifteen minutes or so," Rashanda said.

"That's about right for a first major bowling session," Tanisha squealed. "Did his friends know that you went bowling?"

"No. They were so busy playing games and listening to music that they thought we'd just gone for a walk," Rashanda said. "Thank, God. I would have been too embarrassed."

"Wow!" Tanisha said. "Welcome to the bowling league! You've been officially initiated. Have you told anybody else?"

"I was trying to set-up a three way call, but no one else is home. I've called Grace, Maria, Justine and Lori," Rashanda said.

Tanisha flopped on her bed. "Lori and Justine were hanging out at the mall together," she said. "Maybe they decided to go to a movie." She fluffed her pillow and settled in. "I know I just met him, but I am so ready to go bowling with Glen," Tanisha groaned. I hope he wasn't grossed out by my rotten tooth. I hope that's not why he didn't try to kiss me. Maybe I should tell Rashanda about my tooth and get her opinion.

Tanisha heard a click on her line. "This is the operator," the voice said. "I have a Maria Wesley trying to interrupt this call for an emergency. Will you release the call?" the operator asked.

Tanisha giggled. "Yes, operator. I'll release the call. Maria's ears must be burning, Rashanda. She's trying to break into the line. I'll hang up and call her right now, and then she can three-way you from her phone so you can tell her your story. Plus, I have more questions about your bowling experience."

"Don't say anything to her about my bowling, okay? I want to tell her myself," Rashanda giggled. "I wonder what her emergency is."

"You know how dramatic Maria is," Tanisha teased. "She probably wants our advice on something having to do with Todd," Tanisha groaned. "She breaks into my line at least once a week for some drama or another," she finished. "I'm going to get call waiting on my phone soon."

"You're probably right," Rashanda agreed. "She was talking to him when Ian picked me up at her house. You better hang up so she can call you. I'll wait for you guys to call me right back."

Chapter 20

No More Tears

Clouds. Slender clouds wearing make-up is how they were best described. No. They looked more like cotton candy or marshmallows; a row of shapely, tanned marshmallow cotton candy that's been lightly scorched to make s'mores. If there was such a thing as marshmallow cotton candy, that's what they would be. In a sea of black and blue, they wore marshmallow cotton candy white, sleeveless ensembles.

With their tanned brown skin lying against the starch crisp white, they could have posed for a suntan lotion advertisement. The mission was uniformity. Close enough. Three of the girls wore the same identical sundress, and two of the girls wore matching skirts and sleeveless blouses. The girls had searched several stores trying to find five identical white dresses, but because it was so close to Labor Day, the official last day for wearing white, they had only found dresses for three of them. Miraculously, they'd managed to find two identical sleeveless blouses and skirts, which was a good thing since the old church was not air conditioned. So instead of quintuplets, they were a set of triplets and a set of twins. The pink rose attached to their hearts added a spice of color to their uninterrupted white and capped off their uniformity like a pink cherry atop a vanilla ice cream sundae. White sandals draped their feet with toes painted the same soft shade of pink as their flower.

It was Maria's idea. She thought it would be a nice tribute to Lori to wear a bright color to her funeral. She'd originally suggested pink, since pink was Lori's favorite color. But Tanisha thought that pink was too bright, and it would be too difficult for all of them to find appropriate dresses in the same bubblegum shade of pink that Lori favored. So Tanisha suggested that they wear white. Everyone could find a white dress or skirt blouse combination in the summer. And they had. They'd painted their toes bubble gum pink. They looked like a row of marshmallow cotton candy. They were Lori's angels.

Mrs. Wesley had come through again. Arranging for a white stretch limousine to take them to the funeral had been brilliant. The girls met at Maria's house, and even Maria managed to have herself ready when the limousine pulled into her driveway.

The limousine driver helped Justine into the limousine, folded her wheelchair and placed it in the expansive trunk. They quietly primped their hair and make-up in the long limousine mirror and nibbled the peanuts and pretzels that the driver told them had been arranged by Mrs. Wesley. The excitement of riding in a limousine for the first time was eclipsed by the reason for the limousine. They were going to their friend's funeral.

Once at the church, a collective exhale occurred as the girls squeezed each other's hands before getting out of the car. As if on cue, the limousine driver hopped out and set up Justine's wheelchair before opening the door for the girls. They watched as Mrs. Wesley exited the front seat of the limousine and whispered something to a gentleman dressed in a dark suit. The gentleman smiled knowingly and quickly escorted them past a long line of mourners and into the church.

A reserved pew with a pink ribbon on the end welcomed the girls to Lori's funeral where they found themselves seated directly behind the Perkins' family pew. Grace exhaled loudly and looked around.

She studied her surroundings. The church was beautiful. Stained glass covered each of the windows, and a large wooden cross hung on the wall. Is it called a stage? No, it's called the altar. She counted sixteen ceiling fans whirring non stop and six tall misting fans. The misting fans had yellow rental tags hanging from their poles. They must have been rented by the funeral director to cool off the sanctuary. Even with the fans, the temperature in the church was almost unbearable. Every now and then, a warm breeze moved the thick air. Grace squeezed Justine's hand as she adjusted her friend's wheelchair. She picked up a wooden handled church fan with a picture of Reverend Dr. Martin Luther King, Jr. on the front, and an advertisement for the funeral home on the other side. She turned the fan over and fanned Justine.

"My hands work fine, Grace. You don't have to fan me," Justine whispered. She grabbed the fan and tucked it behind the pew next to a hymnal and Bible.

Grace folded her hands in her lap and watched the line of people parading by the open caskets. She adjusted her body behind Mr. Perkins' large girth so that she wouldn't see her friend laid out in the casket. The girls had agreed that they would not walk up and view the bodies. They all wanted to remember Lori and Charlotte alive and vibrant. She wondered if her friends had obstructed views as well.

Being inside of a church was a new experience for Grace. Her parents never attended church, so she never attended. This was her first funeral. She'd never seen a dead body before and now she was seeing two laid end to end. She read the obituary for the fifth time, and studied Lori's photo on the front. This is how Grace wanted to remember Lori, smiling and full of life, not ashen and gray lying in a casket. She shook her head softly as she heard two ladies whispering by the casket while mourners embraced the Perkins' family.

"They look good don't you think?" a lady in a large black hat asked, her voice louder than she probably realized.

"They sure do," her friend replied even louder, wearing a larger black hat that looked like it could have given birth to her friend's hat.

"I wonder how the undertaker got their heads back on their necks," big hat wondered.

"He probably didn't," bigger hat replied. "He probably just stuck them back on their bodies or stapled them to their necks," she continued. "That's why they're wearing turtlenecks in this heat," she added. "I heard that undertakers will do whatever is the easiest and the cheapest, so they're probably stapled on," she finished.

Grace frowned as she watched big hat and bigger hat hugging the Perkins' family and sobbing. She wondered if they were melting in the dark stockings that they wore. Big hat wore white shoes with her dark stockings. Their heads might be stapled on? I could have done without that visual. Why would anyone wear panty hose in ninety eight degree weather? And even I know that you never wear stockings that are darker than your shoes! When big hat and bigger hat walked past their pew and smiled at the girls, Grace rolled her eyes and looked over her shoulder. She stretched her neck and could still see a line of mourners out the door.

The article in the local paper explained that Charlotte and Lori had been decapitated when they were thrown from the windshield, but Grace had not considered what that actually meant.

So many questions spun through Grace's mind. How does anyone look good after their head is cut off from their body? She closed her eyes and tried to remove the image that she'd been thinking about constantly since Lori's death. Did they feel it? Or did they die on impact when their heads slammed through the glass windshield? She couldn't stop the questions from coming. Did the police find their heads right away? Were their heads cut all of the way off or just sliced halfway from their neck? Were they actually stapled back on their necks? Grace wiped a tear from her eye and shook her head from side to side, glad that her hair was no longer on her neck. She ran her hand through her short hair and fluffed out her curls before casually picking up the Bible behind the pew in front of her and flipping through the pages. She stopped at Matthew chapter seven, verse thirteen. She liked the name Matthew and July thirteenth was her birthday. She read. She continued and read verse fourteen. She closed the Bible.

Grace never read the Bible. She'd tried to read it once after Lori told her that it was the best book in the world. She'd read Genesis and half of Exodus and stopped. It had taken her several hours over the course of several days to read that much. She understood some parts of it: The Garden of Eden story and the part in Exodus that reminded her of the Ten Commandments movie that she saw each Easter Sunday. But the rest had been confusing. And the names were lengthy and difficult to pronounce. Lori had laughed when Grace told her what page she was on in the Bible and asked her how long it had taken her to read the whole thing.

"You don't have to read the Bible from front to back, Grace," Lori offered. "You can skip around and read different passages and books of the Bible whenever you feel like you need motivation or inspiration," Lori said tenderly. "Just pick it up and skim it and flip around until you read something that makes you think about your life," she advised. "You should come to Sunday school with me. It will really help you learn how to study the Bible. You never finish reading the Bible. It's the one book that you will study forever."

She regretted that she'd never accompanied her friend to Sunday school. And now it was too late. Grace picked up the Bible again and turned back to Matthew chapter seven, verse thirteen. 'Enter by the narrow gate for the gate is wide that leads to destruction and those who enter by it are many. But the gate is narrow that leads to life and those who find it are few.' she read. Grace read the passage again. She wished that Lori were here to explain what it meant.

Her thoughts were interrupted by the organist. Grace looked up as the funeral directors proceeded to the front of the church.

"What are they doing now?" she whispered to Justine.

"The viewing is over so they're about to close the caskets," Justine explained.

Holding Teenie's hand, Maria reached for Grace's hand so she instinctively reached for Justine's hand. Mrs. Perkins sobbed loudly and had to be restrained by Mr. Perkins as the funeral directors ceremoniously closed Charlotte and Lori's caskets simultaneously. The soloist sang Eye on the Sparrow and the funeral directors and ushers walked the aisle with boxes of tissues.

Mrs. Perkins had invited the girls to give a tribute to Lori. They had worked on it together, and the girls had decided that Tanisha would read the tribute at the service. When the soloist finished, the minister invited the girls to the microphone.

Sitting on the edge of the pew, Rashanda stood first and Teenie & Maria walked to the left as Grace wheeled Justine to the front of the church and turned her around to face the audience. Tanisha ascended the stairs with Rashanda and Maria. Grace stood near Justine and watched as the guests smiled and stared curiously at the girls in their white ensembles.

Tanisha tilted the podium microphone toward her and cleared her throat.

"My name is Tanisha Carlson and this is Rashanda Jordan and Maria Wesley," she pointed. "Grace Dudley is standing below the podium, and Justine Wellington is seated in the wheelchair." Tanisha's voice cracked slightly when she said wheelchair. She cleared her throat again and continued.

"We stand before you today as Lori's angels. All of us have been classmates and close friends of Lori's since seventh grade. Some of us have been friends of hers since third grade. We've experienced puberty together and were looking forward to going to prom and college together," she read slowly. "We stand before you to tell you that Lori will experience all of those things through us," she paused. "Lori was the beacon of light in our group that beckoned us to be better. We will ensure that her light continues to shine. She corrected us when we spoke the Lord's name in vain or when we forgot to bow our heads and give thanks for our food, something that she always did instinctively and unashamedly," Tanisha read. She took a deep breath to compose herself before continuing. "She was always looking to help others and motivated us to be the best we could be," she explained. "And even though we nicknamed her the church girl and teased her about her faith at times, we all admired Lori's faith and strong religious beliefs. And she was a lot of fun. Some of our best schemes were crafted by Lori. And trust me when I tell you, even though she was a church girl, she usually had the craftiest schemes," Tanisha giggled. "And because she was an unlikely suspect, her schemes usually worked." She took a sip of water from the glass that Rashanda offered her as the congregation chuckled softly.

"But seriously, we will miss Lori like we would miss our own sister, because we loved her like a sister," Tanisha said. "She was our sister. We decided to wear white to represent the light that was Lori. And even though Lori's light was dimmed much too soon, we know that Lori's light was not extinguished because it will continue to live through the friends who loved her, and we loved Lori," Tanisha sobbed softly as tears streamed down her cheeks. She took another deep breath and continued. "Like all of you, we've cried a lot but we have decided to live our lives and honor Lori's memory. We know that she is with us in spirit, and if she were with us physically she would tell us to stop crying. 'No more tears. God doesn't make mistakes.' Lori would say. 'I'm in a better place.' She would lead us to a scripture that would help patch the huge hole in our fragile hearts," Tanisha explained.

"So we stand before you committed to living our lives so that Lori would be proud. We are Lori's Angels. Thank you," Tanisha finished.

Tears flowed freely as the girls embraced. They smiled through the tears and slowly returned to their seats. Grace pushed Justine's wheelchair back to the end of the aisle and exhaled loudly. She smiled at Tanisha's dad as he reached over the pew and rubbed Tanisha's back, surprised that she hadn't noticed him before.

Mr. Carlson was seated next to a woman that looked just like Tanisha, but Grace knew that it wasn't Tanisha's mom. Grace knew Tanisha's mom and this woman wasn't her. Besides, Tanisha had told the girls that her mother did not believe in attending funerals. Mr. Carlson is dating someone that resembles his daughter?

Grace listened to the pastor's sermon and wished she had eaten breakfast. Her stomach growled with hunger. I should have stuffed some of those pretzels from the limousine into my purse. She fished in her purse and ate a mint. She looked around at the sobbing mourners. She'd cried so much over the past several days that she really didn't have any more tears left. She would miss Lori, but she couldn't cry anymore. She had no more tears.

Her stomach growled loudly through the brief service. She was glad that the whir of the fans, plus the singing and pastor's comments drowned out her noisy stomach. Mrs. Perkins had decided that she wanted the service to be swift. After the girls' tribute, the pastor performed the eulogy. He called the death a celebration because the girls were home with the Father, God Almighty. A chorus of "Amens" filled the church as Grace struggled to understand how the tragic death of a sixteen year old girl and her sister could be described as a celebration. She watched as even Mrs. Perkins nodded in agreement and rocked in her seat. Another song was sung before the pall bearers wheeled the caskets outside and into the waiting hearse. She felt sorry for Lori's ex-boyfriend Doug. He had to be restrained when they wheeled Lori's casket by his pew. On the program, he was listed as a pallbearer, but he was too upset to perform this role so Teenie's brother Jack stepped in at the last minute. Doug must have really loved her.

Once outside, Grace noticed that the flowers were being loaded into a separate pick-up truck. There were so many funeral sprays. She hadn't noticed how many flowers were inside of the church, most of them different shades of pink. She wondered if the flowers had been sent to both sisters or if one sister had received more flowers than the other. In the processional, the girls' white limousine was directly behind the truck of flowers. They piled into the white limousine for the ride to the cemetery. Grace was glad that the limo driver had turned on the air conditioning. No one spoke for several minutes as they watched the mourners milling about on the church steps holding the orange funeral stickers that would be affixed to their windshields. Many of the mourners embraced and posed for pictures before scurrying to their cars as the funeral processional pulled away from the curb.

"Is the cemetery far?" Justine asked.

"Nope. It's less than ten minutes away," Tanisha answered.

"I wish Lori could be with us," Maria said.

"She is with us. She'll always be with us," Rashanda reminded.

Tanisha wiped her eyes and carefully reapplied her eyeliner in the slow moving vehicle. "Let's make a pact," she suggested. "Let's agree to be happy. We can't let Lori's death keep us in a constant state of mourning. Let's laugh and live and love Lori."

The girls placed their hands one on top of the other and smiled as the limousine pulled into the cemetery.

"That was fast," Grace stated.

"I told you it was less than ten minutes away," Tanisha smiled.

Grace stared out of the window at all of the tombstones and grave markers. Many were adorned with flowers. She wondered if the flowers were real or plastic. The limousine pulled to a halt behind the family limousine and flower car.

Climbing out of the car, the girls slowly followed the Perkins' family to the gravesite. They helped Justine who used her walker to maneuver carefully over the grassy area. The pink funeral spray that Mrs. Wesley had ordered was near the head of the casket. Each of the girls gently pulled out two of the pink roses. The minister said a prayer and the girls tossed one rose atop Lori's casket as it was lowered into the ground. Clutching one rose, they embraced before slowly walking back to the limousine.

Grace trembled as she climbed back into the car.

"Now remember, no more tears," Tanisha said tearfully.

"What is a repast and are we going?" Grace asked. "They're going to have food at this thing, right? I've never been to a funeral before and I'm starving. I'm so hungry that I'm shaking," she groaned.

The girls giggled loudly.

"A repast is just a funeral reception and there will be a lot of food. Of course we have to go, we're Lori's angels," Maria stated firmly. "Besides, my mom hired the limousine to tote us around all day."

"I can't believe that you've never been to a funeral, Grace," Rashanda said. "But I guess since your parents were only children and you never knew your grandparents."

Grace lowered her head for a moment. "I guess I probably went to my mother's funeral when I was little, but I don't remember it. I'll have to ask my parents."

Rashanda rubbed Grace's arm as the limousine pulled in front of the church. "I bet you did. You should ask your mother when you get home."

As they ascended the steps of the church, Tanisha's father walked up with the woman from the pew. He embraced Tanisha and hugged the other girls warmly.

"Girls, of course you know my dad. And this is my Aunt Helen. Aunt Helen, these are my best friends," Tanisha said.

"It's nice to meet you ladies. I'm so sorry about your loss," she offered sincerely. "You look lovely in white," Aunt Helen added. "Tanisha, may I speak with you privately for a moment?"

Grace accepted Mr. Carlson's offer to wheel Justine up the

small plywood that served as the church's wheelchair ramp. She held the door and led him to the plywood ramp leading to the basement.

"Tanisha, I am so sorry about Lori's passing," Aunt Helen said.

"Thank you, Aunt Helen. And thanks for coming to the services," Tanisha said.

"Friends are such important treasures," Aunt Helen stated. "I personally believe that sometimes your friends can be closer to you than your family," she continued. She squeezed Tanisha's hand softly. "She seemed like such a nice girl. You know she called me about the Delta literacy program?"

Aunt Helen looked over her shoulder to ensure that the other girls were inside before she continued. "She also asked me to do some research about an African American professor at Northwestern," Aunt Helen explained. She studied Tanisha's face. "Now, she told me that she was doing a paper on African American professors who taught during the Civil Rights movement," she paused. "But my instinct tells me that there is more to the story. Do you know what she was up to?" Aunt Helen asked.

Tanisha blushed. She couldn't lie to her favorite aunt. "She was trying to help Grace," Tanisha whispered. "Grace is the girl who was pushing Justine in the wheelchair. We think that the professor was her father. In fact, we're certain that he was. Lori really wanted to help find him so Grace could contact him."

"Bingo. I knew it." Aunt Helen rubbed her hands together. "I knew there was more to the story. The professor's name was Charles Lovett," Aunt Helen said softly. "My intern spoke with him briefly on the telephone last week." She pulled out a slip of paper from her purse. "He said he sounds like a really nice man.

Here's his information."

Tanisha's mouth dropped open in disbelief. She studied the sheet of paper, and stared at her Aunt Helen. "I can't believe that you were able to reach him," she stammered. "This is awesome!" she squealed staring at the paper in her hand.

"Why don't you put that away and share it with your friend at a better time," Aunt Helen coached. "Today is about Lori and her sister."

Tanisha nodded her head in agreement, folded the paper and placed it in her purse as her dad walked up and pulled Tanisha into a bear hug.

"Hey, Booger. You did a nice job with Lori's tribute. I know that was difficult, and I'm very proud of you," he said.

"Thanks, Dad," Tanisha smiled. "But don't' call me Booger in public!" she scolded.

"No one heard me," he chuckled. "We can't stay for the repast. You sure you're going to be alright?" Her father asked.

"But someone might hear you next time," she whined like a six year old. "I'm going to be fine, Dad," she smiled.

Grace stood at the top of the church steps. "Teenie, your friend Glen is here. He's sitting with Rashanda's friend Ian. Did you know that Glen was coming? He wanted me to make sure that you knew that he was here so you didn't leave."

Glen came? He's here? I can't believe that he came to the funeral.

Her father studied Tanisha's face. "Who's Glen, Tanisha?" he asked sternly.

"He's just a friend, Dad," she shrugged. "I'll talk to you later," she blushed. She gave her dad a kiss and hugged her Aunt Helen who winked knowingly at Tanisha.

Chapter 21

Tulips in October

"Billie Mae, I cannot believe that you would lie about something like that," Jackie growled. "You've sunk to a new level of low!"

Tanisha tiptoed out of her room and crouched at the top of the stairs to listen. Upon returning from their Saturday afternoon outing with their dad, Byron and Allen had turned on the television and shut the door to their bedroom as instructed. By the distressed look on her dad's face, Tanisha knew that her parents were about to have an argument. She'd gone to her room as ordered, but her curiosity convinced her that eavesdropping was in order.

"What did you do with the two hundred dollars that I gave you last summer?" Jackie demanded.

"I used it to pay my car note," Billie replied casually.

Tanisha could hear Billie inhale slowly. She imagined the small smoke circles that Billie expertly exhaled.

"You used it to pay your car note?" Jackie asked. "Ain't that but nothing. You used it to pay your car note," he repeated. "That was your plan all along wasn't it? You had no intention of taking Tanisha to the dentist. You tell me that you need money to surprise our daughter and have her tooth removed, and you use the money for yourself. You are so selfish!" he growled. Tanisha imagined his thick eyebrows furrowed into a scowl. She placed a hand over her mouth to mask her breathing.

Tanisha felt a sneeze coming on and squeezed her nostrils to suppress it. *Shoot! I missed Billie's comment.*

"Do you know how I felt when Tanisha asked me about that tooth today? I felt like a fool, that's how," he continued. "But you don't care about that. You just care about yourself. I can't believe that you'd rather drive around in a big car that you can't afford instead of paying for insurance for our children. Well, you're putting the kids on your dental plan now. I'm going to see to that. I don't care if you lose that car and have to take the bus to work. You are covering my kids on your insurance plan, or I'm taking you to court and filing for custody myself," Jackie threatened.

"Jackie, let me explain," Billie pleaded. "And please lower your voice. The children will hear us."

"What's there to explain, Billie?" Jackie asked. His tone was softer and barely above a whisper. Tanisha had to lean across the top stair to hear. "You lied to me about our daughter and took money from me to pay your car note. It seems pretty cut and dry to me," Jackie paused. "Put the kids on your insurance plan next week, Billie, or I will hire an attorney and drag your butt to court and take custody of them myself. I mean it. See if I won't."

Tanisha could hear her father jangling his keys. She ducked behind the banister and crawled on her belly to her bedroom as his heavy footsteps approached the stairs.

"Tanisha, Byron, Allen. I'm leaving now," Jackie yelled.

Tanisha walked out of her room and stood at the top of the stairs. "Bye, Dad. I'll be right down." She thought about tapping on Byron and Allen's bedroom door, but changed her mind. She raced down the stairs and gave her father a hug.

"Where are your brothers?" Jackie asked.

"They're engrossed in a rerun of Star Trek. They told me to tell you bye. And thanks for taking us out to dinner, Dad."

She waved and stared out the window until her father's car was no longer visible. She braced herself to confront her mother. I don't even know what I'm going to say to her, but it's not going to be pretty. I can't believe that she would lie about something like that when she knows how much I hate this tooth in my mouth! Tanisha turned slowly and tightened her face into an angry scowl. "I heard the whole thing, Mom. How could you?" Her expression softened at what she saw next.

With both hands covering her face, Billie rocked back and forth on the tattered sofa. Her shoulders trembled in a rhythmic motion. Her voice was but a whisper. "I'm so sorry, Tanisha," Billie Mae whispered. "I'm such a horrible person. I don't know what's wrong with me," she sobbed quietly.

Tanisha was frozen in her tracks and stared in silence. She'd never seen her mother cry.

"Mom," she said softly. "Are you okay?"

Her mother tilted her head slightly. "No, I'm not okay," she sobbed. "I need help, Tanisha."

"Can I get you anything?" Tanisha asked.

"No. I really need help. I need professional help. I'm so sorry for everything," Billie whispered. "I have a mental illness, and I'm so ashamed of myself."

"Mom, you don't need to be ashamed. A lot of people have mental illness," Tanisha comforted.

"I know, baby girl," she said softly. "I know I need to take medication, but I just can't accept that I have to take it for the rest of my life." Billie wiped her eyes with her hand and sat up straight.

"It's hard accepting that something is wrong with your mind."

Tanisha walked over and sat on the sofa next to her mother and listened.

"When your father lived here, he made sure that I took my medication. It was our morning ritual. He would get dressed for work, bring me my pills and a glass of water and watch me take my prescription. I've been on medication since Jack was born so this routine that your father and I had has gone on for over seventeen years," Billie explained. "That's a long time. I felt like your father was taking care of me," she paused. "But once he moved out, I just didn't feel like taking the medicine anymore. Taking the pills without your father made me miss our routine and miss him."

"But Mom, aren't you the one who wanted the divorce?" Tanisha asked.

Billie took a deep breath before responding. She had stopped crying. "I was. We both wanted it, but I'm the one who filed," she explained. "Anyway, I thought that maybe your father was the source of my mental anguish and with him gone I didn't need the pills anymore. I just couldn't accept that my mental health was not one hundred percent," she admitted. "When my head started spinning out of control, I turned to Buddhism. I thought that if I could learn to center my thoughts I could control the restlessness in my head. But that didn't work either," she paused. "When I started taking the pills again, it felt strange. I felt better, less angry and more in control. I even considered contacting your father to try and reconcile and that scared me," she confessed. "I stopped taking the pills again so that I could continue being angry at him. I know it sounds stupid, but it gave me a place to channel my anger," Billie whispered softly.

Tanisha listened intently. She'd never heard her mother talk so freely before.

"I heard you say that you heard everything," she sniffled. "I'm so sorry that I lied to your father about the money," she sobbed. "For the first time he looked at me like he hated me, like I was an evil, despicable person. I've known your father for over eighteen years, and I've never seen him give me the look that he gave me today. I really let him down. Maybe I am a despicable person," she whispered.

"You're not despicable, Mom. You just need to take your medication," Tanisha said.

"Will you help me, Tanisha?" her mother asked.

"Of course I'll help you, Mom. What can I do?"

"Can you bring me my medicine and a glass of water in the morning before you leave for school or work?"

"I can do that," Tanisha assured. "But what if you're still asleep when I leave? Do you want me to wake you to take your medication?"

"I'm usually awake when you leave in the morning. I'm generally just lying in the bed thinking. Just knock on the door and bring them in. Can you do that for me, sweetie? It would help me feel like I'm not going through this alone. It would mean so much to me," Billie said.

Tanisha smiled. "Sure, Mom. I can do that for you." She's never called me sweetie before.

Billie squeezed Tanisha's hand softly. "Tanisha, I'm so sorry. Let's start over. I'm going to try to be a better mother starting today. I really am going to try. I know you and your brothers deserve the best that I can give you, and I'm going to try to improve. Please be patient with me," Billie pleaded.

Billie inhaled deeply. Her eyes, rimmed with tears, bore into

Tanisha's. "I can't do this alone, I just can't."

"I'll help you, Mom." Tanisha squeezed her mother's hand. Watching her mother's eyes fill with tears, she felt her eyes misting too. *I actually feel sorry for her. For the first time that I can remember, I feel sorry for my mother.*

A few weeks later, as ordered, Billie added her children to her dental insurance plan. Much had happened since Jackie's threat to Billie. She traded in her beloved Chrysler New Yorker for a much less expensive Ford Escort in order to afford the monthly insurance premium. She had finally taken Tanisha to an oral surgeon to have her decayed fang removed.

Tanisha ran her tongue to the now empty spot where her dental shame had lived for as long as she could remember. Her tongue traced the small chip of hard enamel from the new tooth that slowly pushed through the roof of her mouth. The dentist had informed her that she would most likely need braces in order to guide the tooth into its proper position.

"Are you in pain?" Billie asked on the ride home from the procedure.

"A little, but I'll live," Tanisha mumbled. The bloody cotton gauze hung loosely from her mouth and rested on her still numb lip.

"Sweetie, my insurance doesn't cover braces," Billie Mae explained.

"Don't worry, Mom. We'll work something out," Tanisha replied.

She studied her reflection in the mirror. *Well, at least it's just a blank space in my mouth, and not a rotten tooth. Plus, most people have to have teeth extracted in order to get their mouth ready for braces. There's no shame in that.* Tanisha was glad that she and her mother were working on their relationship. She'd feared that when Jack moved away to college that summer, her life with her mother would get exponentially worse. But instead it had gotten remarkably better. She wondered how Jack Jr. was doing in school.

The anesthesia made her sleepy. She wished she had time to take a nap before dinner. Tossing her purse on her dresser, the small card fell to the floor. Bending to pick it up, she smiled.

Teenie,
I'm so sorry about Lori. I didn't know.
I would have been there. Call me!
David

She tucked the card into her top drawer. Bad idea. Mom may look in there to borrow something and ask me who David is. Our relationship has improved, but I don't feel like going there with her just yet. Tanisha removed the card and slipped it underneath her mattress. She was glad that Billie hadn't been home when the flowers were delivered or she probably would have stood over her as she read the card. If her mom saw the flowers in her room and asked any questions, Tanisha was prepared to tell her that they were from her friends at Save Mart to cheer her up over Lori's death. It was partially true. David was a friend. He was a very special friend.

Gently fingering the yellow, white and pink tulips, she leaned over to smell them again. How did he order tulips in October? Aren't tulips a spring flower? Her thoughts were interrupted by the phone.

"Hello," she said. "Hey, Glen!" she smiled. "It doesn't hurt now, but the anesthesia made me sleepy," she yawned. "I'm not going to take a nap. I'm getting ready now," she paused. "I'll be ready. I'm always on time," she laughed. "Listen, I have a question for you. How can someone send tulips in October?" she asked. "No, it's not a riddle. I'm serious." Tanisha twirled the phone cord and listened. "Okay. I hadn't thought of that. I'll see you in twenty minutes by the pool clubhouse."

Glen understood that she wasn't allowed to date officially for two more months, so whenever they got together on a day that she wasn't working at Save Mart, he picked her up at the pool clubhouse. Tanisha would tell her mother that she was walking over to her friend Vicky's house for a visit. Vicky always covered for her. Since her mom was taking her medication regularly, Tanisha wasn't worried about Glen meeting her mother in a few months. He liked me even after seeing my rotten tooth, so even if Mom isn't having a good mental health day when it's time for them to meet, I don't think Glen will hold her behavior against me.

The phone rang again. "How am I supposed to finish getting ready if you keep calling me?"

"Getting ready for what?" David asked.

Tanisha took a deep breath. "David?"

"Who'd you think it was, Teenie?"

"I was waiting for Maria to pick me up," she lied.

"Maria has her license already? I thought that you were older than she is," he said.

"I am. But her mother lets her take the car sometimes to go to the mall. We were just going to the mall," she stammered.

"Did you get the flowers that I sent you?"

"They came yesterday, and I'm looking at them right now. They're beautiful, David," she squealed. "I was going to write you a letter tomorrow. You didn't have to send me flowers."

"I know how much you like tulips," he said.

Tanisha smiled. I can't believe that he remembered my

favorite flower. He is the most thoughtful boy in the world! "I love tulips! How were you able to order tulips in October?"

"I had them sent from Holland," he explained. "They're not out of season in Holland."

Glen was right. "Holland!" Tanisha repeated. "That must have cost a fortune, David. You shouldn't have done that," she scolded.

"Don't tell me what I shouldn't have done, bossy lady," he teased. "I wanted to do something special for you, and I wanted you to know how sorry I was about Lori. I still can't believe that you didn't call me and tell me yourself," he said. "The only reason I found out was because Todd told me." Tanisha could hear that he sounded hurt. "Why didn't you call me and tell me what happened, Teenie? You know I would have come up there to attend the services with you."

Tanisha plopped on the floor. "I didn't want you to do that, David. You just started college, and I didn't want you turning back around and buying a plane ticket to check on me," she explained.

"Don't be silly. I have a credit card with a high limit, and my dad would have understood an emergency plane trip home for a funeral. Did you get my letter?"

"I did. But I didn't open it until last week because everything happened so fast with the funeral that it got buried on top of some papers on my dresser. I'm sorry I haven't written you back," Tanisha said.

"I understand," he said. "I called you a few times late at night and your phone was busy every time I called."

"We were planning our comments for the services so I was on the phone a lot with Maria, Rashanda, Grace and Justine," she lied again. "At one point, I felt like the phone was growing out of my ear." She decided to change the subject and gave him details on the funeral service and the Lori's angels' speech.

"Teenie, when you're going through something, I want you to call me and let me decide if I can get away or not," David said. "I care about you, and I know how close you and Lori were. I wish I could have been there to give you support," David comforted.

"Thanks, David. That means a lot to me. Your friendship means a lot to me," she paused. She felt a knot in her stomach. "David," she paused. "There's something that I need to tell you," she inhaled deeply.

"What's up?" he asked. "You sound serious."

"I met someone last month," she said.

There was silence on the other end of the phone.

"David, did you hear me? I said that I met someone," she repeated softly.

"I heard you twice the first time," he said. "Is that why you didn't let me know about Lori?"

"No. I really didn't want you to worry and feel obligated to come to the funeral all the way from Georgetown."

"What's his name and where'd you meet him?" David asked tersely.

"His name is Glen Horton, and I met him at the mall. He's a junior at Morgan Park Academy. It's nothing serious, but we've been out a few times, and I just wanted you to know." Tanisha traced her finger along a flower pattern on her bedspread.

"Did your new friend go to the funeral?" David asked. His words dripped with sarcasm.

Tanisha took a deep breath before responding. "Yes. I didn't ask him to come though. He just showed up and surprised me. Lori was with me at the mall when I met him, so he wanted to come to pay his respects."

"I see. So is he picking you up tonight, Teenie?"

Tell the truth, Teenie. Don't lie to him. You're just friends, remember? "Yes," she whispered. "I'm sorry I lied to you about Maria picking me up, but your call caught me off guard, and I didn't know what to say."

"Do you like this guy?" David asked softly.

"He's nice, and we have fun together. He's very spiritual, and he's been helping me deal with Lori's death. I've had a rough couple of weeks."

"I know you have," he sighed. "Do you talk to him on the phone late at night like we used to do?"

"We don't talk on the phone as much as you and I did, but I really was on the phone a lot with my girls planning our tribute comments." Tanisha squeezed her eyes shut and curled her toes. "David, I wanted to call you and tell you about Lori, but I didn't want to distract you from your studies. I should have called you. I was going to write you tomorrow and tell you about Lori's death and mention Glen. Don't be mad at me, David. We have a deal. We're friends and we can talk about other people with each other, remember?"

"I remember," David said. "I also remember that this was your idea, and I really didn't like it. I still don't like it," he stated flatly.

"Have you met anyone at college?" Tanisha asked cheerily hoping that a change of subject would soften his tone. She slowly counted to five. "David, I asked you a question. Have you met a girl that you like at college?"

"There are a lot of girls here, but I'm not dating anyone if that's what you mean," David said somberly.

"How's Patty? She's at Howard, right?" Tanisha asked cheerfully. He's mad at me.

"Patty's fine. She's pledging Alpha Kappa Alpha next semester, so she's busy doing all of the sorority rush activities."

"I knew she would pledge AKA. She just looked like the AKA type," Tanisha giggled nervously.

"Yeah, whatever. Listen, I need to get off the phone, Tanisha," David stated.

"David, you're mad. That's so not fair. I knew this would happen," she sighed. "I shouldn't have told you about Glen. I'm not tripping that you're dating Patty, so why are you mad that I've met someone that I like getting to know?"

"I can't stand the thought of you dating someone other than me! That's why!" David growled. "I knew you would meet someone eventually, but I just wasn't prepared to hear this news today."

Tanisha took a deep breath. She knew that he wouldn't be excited for her, but she hadn't expected him to be angry. "You're not being fair. I could have just lied to you, but we're friends, and I wanted to tell you the truth," she said softly.

"I wish you had just kept that information to yourself. I really do," David admitted.

"Well, I'm not sorry that I told you, David," Tanisha sighed.

"I am," David replied.

There was a long silence. Tanisha could hear David inhaling deeply. She heard his heavy exhale.

"What happens now?" Tanisha asked.

"You enjoy your date, but spare me the details," David instructed.

"Are we still friends?" she asked timidly.

"Of course, we're still friends, but I need to chill for a minute, Tanisha," David said.

He's really mad at me. He only calls me Tanisha when he's pissed. "That's fine. I understand," Tanisha mumbled softly. "But David, I treasure your friendship, and I need to know that you'll be there for me if I need you."

She could hear David inhale deeply. "Teenie, of course I'll be here for you. But right now, I need to digest all of this."

"That's all I needed to hear," Tanisha smiled.

"Take care," David stated.

"Take care?" Tanisha repeated. "You make it sound like you're going off to war, and we're not going to see each other again," she teased. "What day are you coming home for Thanksgiving break?"

"I'll be home the day before Thanksgiving," David said. "My flight gets to Chicago at eleven o'clock in the morning."

"Perfect!" Tanisha squealed. "I'm usually scheduled to work the Wednesday before Thanksgiving. When you get back in town you can stop by the store and we can have lunch together," Tanisha suggested.

"We'll see," David replied.

"We'll see? You should be flattered that I want to break bread with you," she teased. "In fact, I'm going to stop eating on Tuesday so that I'm super hungry on Wednesday," she giggled. "And I won't eat again until you take me somewhere and feed me. So if I die of starvation, it'll be on your head!"

"Slow down there, sporty. We don't need you passing out. Remember, black girls eat, white girls don't," he laughed. His tone had softened. "But some of the white girls that I see eating in the Georgetown cafeteria can really eat, so you may have to change your theory."

"I can't believe that you remember my silly theory," she giggled. "But you're right, I'm going to have to modify my thesis because I've noticed a lot of white girls at school eating like normal people. Plus, now I'm in love with diet soda. Go figure," she laughed. "But more importantly, you really do listen to me when I'm talking to you."

"I hang on your every word, Princess," David teased.

He's not mad at me anymore!

"So you better tell that Patty babe that you have plans with me the Wednesday before Thanksgiving," she instructed.

"You are just giving out all manner of marching orders today, boss lady!" David chuckled.

"And bring Mr. Belvedere with you so I can see him," Tanisha paused. "I miss that big black fur ball," she sighed. "Now I wish that I'd met your mom so I could stop by your house and visit Belvedere. I think I actually miss him more than I miss you," Tanisha confessed.

"You miss me?" David asked startled.

"Of course I miss you, knucklehead," she giggled.

"You've never said that before," David said.

"Well, you've only been gone about six weeks, so it's never come up. But yes, I miss you and your bad breath," she laughed.

There was a long pause on the telephone.

"Hello. David, are you still there?" Tanisha asked.

"Yeah, I'm still here. Teenie, let me ask you something. If you miss me, how can you be dating this Glen guy?" David asked.

"David! Let's not go over this again, okay?" Tanisha moaned. "Hey, I don't ask you how you can canoodle with Patty when you supposedly like me so much."

"But that's different," David protested.

"How's it different? I'm just dating someone. I haven't even kissed him and you're canoodling with Patty," Tanisha teased.

"But I'm a man. It's different," he explained. "And, I was canoodling with Patty before I met you," David insisted.

"That's a visual that I don't need! I am hanging up this phone on you right now, Mr. Double Standard!" Tanisha squealed. "And I don't even want to remind you that you shouldn't be canoodling with anyone until you're married," Tanisha scolded.

"Please save the lecture. I remember the last one you gave me," he groaned. "Okay, okay. You win. Again," David conceded. "You should be a lawyer because you know how to argue and break a brother down and make him give in without even being mad at you," he laughed.

"Good! I'm glad that you're not mad anymore. And thanks again for the flowers, they're beautiful. I can't believe that you sent me tulips in October," Tanisha gushed.

"You're welcome. But I really need to go now. My roommate has been hovering in the hallway waiting to use the phone," David explained.

"Okay. I'll write you a letter tomorrow and share the details of my date," Tanisha teased.

"Tanisha Denise Carlson, don't even think about it! That's not even funny," David ordered.

"Tanisha? You only call me Tanisha when you're mad at me," she laughed.

"I do not," David defended.

"Yes you do," Tanisha explained. "When I told you about Glen, you called me Tanisha instead of Teenie. That's how I could tell that you were angry," she said. "And now you're using my whole name," she laughed. "You must be pissed. You sound like my dad when he's trying to be stern," she finished.

"But don't write to me about your date, Teenie," David said. "Spare me the details."

"That's better," Tanisha smiled. "I was kidding about that anyway. Go have some fun, David Barton. Go on a panty raid with your roommate."

"Bye, Teenie." She could hear a smile in his voice.

"Bye, David," Tanisha replied.

Tanisha smelled the tulips and smiled at her reflection. *David knows the truth, and he still wants to be my friend. Maybe Lori was right. The truth does set you free.* Tanisha glanced at her watch. She rinsed her mouth with mouthwash, brushed her hair, spritzed perfume on her wrists and raced downstairs. *I still have three minutes to scoot to the clubhouse before Glen can say that I'm late.*

Racing down the stairs, she grabbed her purse to meet Glen for their date.

Chapter 22

The Migration of Maturity

"I think we should agree to do the deed on prom night," she blurted.

The other girls stared at her dumbfounded. Their eyes shifted from one to the other in stunned silence. Tanisha was the first to respond. "Why wait until prom night, Maria?" Tanisha asked sarcastically. "Let's all do it New Year's Eve so we can go out with a bang!" She threw her hands up in the air and waved her fingers wildly before continuing. "You've lost your mind this time, dingbat," she laughed. "Where in the world did this cockeyed scheme originate?" she paused as Maria opened her mouth to speak. Tanisha held her hand in Maria's face to silence her friend. "Don't answer that. Let me guess. One word. Todd."

"Todd told me that it's old fashioned to wait until marriage to do the deed," Maria explained.

"Bingo!" Tanisha giggled. "I knew it!"

"You're making fun of me, Teenie, but Todd said that you wouldn't buy a car without driving it first, and that no man is going to marry a woman until he's test driven the vehicle," Maria defended.

"Maria! You're twisted!" Grace waved her hands in the air. "Count me out of this one."

Rashanda took a deep breath. "Maria," she said. "Have you considered that Todd is just telling you this so that you'll do the deed with him?" she asked.

"Agreed," Tanisha concurred. "He's trying to fill your head with foolishness and the Todd rules of the world," she said. Her hands made quotation marks in the air. "Don't believe him. Boys will say anything to get what they want. I'm not going to compromise my values just because it's prom night. I like the idea of waiting until marriage."

"Me too," Grace agreed. "I don't even have a boyfriend yet. It's actually the furthest thing from my mind these days."

"Come on Gracie-Wacie, even though you don't have a boyfriend, you can just flirt with someone at school and see what happens. You don't have to be in love with them to do it. I think we should all try it so we can talk about it and compare notes," Maria explained. "No one else has to know. It'll be our little secret."

Rashanda shrugged her shoulders. "I wouldn't say that I agree with that, Maria. I think you should be in love and committed to the person that you share your body with. That's what the Bible says," she paused. "I'm waiting for marriage too.

Maria sighed loudly. "Our circle is getting smaller since Lori died and Justine moved to Chicago. We're going to run out of things to bond over," Maria whined. "If we all agree to do it on prom night, it'll be like a secret club. It'll be our own little rite of passage," she squealed. "Besides, I'm really curious, and there are so many people at school who are already doing it," she finished. "We're the only girls at River North High School who are holding out."

"First of all, you don't know that for sure," Tanisha stated. "And even if we are, who cares? I'd rather be in this club, than that group. I think the girls who are going all of the way are making a mistake that they'll regret later. They're too young to be trading their bodies like baseball cards. Frankly, I think it shows low self esteem and self worth."

"I agree with you, Teenie," Grace said. "I always get uncomfortable when I hear the girls whispering about their exploits during study hall. Half the time they're only doing it in order to keep their boyfriend," Grace said. "They do it, the guy dumps them anyway, and the following week they're whispering about how the guy used them. I think it's pathetic."

The girls stretched an old blanket across the floor in Maria's room and spread out to paint their toenails. Maria's new cat Sugar nudged her bedroom door ajar and hopped on her bed. A fat, black cat that acted like a dog, Sugar had only been a part of the family for three weeks, but he greeted guests when they came over and sat at their feet to be petted. And he didn't hide from visitors like most cats. Sugar curled up on Maria's yellow comforter and purred softly.

"You're allergic to dogs and you hate them, but you like cats?" Tanisha asked. She walked over and petted Sugar gently.

"It's strange, but Sugar doesn't trigger my allergies," Maria explained. She took a deep breath. "I don't care what you guys think," she stated. "I'm going to call Todd tonight and tell him that I'm ready to do it!" she smiled. "He'll be so shocked. He's been bugging me about it for the past two years. I know I said that I was going to wait until marriage, but I'm scared that I'll lose him if I don't do it."

"Maria, I don't think you should rush into anything right now. Especially with what's going on with your parents. It's only been a few weeks since your dad moved out. How's that going for your family?" Rashanda asked softly.

"It's cool," Maria shrugged. "It seems like it happened really fast, but I saw it coming several months ago. I think my mom got tired of pretending like she didn't know what was going on and just wanted to finish her degree before filing for divorce. She just got a job at a large bank downtown, so she's focused on doing well at work," she sighed. "I miss not having her here when I get home from school, but I'm excited for her. She seems happier now that she's working." She waved a magazine over her toenails. "I like this color," she smiled. "I miss my dad, but he wasn't around that much, anyway. He was either working late or gone all day on the weekends. Or at least he said that he was working late, but now I suspect that he was probably spending time with his girlfriend," Maria shared.

"Did your mother confront your dad about his girlfriend?" Tanisha asked.

"Confront him?" Maria repeated. "Girl, Liz handled it like an academy award winning actress," she chuckled. "My mother was as smooth as butter," she sighed deeply. "At first, I was ashamed to tell this story, and my mother told my brother and me that it was 'family business' and that I shouldn't talk about the details of their breakup," she paused. "But you guys are my closest friends, and I know that you won't blab my business all around the school. I told Rashanda bits and pieces of the story, but since we're all here together, I'll just tell everyone the whole story. She sat up and leaned her back into her bed frame.

"After Liz got her first paycheck, she suggested to my dad that the four of us go out to dinner to celebrate. But my dad said that he had a poker game that night and couldn't go, so my mother took Neal and me to her favorite restaurant. We had a nice time, but she seemed distracted during dinner," Maria explained.

"When we came home, my brother walked to his friend's house for a sleepover, and I was chilling in the family room watching television. The next thing I know, Liz was walking downstairs with a large suitcase. She dragged the suitcase into the garage and said she'd be right back. I thought that maybe she was taking some clothes to the Goodwill box at ten o'clock at night," Maria shrugged. "She came back about thirty minutes later, opened a bottle of wine and poured herself a glass. Now, I thought this was strange because my mom never drinks alone. The only time I ever see her drinking alcohol in the house is when we're having a party or my dad is here and they're having a drink together," Maria explained. "Liz didn't say a word to me. She just sat at the dining room table, quietly flipped through her magazine and sipped her wine." Maria paused as Sugar crawled into her lap. She gently stroked the cat and nuzzled her nose into his sleek black fur.

"A few minutes later, my dad stormed into the house and told me to go to my room," she continued. "I did, but I kept my door open. Apparently, my mother had driven by my dad's girlfriend's house and saw his car parked down the street. She rang the bell and left the suitcase on the porch."

"How did your mom know where his girlfriend lived?" Grace asked.

"Just listen. I'll explain that in a minute," Maria said. "Anyway, I heard the entire fight. I think they must have forgotten that I was upstairs or they didn't care, because they weren't even whispering," she shared. "I've never seen my mother that angry. But there was nothing my dad could say. He was caught. Liz told him to move out, and said that she was filing for divorce. He said something about divorce not being allowed in the Catholic faith and then I heard glass breaking. I ran downstairs and saw my mother's wine glass on the kitchen floor. Liz was holding the wine bottle over her head ready to throw it," she explained. Maria's expression was distant and soft. She took a long, deep breath before continuing. "I was really scared. I've heard them argue, but I've never seen anyone throw anything at the other one," she paused. "I didn't know what to say so I just stood there and cried."

"My mother ran over to me and gave me a hug and told me that everything was going to be okay," Maria sniffled. "See, even talking about it now makes me want to cry," she said.

"Maria, you don't have to talk about this anymore if it's upsetting to you," Rashanda coached.

Tanisha handed Maria a box of tissues from her nightstand. Maria blew her nose and dabbed at her eyes before continuing.

"Honestly, it feels better to get this out in the open. And I want my friends to know exactly what happened," she paused. "Anyway, my mom started picking up the broken glass and my dad walked over to me and gave me a hug. He had this guilty look on his face like he didn't know what to say," Maria explained. "I think he was embarrassed and afraid to say anything since he suspected that I'd probably heard the entire fight," she finished. "After he hugged me, he went upstairs to get something and left. I helped my mother pick up the glass and clean up the mess. The only thing my mom said while we were cleaning is that she was glad that she'd been drinking chardonnay instead of merlot," Maria giggled.

"What's the difference?" Grace asked.

"Chardonnay is white wine, and merlot is a red wine," Tanisha explained. "Red wine would have left a stain on the wall."

"Exactly," Maria agreed. "Liz stayed up all night packing my dad's clothes, drinking wine and talking to her sister on the phone. Actually, she stuffed most of his clothes into suitcases and bags and dragged them into the garage. The next morning, Neal walked home from his sleepover, and my dad came back around lunchtime. My parents talked in the garage for a few minutes and then they sat us down and told us that they were separating for a while. My dad said that they were going to try to work things out. When he said that, I looked at my mother, and she rolled her eyes at my father. But other than the look that I caught her giving him, it was very civilized and orderly. Nobody cried. Nobody raised their voice. But every time my dad spoke, my mother looked like she wanted to cut his liver out and feed it to him," she finished.

"Maria! That's so gross," Rashanda scolded.

"Well, it's true. She stared at him like she wanted to kill him," Maria defended. "As soon as they finished talking to us, Liz left to go to the grocery store and my dad made a phone call. He pulled his car into the garage and packed his things in the car and pulled it onto the driveway. When we got outside, his secretary was parked in the driveway, and he put a few things in her car. At first I thought that it was a coincidence that he'd called her to help him move out, and then it hit me. His secretary was his girlfriend!" Maria exclaimed. "That's how my mother knew where he was. My dad put some things in her car and she drove away. He hugged us and then he drove off. Liz came back about two hours later with groceries and our new cat, Sugar," Maria finished. "And the rest is history. That's the whole sordid story."

"Wow! Did you know that your dad was having an affair with his secretary?" Grace asked.

"I didn't know who it was, but I suspected that he was seeing someone," Maria admitted. "Now that I think about it, the signs were all there. He was never home for dinner. He routinely missed my brother's baseball games. We never did anything as a family anymore. He and my mother never went on dates. He'd just checked out of our lives," Maria shrugged. "It's been a few weeks now, and I don't even really miss him. I was so accustomed to him not being here. And when he was here, he and my mother just fought all the time or he was snapping at me and Neal over silly stuff," Maria continued.

She stretched her arms over her head and inhaled deeply. "I never told you this, but when they first started fighting about a year ago, I did crazy stuff to get attention like take money from my mother's purse. It was wild. I knew that if I did something bad and got caught then they'd have to sit me down and talk to me," she sighed. "I thought that if I could shift their focus from them to me, that it would make their relationship better. They'd see that they needed to be together for my sake. My mother never missed the money that I took from her purse," Maria paused. She took a deep breath and stared into space. "One time, I even tried to take something from a store, but I got caught. Fortunately, the security guard gave me a break and didn't call my parents. I had the money to pay for it, but I just wanted the attention. It was so stupid," she admitted. "I'm embarrassed to share this story," she sniffled. She felt tears welling in her eyes again.

"Don't cry, Maria," Tanisha offered gently. "You've had a rough couple of months." She stroked her friend's arm gently.

Maria took a deep breath and continued. "Now that my dad is gone, I haven't felt like taking money from Liz or stealing anything from a store. And when I see my dad now, he's super nice," she smiled. "I think he feels guilty for destroying our family. But truthfully, I like the new family that we have now better than the old one. Everyone just seems happier," Maria finished.

"I know what you mean. When my parents split up, I lied

about stupid stuff. It's crazy what you do when you're going through some serious drama," Tanisha groaned. She sat up and hugged her knees into her chest. "This conversation keeps getting deeper and deeper. How's your mom doing now that your dad has moved out?" Tanisha asked.

"I think she's doing great," Maria replied. "We're going to family counseling once a week so the three of us can talk about our feelings and our new family structure. And Neal and I meet with a child psychologist individually once a week. It's the same psychologist that worked with me when I was bulimic. She's real cool so I told her about my little kleptomaniac phase. She said that it's not uncommon for kids to act out when they see their parents are having marital problems," Maria paused and studied her toe nail. "I changed my mind. I don't like this color," she said. Grabbing a cotton ball, she soaked it with nail polish remover and wiped off the polish. "This may sound insensitive and cruel," she continued. "But I really think that my mom is better off without my dad. She's happier now," Maria smiled. "I like seeing her happy. Did you guys go to counseling when your parents split up, Teenie?" Maria asked.

"No. We should have. I was closer to my dad than I am to my mom, so I was really sad when he moved out. But I see him every weekend, and now Billie and I have gotten a little closer," Tanisha shared.

Maria nodded her head. "Since my dad moved out, my grandfather has been visiting a lot more now. He's just glad that my mother seems happier. I think he knew what was going on too," she paused. "In one of the family counseling sessions my mother reluctantly shared that she's known about my dad's girlfriend for a long time, but she hung in there for us."

"A lot of people stay together for the kids," Rashanda stated.

"I'm so glad that my mother had enough dignity and self respect to take a stand. It sounds like she tried to give my dad a second chance, but he wouldn't stop seeing other women, so she just got fed up. I'm proud of her. She's a strong woman," Maria boasted. "She even said that she still loves my dad, which I was surprised to hear. I expected Liz to say that she hated him, but she said that she hates what he did, but she still loves him," Maria explained.

"That's deep," Tanisha mumbled. "I don't know if I could still love someone that betrayed our marriage like that."

"Me either," Maria echoed. "But that's what she said. She said that she'll always love my dad. He was her husband for over sixteen years, and he will always be the father of her two children. And she also said that she didn't want us to be mad at him. They were young when they got married and now they have a chance to find happiness with other people."

"Your mom is my hero," Tanisha squealed.

"I second that," Rashanda agreed.

"Third," Grace echoed.

"Do you think Liz will remarry?" Grace asked.

"I don't know, but it's too soon to tell. I think she's just enjoying her new life right now. She's ordered herself some new bedroom furniture, and she just picked out a new sofa for the living room. She's taking tennis lessons and just got a new haircut," Maria shared.

"It seems like more people are splitting up than staying together," Rashanda observed. "It's sad and scary. I always thought that your parents were so happy, Maria," Rashanda stated.

Maria shrugged her shoulders and tossed her hands into the air.

"I think they wanted people to think that they were happy," she said. "They had me fooled for awhile. But over the past year or so, I really noticed that they never did anything together, and they didn't seem like they were friends," she paused. "They were only nineteen when they got married, and I think they just grew apart," Maria finished. She painted her pinky toe and fanned her toes out before continuing.

"Last week, I overheard my mother on the phone with her sister, and she referred to this time in her life as the intermission. She said that the time with my dad was Act I, and she's going to refresh herself during this intermission and prepare for Act II because the Liz Wesley play isn't over yet," Maria finished. "She also said that Act I wasn't so bad. She had a good marriage for a number of years and had her children," Maria shrugged again. "I like that analogy. If life is a play, sometimes Act II is better than Act I. You never know. My mother is handling the divorce well which is helping me deal with it."

"I admire your mother's strength," Tanisha said.

"Me too," Maria agreed. "I'm seeing a different side of my mom, and I like it. I heard her crying in her room one night, but I didn't want her to know that I heard her, so I didn't disturb her." She glanced out the window briefly before continuing. "She really loved my dad, and I think she thought that they'd be married forever," Maria sighed. "She's a lot stronger than I ever gave her credit for being, and watching her handle this divorce has made me respect her as a woman instead of just looking at her as my mother," Maria said.

"That's deep. But it makes sense," Grace offered. "It's easy to forget that our mothers are women and have feelings."

"I guess that's true," Tanisha offered. "But most of the time, I swear that Billie Mae is the sister of the tin man from The Wizard of Oz or the cousin of the Wicked Witch of the West, and she needs to fly on her little broom and head to Oz to get a heart."

"Teenie! Let's keep it positive," Rashanda coached.

"That was just a joke," Tanisha giggled. "But seriously, does it bother you that your dad's girlfriend is white, Maria?" Tanisha asked.

Without hesitation, Maria shook her head rapidly from side to side. "Not at all," she said. "She's actually very nice," Maria offered. "She's only twenty six, so she's only ten years older than I am. I think she's cool. But of course I don't let my mother know that."

"Good strategy. Liz might not appreciate you bonding with the mistress!" Tanisha laughed.

"I'd be so devastated if my parents got a divorce," Rashanda admitted.

"Don't even put that negative energy into the universe, Rashanda," Tanisha said seriously. "But if anything did happen to your parents' marriage, you'd keep living and would keep doing you, just like Maria and I are doing," Tanisha said.

"This divorce talk is getting too depressing. What were we talking about before?" Grace asked.

"Doing the deed. Maria was trying to convince us to do the deed on prom night so that we can continue to be close and bond," Rashanda offered.

"We do not need to 'do the deed' to bond us," Tanisha stated. "That's absurd. I still feel close to you guys," she said carefully, crossing her legs so as to not smudge her toenail polish. "It's different with Lori being gone and Justine living far away, but it's still cool," Tanisha said.

"I think you're right, Teenie," Maria sighed. "After sharing my family saga with you guys, I feel one hundred percent better." Maria sat up straight and smiled at each of her friends. "And you'll each be happy to know that after this fifteen minute girl therapy session, I've changed my mind. I'm going to continue with my abstinence until marriage campaign," Maria boasted. "The last thing I need is more drama in my complicated young life."

"Agreed!" Rashanda squealed. "You definitely don't need any boy drama in your life right now, and doing the deed before you get married has drama written all over it."

"Speaking of boy drama," Tanisha said. "Glen hasn't tried to kiss me yet. What do you ladies make of that?" she asked.

"You are kidding me," Maria squealed. "What's he waiting for?"

"I have no idea. We've been dating for almost two months, and he hasn't tried anything," she sighed. Tanisha pulled a pillow sham from Maria's bed and squeezed it against her chest. "At first, I thought that maybe he was turned off by the cavity in my tooth, but he hasn't tried to kiss me since I got it pulled either," Tanisha moaned.

"I didn't even notice that you had a cavity in that tooth until you told me that you had it pulled," Maria offered. "Smile so I can see the space where it was."

Tanisha smiled widely. "A lot of people never noticed it because I was really ashamed of it, so I learned how to hide it when I talked and smiled," she explained. "The dentist wants to wait six months and see what the permanent tooth does on its own. If it hasn't moved into the proper position by then, I'll have to get braces," she paused. "I'm stressed about that because Billie's insurance doesn't cover them. My mom and dad said they'll see what they can do, but I know that they're struggling to send money to my brother in college," she sighed. "My mother has even offered to ask her father for a loan for my braces," she paused. "My grandfather would probably loan her the money, but my father doesn't want her to do that. They said they'll figure out how to pay for my braces together.

It's weird. Now that they're divorced, my parents are being civil to one another, which is nice to see," Tanisha finished.

"I think it's cool that you and your mom are working on your relationship," Maria said.

"Me too. Billie Mae really isn't so bad after all," Tanisha admitted. She blew on her toenails and thought. I'm not ready to tell them about Billie's bipolar disorder yet. I need to make sure that the new and improved Billie is for real. Besides, this girl chat topic has been serious enough for today.

"Anyway, I'll figure something out even if I have to pay for them myself with my Save Mart money," Tanisha finished. "I'm not going to prom next year with a hillbilly smile," she grinned widely. "Hi! Just call me Ellie Mae Clampett!" she teased. "I live in a double wide trailer, we don't have indoor plumbing and I ain't never rode a plane before!" The girls giggled and laughed at her joke. It's so good to not have to hide that tooth from my friends anymore! She smiled widely. The gap from her recently pulled tooth prominently displayed.

"I'd rather have the photo taken with braces in my mouth than a missing tooth," she continued. "Plus, the sooner I get the braces on, the sooner they can come off," she continued.

"Or you could just smile without showing your teeth, Teenie," Grace suggested.

"Good point, Grace," Rashanda said. "My parents had trouble paying for my braces too, but my orthodontist worked out a payment plan with them. He'll work with you if you ask him to," Rashanda suggested.

"Thanks, Rashanda," Tanisha smiled. "I think my parents are thinking that they'll have to pay for the braces all at once. I'll tell my mother to talk to him about setting up a payment plan."

"I'll tell you what you need to do," Maria offered. "You need to let that rich, fine David Barton help you pay for them! He's in love with your narrow butt," Maria gushed. "He'll give you whatever you need."

"That's very funny, kleptomaniac! I'm not asking David for money to help pay for my braces. It ain't gonna happen," Tanisha stated firmly. She threw a pillow at Maria's head. She missed. "Besides, he's not wealthy. His parents do well for themselves, but he's just a struggling college student. And move over, you're going to smudge my toes."

"Teenie, do you still keep in touch with David?" Grace asked.

"I do. In fact, I talked to him last week, and he sent me tulips from Holland after Lori's funeral. I wrote him a letter a few days ago. He'll be home for Thanksgiving so we'll see each other then," she explained. "But we're just friends. He's still dating this girl named Patty from his high school. She attends Howard University. I told him about Glen," she finished.

Maria shook her head sarcastically. "He tripped out too. He probably wants to kick Glen's butt, which confirms that David really likes you, Teenie," Maria teased. "You need to go ahead and claim that boy and call yourself his girlfriend before he meets someone else and drops you like a hot potato!"

"You are so twisted, Maria. It's not even like that and you know it. We're friends for now, and we're going to stay friends until I graduate from high school and then we'll see what happens once we're both in college," Tanisha stuck her tongue at Maria. "So I'm working on Glen as the possible high school boyfriend."

"Let's get back to Glen. I can't believe that he hasn't kissed you, Teenie. Why don't you just kiss him?" Rashanda suggested.

"I thought about kissing him first, but I'm too nervous," Tanisha gushed, "He's older, and he's supposed to have more experience. I don't want him to think that I'm fast. He might get the wrong idea, so I'm trying to chill," she explained.

"That's what I did with Ian. I kissed him first," Rashanda admitted. "I wanted to find out if he was a good kisser, so I went for it."

"And we all know what happened after that!" Grace laughed. "You guys made out like dogs in heat."

"Very funny, Grace. We did not! Ian and I are totally cool. We talk on the phone regularly, and we write letters weekly too. It's awesome having a boyfriend," Rashanda boasted. "I really like him. He's so smart and he's just a nice guy," Rashanda smiled. "He wants me to come to Northwestern for a campus visit after his fall midterms are finished. My parents have already said that I can spend the weekend with Justine, so he'll just pick me up at her new apartment since it's only a few minutes from campus and we can spend the day together. By the way, Justine doesn't use her walker anymore. She still has a limp from the accident, but she doesn't use the walker," Rashanda shared.

"Praise the Lord!" Grace said.

"Wow! You sound like Lori," Maria observed. "That's what she would have said."

"You're right. That was Lori's favorite celebration phrase," Tanisha sighed. "That's good news about Justine," she continued. "I miss Lori and Justine," she shared. "But let's not go into our dark mood again. Let's keep talking about boys," she finished quickly. "Do you love Ian, Rashanda?"

"I think I do," Rashanda replied.

"Why do you think that you love him?" Maria asked.

Rashanda shrugged her shoulders. "When I'm not with him

I really miss him. I miss studying for my advanced placement test with him. And when I think about something bad happening to him, like a car accident or death, I get really sad. Sometimes, I cry thinking about it," Rashanda explained. "I just think that I love him."

"Have you told Ian that you love him?" Tanisha asked.

"No. I don't want him to think that I'm just infatuated with him because he's my first boyfriend," Rashanda said.

"Does he know that he's your first boyfriend," Maria asked.

"He does," Rashanda replied. "I told him when he left for Northwestern."

"Is he a virgin?" Maria asked.

"Maria!" Grace squealed. "That's none of our business."

Maria furrowed her eyebrow at Grace and scowled. She waved her hand dismissively. "It is so our business," she said. "I sat here and told you guys all of the sordid details of my parents' break-up. The least Rashanda can do is spill the beans on Ian's virginity."

Rashanda laughed out loud. "I don't mind telling you guys. He's not a virgin. I asked him one night when we were on the phone. He told me that he did the deed with his prom date."

"See!" Maria screamed. "Everyone does it on prom night!"

"Calm down, Maria," Tanisha said. "And just because everyone does it, doesn't mean it's the right thing to do. Stay focused. Go ahead and continue, Rashanda."

"We didn't go into any detail," she shared. "But he told me that he's only done it that one time."

"And you believe that?" Maria asked sarcastically. "He's probably teaching a sex clinic after his chemistry classes," Maria giggled. "He's in college, Rashanda. Do you really believe that he isn't doing it with someone in college? Puleeeze!"

Rashanda stared at her friend curiously. "I have no reason not to believe him," she shrugged. "Besides, I told him that I'm waiting for marriage."

"And he still wanted you to be his girlfriend?" Maria asked. "Have you heard from him since you dropped that bomb?"

"Maria! Stop it!" Tanisha scolded. "Just ignore her, Rashanda. The nail polish fumes are making her say silly things."

Rashanda stuck her tongue out at Maria. "We've talked on the phone at least twice a week, and he's written me three letters," Rashanda gushed. "He thinks it's cute that I'm saving myself for marriage."

"Good for you, Rashanda," Grace cheered. "I think you should hang in there with Ian. He sounds like a keeper."

"I wonder what Lori's advice would be if she were here," Rashanda stated.

"She'd probably quote a scripture or say a prayer for our wayward souls," Maria laughed.

Tanisha swatted Maria playfully on the thigh. "You're wrong for mocking Lori's faith, you heathen! But you're right, she would quote a scripture. She would probably quote Matthew chapter seven verses thirteen and fourteen and remind us to enter by the narrow gate," Tanisha said. "That was her favorite scripture."

Grace's chin dropped when Tanisha said that scripture. She stared at Tanisha. "That was Lori's favorite scripture? I didn't know that," Grace said. "I was just flipping through the Bible at Lori's funeral and stopped in Matthew and picked chapter seven, verse thirteen because it's my birthday, the thirteenth day of the seventh month," Grace said. "That is so weird."

"That was one of Lori's favorite scriptures from the New Testament," Tanisha said. "She memorized it because she said that it reminded her to do the right thing and choose the right or harder way even if she was tempted by the world to choose the popular or easier way," she explained. She stared squarely at Maria. "For instance, an example of what it means is NOT doing it on prom night even if it seems like everyone else is doing it and it would be easy to do. That's entering by the narrow gate," she finished.

"I hear you, Teenie," Maria groaned. "Are we going to crown you the new church lady?" Maria giggled. "Here's my new thing. I think I want my husband to also be a virgin on our wedding night so we can figure it out together."

"Good luck with that," Tanisha groaned. "Most boys these days cash in the virgin chip as soon as they learn where to put their little missile."

The girls giggled loudly.

"Maria, where is Liz?" Rashanda asked.

"She's at her tennis lesson, and then she goes to her standing Saturday afternoon hair appointment, so she won't be home for hours."

"So if that's your latest rule, then you won't be marrying Todd because we all know that he certainly ain't no virgin," Rashanda laughed.

"Exactly. I don't plan to marry Todd. I don't think that I'm in love with Todd," she said. "In fact, I know that I'm not in love with Todd," she clarified. "I just like hanging out with him because he's fine and he drives a nice car."

"Girl, sometimes you are so shallow. But I appreciate your honesty. At least you know who you are," Tanisha laughed.

Rashanda twirled the fringe on Maria's pillow sham. "I've never told anyone this, but when Ian and I were making out, I kept wondering what Lori would think since she always said that you shouldn't kiss a guy until the third date," Rashanda explained. "Since it was our first official date, I felt guilty kissing him," she confessed. "I was more worried about what Lori would say and think than my own parents," Rashanda said. "I didn't even think about my parents, but I kept wondering what Lori would say," she sighed, fighting back tears. Her words were slow and deliberate. "I can't believe that she died on the same day that I became Ian's girlfriend and had my first major kissing session," she struggled to speak. "While---I---was---making---out---with---Ian---and---worrying---about---what---Lori---would---think," Rashanda stammered. "Lori---was---dying!" She buried her head in her hands and cried.

"Don't cry, Rashanda," Tanisha said softly. "You just said that you love Ian, so Lori wouldn't have judged you. She probably would have dragged you to church on Sunday to confess your sin at the altar, but she wouldn't have judged you," Tanisha smiled. She handed Rashanda a box of tissue.

"I agree with Teenie," Maria offered. "But I know what you mean, Rashanda. Usually, I spend more time wondering what you guys will think about something that I've done than I do worrying about what my parents will think when they find out," she agreed. "For instance, today I was scared to tell you guys that I'd been stealing money from my mother's purse, and that I tried to steal something from a store," she admitted. "After the counseling session, the therapist told me to tell my parents what I'd done, and I did. But I wasn't nervous. I told them, we discussed it, and life went on. It was no big deal. But sitting here talking to you guys, I was really nervous about what you'd think about me," Maria paused. "I know that my parents love me unconditionally and will forgive me, but sometimes I'm afraid that you guys won't want to be my friend anymore if you see my flaws," she finished.

"You have far more flaws than good qualities, kleptomaniac. We're drawn to your flaws like a fly to honey," Tanisha teased. "By the way, thanks for telling us that you're a thief, now we know not to leave our purses anywhere near you," she giggled.

Maria cut her eyes at Teenie and playfully kicked her in the foot. "But seriously, your approval is more important than my parents' approval. Peer pressure is a trip. Good thing you guys aren't knuckleheads."

"Amen to that," Tanisha finished. "But I can relate. I was afraid that you guys wouldn't want to be my friend anymore if you saw that I had a cavity in my tooth," Tanisha admitted. "I lost sleep sometimes wondering what you'd do if you saw it."

Rashanda wiped her eyes with a tissue and blew her nose. "Thanks, guys," she said. "That makes me feel a little better," she sighed. "But I still feel guilty that I was having the time of my life, and Lori was probably dying at that moment."

"Don't feel guilty, Rashanda," Maria coached. "We have to live our lives. That's what Lori would want us to do, and that's what we promised to do at her funeral. Let's live our lives but still keep her memory alive by including her in the discussion like we did today."

"New topic!" Grace groaned loudly. "Talking about Lori is making me sad. Let's talk about something else," she suggested.

"Technically, we were talking about boys and we segued to Lori," Maria corrected. "Besides, if we aren't talking about boys, what else is there to talk about?" Maria asked. "Talking about boys is so much fun. What do you want to talk about now, Grace?" Maria asked as she delicately waved a magazine across her toenails.

"I think I'm ready to contact Charles Lovett," Grace said.

"Who's Charles Lovett?   I've heard that name before but I don't remember who it is. Is that the new boy that just transferred to River North High? Maria asked casually distracted once again by her toe nail polish. "I haven't seen him yet. Is he cute? Do you have a crush on him, Grace?" Maria finished.

Tanisha coughed into her hand, and enlarged her eyes before gently nudging Maria's knee. "Ouch! Why'd you bump my knee, Teenie?" Maria whined. "That hurt!"

Grace took a deep breath and blew the air out of her lungs slowly. "Charles Lovett was my biological father," Grace finished. "I'm ready to find him."

ABOUT THE AUTHOR

A native Chicagoan, JC Conrad-Ellis now lives in the Memphis, Tennessee area with her husband and their three children, all of whom are panting for a puppy.

Available Now!
Dancing with God's Grace
The fourth book in the Black Diamond Series
Sunshine on Sunday
The fifth book in the Black Diamond Series and
Love, Secrets & Pearls
the sixth book in the Black Diamond Series
Visit JC Ellis' website for interactive blogs:
www.blackdiamondseries.com
Follow JC Ellis on Twitter
@dearjcellis
In **Chemistry & Chaos** book three in the Black Diamond Series, Tanisha "Teenie" Carlson and the girls return for more adolescent drama, young love, dating and life lessons. This time,

the reader learns the trials and tribulations that are taking place behind the front doors of the "other" girls: Maria Wesley, Lori Perkins, Rashanda Jordan, Justine Wellington and Grace Dudley while Tanisha's mama drama and boy challenges continue.

At sixteen, wiser and armed with more self confidence, the girls attempt to embrace their fragile teen life challenges with class, confidence and a splash of sass. Layer by layer, the reader will learn that, just like Teenie's character, her friends are fearfully and wonderfully made while still flawed in very believable, relatable and forgivable ways.

The grace and strength displayed by each character will prove encouraging to readers of all ages as the girls confirm that a strong friendship network circle of support is as important as a good bra.

www.ingramcontent.com/pod-product-compliance
Lightning Source LLC
Chambersburg PA
CBHW070925190726
48292CB00004B/1101